ARSENIC AT ASCOT

A FIONA FIGG & KITTY LANE MYSTERY

KELLY OLIVER

B

Boldwood

First published in Great Britain in 2023 by Boldwood Books Ltd.

Copyright © Kelly Oliver, 2023

Cover Design by Alexandra Allden

Cover Photography: Shutterstock and Getty

A CIP catalogue record for this book is available from the British Library.

Paperback ISBN 978-1-80483-186-1

Large Print ISBN 978-1-80483-187-8

Hardback ISBN 978-1-80483-188-5

Ebook ISBN 978-1-80483-185-4

Kindle ISBN 978-1-80483-184-7

Audio CD ISBN 978-1-80483-193-9

MP3 CD ISBN 978-1-80483-192-2

Digital audio download ISBN 978-1-80483-191-5

Boldwood Books Ltd
23 Bowerdean Street
London SW6 3TN
www.boldwoodbooks.com

To all my animal friends...

1

THE TELEGRAM

I knew it would happen sooner or later.

In one week, I'd gone from fearless lady spy to glorified gopher. Well, perhaps not that fearless... and not that glorified either.

I reshuffled the already neatly stacked file folders and arranged them to exactly parallel to the corner of my desk. I may be a mere file clerk, but mine was the tidiest desk in the Old Admiralty. This wasn't saying much, given the manly state of disorder in most of the War Office—especially Room 40, with its rows of drafting tables all overflowing with papers, telegrams, and folders. According to my dearly departed father, outward turmoil concealed inner peace. If so, the men in Room 40 had the souls of monks.

Thankfully, the converse wasn't true, or my mind would be a battlefield. I patted the top of the stack. No. A well-ordered desk was a sign of a well-ordered mind.

A wooden screen kept my little corner separated from the pandemonium on the other side where the codebreakers worked on deciphering German telegrams and secret messages. The room was long and narrow, like the barrel of a rifle. Standing at one end, you could barely see out the windows at the other. At the far end of the room, a few desks held teletype machines. Most of those were operated by women working alone. But the male codebreakers worked in packs like wolves. One such pack—three of the best codebreakers in the business—huddled around a drafting table just on the other side of my screen. They howled whenever they cracked a German code.

A lot of crucial deciphering of enemy telegrams and such happened in Room 40.

Just not by me.

My boss, Captain Reginald "Blinker" Hall, had assured me this wasn't a demotion. I was just back where I belonged. And not because I'd failed on my last mission, or because of my penchant for "silly disguises" as he called them. To be fair, I hadn't had the opportunity to wear a disguise on my last assignment, unfortunately.

As Captain Hall informed me, my singular mission—besides filing and fetching tea—was to follow the notorious German spy and South African huntsman, Fredrick Fredricks, expert in war propaganda and agent provocateur. Over the last seven months, I'd followed him across the globe from Paris to Cairo and back again as he disposed of double agents and undermined the British war efforts. Always one step ahead of me, he'd taunted, teased, and shamelessly flirted. *Cheeky cad.* Captain Hall insisted Fredricks was of more use to us alive. But I wasn't so sure.

Heat spread up my neck as I remembered our one secret kiss in the mountains of Northern Italy. Not a real kiss, mind you. Merely an espionage ruse to avoid detection. We'd almost been caught following a couple of socialists and had to stage a kiss. When I closed my eyes, I could almost conjure his sandalwood scent. *Get a grip, Fiona. He's your enemy, for goodness' sake.*

Trouble was, no one knew where to find the bounder. He'd

vanished without a trace. His trail had gone cold and as a result so had my spying activities.

I gathered the stack of folders and went to the filing cabinet. Balancing the stack on one forearm, I opened the top drawer. A familiar smell hit my nose. The earthy scent of aging paper laced with stale cigar smoke and a hint of lingering futility. At least I could console myself that I'd developed the world's best filing system.

"Miss Figg, be a good girl and bring us some fresh tea." The booming voice coming from the other side of the screen was unmistakably that of Mr. Dillwyn "Dilly" Knox, former papyrologist at King's College, Cambridge, known as much for his dalliances as his codebreaking.

Moving my fingers along the tops of the folders in the drawer, one by one, I slid the new ones into their proper places, and pretended I hadn't heard Mr. Knox.

"Did you hear me, Fiona?" He bellowed so loud, everyone in the building had heard him.

I stacked the remaining folders on top of the filing cabinet and poked my head around the screen. "You rang, sir."

"A spot of fresh tea, if you please." His thick lips parted into a lascivious smile. "Mine has gone cold."

Cold tea. Cold trails. Cold careers. What hadn't gone cold?

I stepped in front of the divider.

"Yes, sir." I bobbed a quick curtsy. "Very well, sir."

He laughed and waved me along.

I'd been right about one thing. Without Fredricks, I was nothing but ordinary, boring Fiona Figg, head file clerk and twenty-five-year-old war widow on her way to spinsterhood. Truth be told, my husband had divorced me before he was killed, which made me neither a widow nor a spinster but something far worse, a divorcee. I sauntered to the kitchenette, making a show of dragging my feet and taking my time. Making tea when I should be trailing spies. *Sigh*. How I missed the adventure already.

"Shake your tailfeathers, Miss Figg," Mr. Knox called after me. "I'm dry as an ancient Egyptian papyrus."

Tailfeathers, my flat feet.

"Oh, go stick your head in a bucket," I said under my breath.

"What's that, Miss Figg?"

I turned and flashed a fake smile.

He was peering over the top of his eyeglasses at me.

"Oh, with a bit of luck it—" I rounded the corner into the kitchenette "—will be ready in two shakes."

"It had better be." He sighed. "Monday mornings are cursed."

The kitchenette was a narrow rectangle with yellowing wallpaper, chipped floor tiles, and a stained counter sporting a Bachelor's Stove. As usual, the small sink was overflowing with dirty dishes. *Really*. Couldn't these brilliant men clean up after themselves? How hard was it to wipe out a cup? I huffed as I stood staring at the mess. Too busy with national secrets to drop an empty biscuit box into the rubbish bin. Shaking my head, I put on the kettle and set to work washing the dishes while I waited for the water to boil. The kettle whistled and I rushed to remove it lest it disturb the codebreakers. They could be a cranky bunch.

I whirled hot water around in a stained porcelain teapot that had obviously seen better days, and then emptied it in the newly cleaned sink. I poured a goodly amount of black tea from a paper bag into the pot and followed with boiling water. After letting it steep into a nice strong brew, I loaded a tray with a little jug of milk and several cups. Anyone wanting a slice of lemon was out of luck. I hadn't seen a lemon since the bloody war began almost four years ago. Thanks to the Defense of the Realm, Cake and Pastry Order, however, tea was declared a weapon of war and thus essential to our troops' success. It certainly was essential to *my* success.

As my grandmother always said, "With a good strong cuppa, you can get through anything."

"I say." A familiar voice came from the doorway. "Fiona, old thing, there you are." Captain Clifford Douglas, good friend, compulsory chaperone, and blabbermouth. With his receding hairline and long face, he looked rather like a horse. A well-groomed horse.

The wet dog at his feet shook itself, spraying me with mist.

Almost anything.

The little beast, Poppy the Pekingese, belonged to my erstwhile espionage partner Kitty Lane. The girl had stayed behind on our last mission to tie up loose ends. Unlike me, she had not been recalled from the field.

"Perfect timing." Grinning, Clifford eyed the tea tray. Why the War Office thought I needed a chaperone was beyond me. Still, I had to admit, I'd come to rely on good old Clifford. He was as loyal as a hound.

"Be a lamb and carry this out, will you?" I handed him the tray.

He stared at me like I'd asked him to walk naked across White-hall. I pushed it at him and reluctantly he obliged. If I could deliver tea, so could he. After all, he had been grounded too. The only place he'd chaperoned me in the last week had been to the canteen for lunch. While he'd enjoyed toad-in-the-hole and suet pudding and nattered on about god-awful hunting adventures, I'd nibbled on buttered toast and sipped tea.

We delivered the tea to Mr. Knox's workstation, where three codebreakers stood, heads together, examining a telegram.

"I say." Clifford shoved a pile of papers out of the way and sat the tray on the table. "Have you broken a code?"

The men clammed up. Mr. Knox flipped over the telegram.

Curses. If Clifford wasn't along, they might have given me a glimpse. I *had* helped solve the Zimmerman telegram that got the Americans to join the war.

I poured a splash of milk into each cup. The men could help themselves to the tea. I wasn't a servant.

"Is it true you have a photographic memory, Miss Figg?" Mr. Nigel Grey slid a cup and saucer off the tray. The other men called him "dormouse," presumably because he was petite with a pointed nose and sleepy eyes. The grandson of the fifth Lord Walsingham, he'd been a whizz at languages at Eton and was recruited by the head of cryptography.

"Let's see a demonstration, shall we?" Mr. Knox chuckled. Glancing around the mess of papers strewn across the table, he plucked one out and thrust it at me. "Take a look and then we'll test you."

"I'm not a trained monkey at a circus." I put my hands on my hips. I wasn't about to humor him with a demonstration. *Ridiculous man.*

"I'll bet you can't do it," Mr. Knox said, a mischievous twinkle in his eyes.

I scowled, determined not to be baited.

He waved the sheet of paper under my nose. "If you can reproduce this word for word, we'll let you see the latest telegram we intercepted." He nodded to his pals. "Right, lads?"

"Don't pester Miss Figg." Mr. Montgomery came to my defense. With his pinched face and spectacles, Mr. William Montgomery still looked more like a preacher than a codebreaker. A Presbyterian minister and an expert translator of German theological texts before the war, now he was the head of cryptography.

Too late. "You're on." I'd already snatched the paper from Mr. Knox's meaty paw.

Good heavens. The document was in German. While my French was passable, my German was rudimentary at best. It was no use trying to read the bloody thing. I stared at it, forming a mental snapshot. That was the way my memory worked. I could commit any document to memory just by looking at it. It truly was as if my mind took a photograph and later, I could reproduce it in full even without comprehending one whit.

Mr. Knox grabbed the paper out of my hand. "You've studied it long enough." He slapped a fresh piece of paper onto the table and then pulled out a chair. "Have a seat, Miss Figg. Let's see what you can do." Smiling, he winked at the other men.

"Fiona has a brilliant memory." Clifford removed a pencil from his breast pocket and handed it to me. "The old bean can probably recreate every document in that bloody filing cabinet." He pointed toward my workstation.

I nodded. At least someone believed in me. "Tea, if you please." If I was putting on a show, I might as well get celebrity treatment.

Clifford fetched a cup from the tray and sat it on the table next to the blank sheet of paper.

"Quit stalling, *old bean.*" Mr. Knox chuckled, causing his ample belly to shake. "Worried you can't do it?"

Even Poppy, the little beast, looked up at me expectantly.

Pencil in hand, I took a sip of tea, and then began transcribing from memory. Once I started, I couldn't stop, lest the text unravel. I had to reproduce it all at once, as fast as I could, or the picture lingering before my mind might vanish. The document was in front of my mind's eye just as it was before my physical eye only moments ago. But this version was ethereal and fragile, like the vapor floating up from my teacup. An automaton, without any idea of their meaning, I wrote out the German words.

"By God!" Mr. Knox said. "She's doing it."

"I told you." The way Clifford beamed, I wondered if he'd put a wager on me.

"There." I shoved the paper at Mr. Knox. "Done."

"She showed you, Dilly," Mr. Grey tittered, his tone high-pitched and tinny. "Good on you, Miss Figg."

Poppy barked in agreement.

"What's that dog doing in here?" Mr. Montgomery's voice was stern.

"She's not just any dog." Clifford scooped up the creature, cuddling her in his arms. "She's Poppy the Pekingese, Britain's premier canine intelligence agent."

"Enough horseplay. Get that dog out of here." Mr. Montgomery scowled. "We've got a war to win."

"The telegram." I wiggled my fingers at Mr. Knox. "I reproduced it word for word." I raised my eyebrows. "Now, you owe me a look at the latest intel."

Mr. Montgomery's lips tightened into a thin line, but he didn't say anything. Of course, it wasn't cricket to allow a lowly file clerk to see classified documents. But Mr. Montgomery had always been one of my most ardent supporters. In fact, he'd recommended me for my first espionage assignment when that poor bloke fell and broke his leg on the way to Ravenswick Abbey. His bad break was my lucky one.

Fortunately, the head of cryptology was too distracted by a dog in the office to worry about me.

"Fair is fair," Clifford said, pinching tobacco out of a pouch and poking it into his pipe.

With a dramatic flair befitting a West End Shakespearean actor, Mr. Knox waved the telegram over his head and brought it down onto the table in front of me. "Have a go at it."

I snatched up the telegram.

He poured himself a splash of milk and another cup of tea. "None of us can make head nor tail of the bugger."

As I read the telegram, an uncomfortable heat crept up my

neck like a venomous spider. The proximity of the men was stifling. "Give me some space, if you please." I waved them away.

Of course, none of them moved, except Mr. Montgomery, who sighed and went back to his own desk. Clifford peered over my shoulder, puffing away on his foul-smelling pipe. Poppy sat panting at his feet. Mr. Grey's beady dark eyes glowed with expectation—I could almost see his mousy nose twitching. Did he know I'd already decoded the wretched text? With an imperious look on his face, Mr. Dilly Knox put his hands in his pockets and leaned back into nothingness as if sitting on a throne. The smirk on his round face made me wonder whether they were having me on.

Was this some sort of joke? It was all too easy. I'd deciphered the telegram in a matter of minutes. Surely the men had too. My face burned and I put a hand to my cheek.

Oh, my word. A terrible thought took hold in my mind. I dropped the telegram and held my hand out in horror. My fingers trembled as I examined and then sniffed them. Could the notorious poisoner have laced the paper with some toxin? Some toxin absorbed through the skin. I glanced up at the men. If that were the case, at least one of them would be feeling the effects by now.

"I say." Clifford removed his pipe from his mouth. "Is something wrong, old girl?"

Poppy tilted her head and squeaked.

"Burn your fingers, Fiona?" Mr. Knox was clearly enjoying my distress. "You dropped it like a hot potato." I glanced up at him and he winked at me. Did he know?

Why had Fredricks resorted to sending coded messages to the War Office? I covered the telegram with one hand and placed the other across my racing heart. "I don't feel at all well." It was true. My stomach roiled and I could feel my pulse pounding in my temples. Either he was in grave danger, or the bounder was taunting me.

"Lady troubles?" Mr. Knox asked with a snide grin.

Why not? That would scare away the men. I nodded and pressed my palm against the rough paper. A strange bitterness rose in my throat.

This telegram wasn't poisoned. Far worse.

It was meant for me. And me alone.

2

THE INVITATION

Later that evening, alone in my flat, I paced the floor, wringing my hands, and wondering what to do. Should I tell Mr. Knox that I'd decoded the telegram? It was so simple. Why hadn't the men figured it out? Maybe they had. Did they know it was meant for me? Although I hardly ever took tea in the evening, I needed to think. And what better way to clear one's head than a strong brew? My heels clacking on the wood floor, I headed for the kitchen. The echoes reminded me I was alone.

Not just alone. Lonely.

Andrew and I had moved into the modest two-bedroom flat on Northwick Terrace just after we were married. We'd been deliriously happy. Before the war. Before Nancy, the husband-stealing tart of a secretary. Before he died in my arms at Charing Cross Hospital from mustard gas poisoning.

The terrible memory sent me into a panic, as it always did. *Breathe, Fiona. Just breathe.* I leaned up against the wall to steady myself. When I'd regained my composure, I continued down the hallway toward the kitchen. Shuffling through the flat alone, only the sounds drifting up from the street for company, for the first time, I thought about moving. Or perhaps getting a cat or a flat-mate or both. The advantage of both would be that the flatmate could mind the cat when I was gone on a mission. Provided I ever got another assignment.

Busying myself with the tea-kettle, I tried to forget about Andrew. Of course, being back in this flat made it impossible. Everything here reminded me of the life we'd shared. Even the kitchen. He'd insisted on the newest appliances. The enameled Smith & Phillips gas stove. The paraffin lamps from Liberty's. The telephone mounted on the wall that looked like a face smiling at me with its two bells for eyes, large protruding mouthpiece for nose, and long wooden lip. He'd said I deserved the best. That was before he'd hired and admired the buxom Nancy. The kitchen had been one of my favorite places to sit with a cup of tea and read the latest Sherlock Holmes stories in *The Strand Magazine*. The black and white mosaic floor tiles and mint-green wallpaper had made for a cheery retreat from the world. At least they used to. Before Andrew abandoned me.

I took my steaming cuppa to the breakfast table and dropped into one of my mother's favorite painted chairs. I'd inherited the dining room set when she'd died, along with her unbridled ambi-tion and unrealistic hopes for my future.

If that telegram meant what I thought it did, I needed to get that cat and take in a boarder *tout suite*. For I was about to get sacked. The telegram had been sent from the War Office. One of our own. Or at least it was typed on War Office letterhead. It read:

6 6. 13 1 3 8 5 18 9 5. 8 5 12 16 13 5. 6 6.

A simple numeric code. Easy to decipher.
Too easy.

It used a plain 1=A cipher. Any schoolgirl could decrypt it. *FF. Ma cherie. Help me. FF.* That was all it said. *FF. Ma cherie. Help me. FF.*

FF. Fiona Figg. Fredrick Fredricks. Yes, we shared initials. The scoundrel. He always insisted on calling me ma chérie, much to my consternation.

Fredrick Fredricks. Asking me for help. Couldn't he have been more specific? Help him how? Help him where? Was he in trouble? Or was he once again trying to enlist me in his *purported* project of ending the war? No doubt by insuring Germany's victory. I didn't trust him. And I wished he'd quit singling me out. Although if he hadn't, I'd never have got assignments taking me from Paris to Cairo. If it weren't for him, I'd never have left London or this dreary little flat. In some ways, I owed Fredricks. The rotter. I should be grateful to him.

FF. Ma chérie. Help me. FF.

I should take the telegram straight to Captain Hall. Trouble was, I had no idea where to find Fredricks or what he wanted. Was he setting a trap? *Deuced vague trap.* And why did he send his message via telegram, which he undoubtedly knew would be intercepted by the War Office and sent to Room 40? How could he be sure I would see it? And didn't he care if everyone else saw it? So many unanswered questions. I aimed to find out where he was and what he was up to. No doubt, no good.

Should I tell Captain Hall or go it on my own? *Should* was probably not the right word. I knew I *should* tell Captain Hall, the question was, *would* I?

I sipped my tea and pondered my future selling chestnuts on the street corner. Conjuring the sweet burnt smell made my stomach growl. I fetched a packet of ginger biscuits from the cupboard. I'd been back over a week, and my cupboard and ice box were still empty. I didn't even have ice in the ice box, let alone milk or meat. I had yet to contact the ice girl and have her start up delivery again. My heart just wasn't in it. Starting up my dreary lonely life again. Biting into a stale biscuit, I realized I'd abandoned our flat after Andrew abandoned me. Now, it was as filled with his absence as it was dust. I felt like I was sitting in a funeral home.

Fiona, get a grip. There's a war on. Men are dying. You've got it good by comparison.

I stood up and tugged on the bottom of my cardigan. Time to quit moping about and lay in some proper food. Of course, the standard for what counted as *proper food* had fallen drastically since war rationing. War bread, made from whatever the baker could find lying around, was ghastly. And we were lucky to get any meat or fresh vegetables. Perhaps I should reconsider Clifford's favorite toad-in-the-hole and suet pudding. At least it was filling. I stared into my empty cupboard.

Tomorrow after work I'd go shopping.

I took my tea and the rest of the pack of stale biscuits into the living room. I sat them on the sheet-covered table and began removing the sheets from the rest of the furniture. With every snap of the cotton sails, great clouds of dust filled the room.

Coughing, I swore I'd pull myself together and put things in order. Halfway through, I gave up. I grabbed the biscuits and dropped into one of the crimson velvet chairs I'd inherited from my grandmother. When I'd visit the farm as a child, she'd never allowed me to sit in them. What would she think if she saw me now, munching crumbly biscuits in her precious chair? Planning my attack, I surveyed the room and nibbled.

I'd piled a few sheets in the center of the dusty Donegal carpet. A carpet brush was in order. The cupboard sported a thin film of grime. And the place needed a good dusting. The oak table and silver candelabra were covered in gray powder. And my grandfather's cuckoo clock on the mantelpiece could use a good wipe down. All in all, the place required a thorough scrubbing.

"A new broom may sweep clean, but the old brush knows all the corners," my grandmother used to say.

Munching the last biscuit, I sat watching the motes dance in the light and the crumbs fall to the floor. A sure sign I wasn't feeling quite myself.

Tomorrow. I'd clean the house tomorrow.

A rap on the door interrupted my melancholy reveries. Who could that be? I wasn't expecting any visitors. Maybe Clifford had dropped by to show me his latest story about our adventures. Yes, he fancied himself a regular Watson, reporting on our forays into crime solving. By *reporting*, I meant exaggerating.

When I opened the door, no one was there. I stuck my head out and glanced up and down the hallway. How strange. Whoever knocked had vanished into thin air. A neighbor's child playing a prank? I stepped back inside, shut the door, and nearly stepped on an embossed card. I bent and picked it up. Heavy linen card stock. Blank. I turned it over.

Crikey. An invitation to a charity house party at Mentmore Castle this coming weekend. Addressed to Lady Tabitha Kentworthy. Obviously, the delivery boy had got the wrong flat. *Lady Tabitha Kentworthy.* Surely there was no lady living in my modest building.

I flipped it over again and stared down at the blank card stock... as if invisible ink would show itself and reveal the sender or the true whereabouts of this Lady Tabitha Kentworthy. Turning the card over again, I re-read the invitation.

Lord Rosebrooke, and his daughter Lady Sybil, request your presence at Mentmore Castle for the annual Rose Charity House

Party to benefit the War Orphan Fund. This year's theme is ROYAL ASCOT. 1–4 February 1918. RSVP Lady Sybil Grant.

The 1st of February. That's Friday. Today's Monday. Golly. Only four days from now.

Of course, I'd heard of Lord Rosebrooke and his eccentric daughter. He'd been prime minister, after all. And I'd heard of Ascot. The horserace track. But who in blazes was Lady Tabitha Kentworthy? And why was her invitation to a charity weekend at Mentmore Castle under my door? I tapped the card stock against my palm. Pacing around the living room, I stepped over dusty sheets and sneezed.

First the coded telegram and now a mysterious invitation. Both no doubt the handiwork of Fredrick Fredricks. I turned the card over and inspected it again, this time holding it up to the light, looking for secret signs or the scoundrel's panther insignia.

Nothing.

How odd. Usually, Fredricks made a grand show of using his insignia seal. It was unlike him to lie low. For a spy, he always was remarkably visible, deploying the Edgar Allan Poe strategy of hiding in plain sight.

That was, until now.

3

THE ASSIGNMENT

The next day at work, I couldn't stop fretting over the telegram. From Fredricks, obviously. Where was he and why did he need my help? Sitting at my desk at the War Office, I pulled the house party invitation from my handbag and stared down at it. Also from Fredricks, no doubt. What was he up to? An uncanny sensation of being watched made me look up. Mr. Knox was peeking around the corner of the screen.

"Don't lurk." I stuffed the invitation back into my handbag and pretended to straighten the pile of file folders on my desk. "Either come in or go away." Mr. Knox was the only one of the code-breakers who received such brusque treatment from me. And with good reason. He deserved it. The cad was always flirting with me and every other woman—and occasional man—in sight.

"Did you crack that code?" He sauntered over to my desk and sat on the edge.

"Is that a trick question?" Any schoolboy could decode it. I narrowed my eyes. "Surely *you've* figured out what it says." And he was supposed to be one of the greatest cryptologists in Britain.

"Of course I know what it *says*." He grinned like a hyena. "But what does it *mean*?"

I shrugged. "Why ask me?"

"Know anyone with the initials FF?" He winked.

Was he toying with me? For all I knew, the whole thing was a rotten prank. I wouldn't put it past him.

"I'm just a file clerk." I plucked a file from the top of my stack and delivered it to the filing cabinet. "Not a codebreaker."

"How far would you go for king and country, Fiona?" He was leering at me again. Blasted man. Using my Christian name and making lewd insinuations. "Should I start calling you Mata Hari?" He chuckled.

That wasn't funny. Not in the least. I'd known Mata Hari. *Poor woman.* We'd become friends, of sorts. Of course, at the time, she thought I was a nun offering absolution to her wretched soul. I'd watched the police execute her outside Paris. Dreadful. Absolutely dreadful. I shuddered at the memory. *Poor, poor woman.* Her only crime was loving men—perhaps a bit too much and a few too many.

Mr. Knox pulled a square of paper from his jacket pocket. "You, too, shall be tested." He handed me another telegram.

6 6.

13 1 3 8 5 18 9 5 13 5 5 20 13 5 21 14 4 5
18 2 9 7 2 5 14 20 15 13 15 18 18 15 23 1
20 14 15 15 14.

4 15 14 15 20 20 5 12 12 1 14 25 15 14 5
13 25 12 9 6 5 4 5 16 5 14 4 19 15 14
9 20.

6 6

I studied it. The same simple numeric code. Quickly, I did the transcription of numbers to letters.

"Love notes from your paramour?" Mr. Knox leaned closer.

I wished he'd get off my desk.

"Secret liaison, is it?" He stabbed the telegram with a meaty finger.

Of course, he'd already decoded it. And he knew these coded messages were meant for me. Did anyone else know?

I glanced up at him. "Who else knows?"

A broad grin split his face. "Why, everyone."

My cheeks burned.

"The codebreakers, that is." He grabbed the telegram from my desk. "Not the upper brass. And, of course, not the secretarial staff."

That was a low blow, even for him.

"What exactly do they know?" I steadied my voice.

"Why, Fiona." He smiled. "Surely you deciphered it." He waved the telegram, taunting me like a naughty schoolboy.

Indeed I had.

FF. Ma cherie meet me under Big Ben tomorrow at noon.

Tomorrow, Wednesday, at noon. As Mr. Knox pointed out, everyone knew what it *said*. But how many knew what it *meant*? Namely, that it was meant for me.

"Are you going?" Mr. Knox stood up.

I shrugged.

Of course I was going. My chief assignment, other than filing and brewing tea, was trailing Fredrick Fredricks to discover his latest plots to undermine Britain. If the sly fox had come out of hiding, I wasn't about to let him slip back into his hole.

"To tell Captain Hall." Mr. Knox stared at me with unblinking eyes.

He was right, of course. I should tell Captain Hall. The telegrams were obviously from Fredrick Fredricks. They were implicitly addressed to me. He claimed to need help and wanted me to meet him tomorrow at noon under the clock tower. And then there was that last line.

Do not tell anyone my life depends on it. FF

Fredricks had forgotten rather important punctuation.

"What makes you think it's addressed to me?" I avoided Mr. Knox's lecherous gaze and straightened the pencil cup on my desk.

"Don't be coy." He came around the desk and stood next to me. Right next to me. The heat of his body made me break out in a cold sweat. He was making me deuced uncomfortable, invading my personal space.

I leaned away from him. "Do you think I should?" I wasn't sure if I was asking whether to tell the captain or go meet Fredricks. No matter. I'd learned the best way to defuse a cocky man was to ask his advice.

"Personally," he bent and whispered in my ear, "I never turn down a secret rendezvous." The rascal put his hand on the back of my chair so that his fingertips touched my shoulder blade.

I felt like an animal caught in a trap.

"I'll tell you what we'll do." His sour breath smelled of coffee laced with nicotine. "I'll go with you, and we'll keep it our little secret."

I twisted in my chair. "It says come alone."

Fredricks always did have a flair for the dramatic. If his life was in danger, why come out of hiding to meet in front of one of the busiest spots in all of London? Then again, Fredricks was a master of disguise. He'd fooled me on more than one occasion. Like when he posed as an Egyptian in Cairo or a British officer in Italy.

"Excuse me." A Girl Guide appeared out of nowhere. The War Office had taken to hiring them to deliver messages and do odd jobs. They'd tried Boy Scouts, but boys had proven too unreliable, always horsing about, and disrupting the coders.

Mr. Knox took a step away from me and my desk.

What must the girl think? Probably not the first inappropriate liaison she'd witnessed at the Old Admiralty. Not that my unwelcome encounter with Mr. Knox was a liaison.

"I'm looking for Miss Figg." Rosy cheeks and pigtails, she looked the perfect darling.

"You've found her." I gave Mr. Knox the evil eye and then smiled up at the girl.

"A message from upstairs, ma'am." She handed me a folded card.

"Miss," I corrected. I took the card.

She curtsied and disappeared.

Oh dear. What now?

Captain Hall needed to see me immediately. *Why?* Had he learned of the telegrams? Was he going to reprimand me? Did he have some papers that needed filing? Or perhaps he just fancied a cup of tea.

"I have to go." I tucked the note into the pocket of my bespoke skirt and pushed past Mr. Knox. "Our little secret," I hissed on the way past, "will have to wait."

On my way up the dark wooden staircase, I thought about the telegrams. Why would Fredricks make these telegrams so easily accessible to everyone? Why would he use a primary school code? Why would he say to come alone when he had to know full well codebreakers in Room 40 were reading his messages right along with me. Indeed, how did he know his messages would reach me at all?

I was just a file clerk, if a darn good one.

When I arrived at the first-floor landing, I stopped and gazed out the window. Late January in London was dreary. Today it was not cold enough to snow, but even through the window the damp penetrated my bones like a melancholy spirit. I wrapped my cardigan tighter around my torso and continued on my way.

Was Fredricks up to his usual tricks? Or was he truly in trouble? If his life was in danger, and the telegram was the only word he could get out of whatever jam he was in, then that would explain a lot. The War Office had a brochure on every situation. No doubt it had one on what to do when your arch enemy summons you to Big Ben.

I climbed the last flight of stairs and arrived at the captain's suite. Captain "Blinker" Hall had his living quarters in a well-appointed flat on the top floor of the Old Admiralty. His office was at the head of a long hallway. My low heels tapping across the bare floor, I covered most of the distance on tiptoe, as if I needed to sneak up on the boss. I quickened my pace. Having spent the last week filing papers and fetching tea, I was ready to get back out into the field—wherever that may be. Any place, except cooped up behind a screen in Room 40.

I knocked and then entered Captain Hall's office suite. His secretary asked me to take a seat. I tucked my skirt under my thighs and sat in one of the high-backed leather chairs. The captain's office was far nicer than Room 40. For one thing, there weren't rows of messy tables and dozens of men crammed into one room. As I waited, I studied the portrait on the wall. A distinguished-looking army officer wearing full regalia stared out of the painting. His expression was stern but there was a sadness in his eyes. War took its toll on everyone, even the most committed, perhaps them especially. Something about the portrait reminded me of Archie. Perhaps it was the lock of chestnut hair peeking out from under his cap. Or the melancholy smile playing on his full lips.

Lieutenant Archie Somersby. I'd met him just over six months ago when I was volunteering at Charing Cross Hospital. We first kissed in Paris when I was dressed as Harold the helpful bellboy. Our second kiss in Vienna was a bit of a haze—all those gin fizz cocktails. In Cairo, we stood under the mistletoe at Shepheard's Hotel. And then in the mountains of Italy, he'd proposed.

I closed my eyes, recalling the scene. We were all alone in the hotel bar. He'd dropped to one knee—that irresistible lock of chestnut hair falling over his forehead—and had proposed: "I think you're a brick... and... Fiona, will you marry me?" He was holding my hand and I felt him tremble. And then the crestfallen look on his face when I'd told him to ask me again after the war.

I picked at imaginary lint on my skirt. *Do I love him enough to marry him?* With this bloody war on, would I ever get the opportunity to find out?

"Captain Hall will see you now." The secretary smiled and gestured for me to enter the interior office.

I took a deep breath, held my head high, and strode into his office.

"Blinker" Hall was a small man behind a large desk. Dwarfed by the giant window directly behind him, he looked like a child playing at being in charge. He glanced up from his paperwork and nodded. Given the nervous fluttering of his eyelashes, his nickname was apt.

"You wanted to see me?" I crossed the room and stood in front of his desk.

He didn't invite me to sit.

"I have an assignment for you." His lashes fluttered. "Infiltrate the anti-vivisectionists and find out who is their mole at Porton

Down. Someone out there is interfering with military research and feeding information to those damn animal defense people."

"Yes, sir." *Anti-vivisectionists. Good heavens. Infiltrate. Moles.* I sucked in air and begged my face not to betray my excitement. "Yes, sir." An undercover assignment. How thrilling. "Who are the anti-vivisectionists and what is Porton Down?"

"They're against vivisection." He shuffled some papers on his desk.

"Right." I nodded. "And what is that?"

"Using animals for medical research. Or in this case, military research." He looked up from his papers. "Specifically, experimenting on them, operating, cutting—"

"Yes, I see." I stopped him before he went into the gory details.

"Your primary target is Emilie Augusta Louise Lind af Hageby." He opened a file folder.

"Target?" Emilie Augusta Louise Lind af Hageby. Quite a mouthful.

"She is leading a campaign to stop our research operations at Porton Down. I need to find out who there is feeding her top-secret information." He read from a sheet of paper. "Lizzy Lind, a rabble-rousing Swedish immigrant who has taken it into her head to protect all of God's creatures." He opened his arms and waved his hands over his desk indicating the horizon. "We need animals for the war effort, horses, dogs, goats, birds. Whatever will help us win this damn war." His lashes fluttered. "She can save all the other animals to her heart's content, but not if they've been commissioned for military service."

"Yes, sir." I wasn't entirely sure what he was telling me. We need more animals for the war? Animals in military service should not be saved? "And what is Porton Down?"

"Top-secret military research facility." He tapped the stack of file folders. "I'll give you a file with the details on your mission. Bottom line. Find the mole and possible saboteur."

"Saboteur?" Goodness. This was a serious assignment. I held my head up high. Yes. I was up to the task.

"Someone is stealing animals." He jabbed his finger at a file folder. "And find out what this Lind woman is up to." He shook his head. "Appalling. She prefers animals to men."

Although I didn't see the appeal of animals myself, stinky creatures, I could understand the sentiment when it came to certain men. Still, after the horrors I'd witnessed while volunteering at Charing Cross Hospital, I couldn't countenance putting animals' lives before the lives of those poor boys on the front lines, coming back in fragments.

"As the granddaughter of King Gustav's chamberlain, we suspect she has German sympathies. Sweden's queen is German, and the king has thrown in with Germany, the fool." He tapped his pencil. "Find out if she's working for the Germans. It's possible that she's getting information from this mole at Porton Down and feeding it to the enemy. We need to know. And the sooner the better."

I narrowed my brows. "I thought Sweden was neutral in the war."

His lashes beat faster. "Yes, but the Swedish aristocracy is decidedly in favor of the Germans, and this Lind af Hageby is a noblewoman, no doubt influenced by her peers and perhaps even working as a spy for the Germans." A spy for the Germans. A spy other than Fredrick Fredricks. How exciting. I wondered what disguises might be appropriate to flush out this Emilie Augusta Louise Lind af Hageby.

"As for disguises." Captain Hall cleared his throat.

He must have read my mind. *Sigh.* No doubt he was about to forbid disguises. To say he didn't like my disguises was an understatement. *I* thought they came in deuced handy. All the great detectives wore disguises. Sherlock Holmes... well, Sherlock Holmes wore disguises. What was good for Sherlock was good for me.

He held up a sheet of paper. "Your cover identity is Lady Tabitha Kentworthy, great-grandniece of Baron Strathbogie of Atholl." He didn't meet my incredulous gaze. "A line of disgraced Scottish peerage that may or may not have died out. We're going with not. And Lady Tabitha is last of the line."

Strathbogie of Atholl. I admit, I wasn't up on my peerage, but I'd never heard of him.

"These anti-vivisectionists are wealthy ladies with too much time on their hands." He shuffled some papers on his desk. "Lady Tabitha will gain your access to them."

"Yes, sir." *Lady Tabitha.* Why did I have to be the descendant of a disgraced line? Wouldn't an honorable line do just as well?

"Did you receive the invitation to Lord Rosebrooke's house party?" Finally, he looked up.

Well, I'll be... Captain Hall was the source of the invitation. Not Fredricks.

"This gives more details of your cover and your assignment." He shoved a folder in my direction. "It has everything you need for the house party and your mission at Porton Down. Miss Lind will be at that party this weekend. I'm hoping you can root out the mole before then."

My mouth agape, I stood up and took the folder. This was not what I expected from my meeting with Captain Hall. Usually, he disdained my disguises. Now, he was authorizing one, ordering it, even. And, somehow, he'd secured an invitation to one of the most famous house parties in England. A house party that I was expected to attend in three days. Disguised as a posh lady. And he wanted me to root out a mole and likely German spy in a matter of days. I took a deep breath. My first solo assignment. I wouldn't let him down. "But what will I wear?" I said more to myself than to him.

"Whatever ladies wear these days." Still tapping his pencil, he went back to the papers on his desk. "The War Office will provide a *modest* expense account." He looked up. "Do your homework, Miss Figg. This is not your school play or idiotic Sherlock Holmes." He stabbed the air with his pencil. "This is war. England depends on you."

Sherlock Holmes is hardly an idiot. The War Office could learn from his deductive techniques. "Yes, sir." My heart skipped a beat. Finally, a real assignment. Undercover. Without Fredrick Fredricks.

"Don't dilly dally." He waved his hand at me. "Get to it." He didn't look up from his papers.

"Yes, sir." I couldn't help but smile.

"Off you go." He waved his hand again as if he were sweeping me out of his office.

"Yes, sir." Should I salute?

Busy with his paperwork, he ignored me. After an awkward moment, I trotted out of his office and back down the hallway. My heart sang as I bounded down the stairs. Finally. I'd arrived. I was a true British agent.

Now, if only I knew what ladies wore at Royal Ascot.

4

CLOTHES MAKE THE WOMAN

I assumed when Captain Hall shooed me out of his office with an "off you go," he intended me to get to work on the case straight away. I wasted no time gathering my coat, hat, and handbag, and saying ta-ta to Mr. Dilly Knox and the others. The file on my assignment tucked under my arm, I tugged on my leather gloves and waved goodbye to the men, the dirty kitchenette, and the heavy tea tray.

I was practically giddy as I left the Old Admiralty. I headed up Whitehall. As usual, the wide street was busy with motorcars and lorries carrying soldiers. With most men fighting, the few shops nearby were manned by women. Whitehall was the center of government but not shopping.

Where to first? I'd need a new ballgown, of course. And some disguises. And some intel on these anti-vivisectionists. *Do your homework, Miss Figg.* Captain Hall's voice echoed through my head. Yes. Yes. My homework. All in due time. First, the most important element of any espionage assignment. My wardrobe. *Whatever ladies wear these days.* What did ladies wear these days? And not just these days, but at the most important social event of the season, Ascot. Too bad Kitty was still in Italy. She was up on all the latest fashions. She'd know what ladies wear at Ascot. I was lucky to have any frock still in one piece after my six previous missions for the War Office. Espionage was deuced hard on the wardrobe. Less than a year in and I'd already ruined three pairs of shoes and several dresses.

I pulled the omnibus schedule from my handbag. The next bus to Brompton left in five minutes. I'd have to hop it. I picked up my pace and made it to the corner just as the bus pulled up. Winded, I dug a two-pence coin from my purse and handed it to the conductor. I took a seat in the back of the bus, far from other passengers. I didn't need prying eyes looking over my shoulder as I reviewed my assignment. *Sigh.* I wriggled out of my coat and made myself comfortable—as comfortable as I could be in the back of a stifling bus. Still, a small price to pay for the beginning of another great adventure. I laid the file folder on my lap, glanced around, and then opened it.

Emilie Augusta Louise Lind af Hageby, aka Lizzy Lind, was forty years old. In 1902, she had enrolled at the London College of Medicine to secretly document the vivisectionist practices there. She wrote a book detailing various surgeries performed on a live dog without anesthesia, including one such operation to remove its pancreas to assess whether the dog could live without it. *Good heavens. How gruesome.* I shuddered. *Fiona, get a grip. It's just a dog, for heaven's sake.* I thought of Poppy the Pekingese and how many times she'd saved my life on a mission. If science didn't tell me otherwise, I'd think she had a mind of her own.

I went back to the file. In 1906, Lizzy Lind had co-founded the Animal Defense and Anti-Vivisection Society, along with Lady Nina, Duchess of Hamilton. *Wealthy ladies with too much time on their hands.* Wealthy women. That meant luncheon parties, tea parties, garden parties, and the like. I'd need a whole new wardrobe. And hats. I'd need new hats, at least three, maybe four. I would love to have one of those new wide-brimmed velvet top hats with plenty of lace and silk. *Concentrate, Fiona.* I forced myself to go back to the file.

The Animal Defense Society had a shop and offices at 170 Piccadilly. I took note. Hopefully, I would have time after my shopping and homework to do some reconnaissance. Lizzy Lind had helped to set up veterinary hospitals for horses and other animals wounded on the battlefield. And she founded the Purple Cross Services for wounded horses. Did the War Office suspect the hospitals were a front for something else? On paper, Miss Lind sounded like a saint, not a saboteur.

"Knightsbridge," the conductor announced as the bus came to a stop.

I closed the file, gathered up my handbag, and prepared to step off the bus. Ah, Knightsbridge. I smiled as I surveyed the bounty spread out in front of me. Debenhams, Harvey Nicks, Harrods. I had my choice of department stores. What did the captain mean by *modest*? Modest was a relative term. Relative to Queen Mary, Harrods was modest. Relative to my salary, it was a queen's ransom. Liberty was more my speed. I doubted the Duchess of Hamilton would be caught dead in Liberty. No, if I was to fit in with wealthy ladies with too much time on their hands, I needed the best.

I strode toward the grand entrance to Harrods. Might as well start at the top. I rubbed my hands together. Harrods' giant dome and scalloped windows gave the regal appearance of a royal palace. Engraved over the entrance were the words *Omnia Omnibus Ubique* (All Things for All People Everywhere). Harrods really did have everything, including the newly opened "Pet Kingdom," where royals stocking their personal menageries could buy exotic pets such as lemurs or lions.

Inside, the bustle of shoppers, along with overflowing shelves of goods reaching to the ceiling, mosaic-tiled columns and intricate patterned floors, was an exhilarating assault on the senses. The entrance was abuzz with a cacophony of laughter, heels tapping, cash registers ringing, and clerks snapping bags and dropping coins. The smells of spices and baked goods mixed with the raw scent of sides of beef hanging in the meat and poultry gallery, which was one of the grandest rooms at Harrods.

I needed to lay in supplies at home. Although, even before the war, the gourmet fare at Harrods was beyond my pocketbook. Still, a little treat to celebrate my new assignment was in order. My first solo assignment. No Clifford to chaperone. At least I hoped not. No Kitty to upstage me with her forensics and foot-fighting. And no Fredricks to tease me with his flirting.

Fredricks. Given my new assignment, should I bother meeting him tomorrow? Big Ben at noon. He was still a priority of the War Office. And finally getting the goods on him, or at least learning his devious plans, could put me in even better stead with Captain Hall. It was only a twenty-minute walk between Big Ben and Piccadilly. I could meet Fredricks and then visit the Animal Defense Society, under cover, of course.

I'd need to stop at Angel's Fancy Dress Shop for some disguises. What disguises were appropriate to infiltrate an anti-vivisectionist organization? A stop at the library was also in order. My homework consisted of learning as much as I could about these anti-vivisectionists, and by extension their nemeses, the vivisectionists.

Waiting my turn, I stepped onto the moving people conveyer. The blasted thing was unnerving. I gripped the handrail and held my breath. No wonder the staff used to greet guests at the top of the bloody thing with a glass of brandy and smelling salts. Once I reached the top, I gingerly stepped off the belt and onto *terra firma*. Thank heavens. Zigzagging through the crowds, I made a beeline for the women's clothing department. By the number of patrons dressed in their finery, you'd never know there was a war on. Unless nearly four years of belt-tightening meant it was time to buy a new wardrobe. The women I passed on my way to the evening gown section were already dressed to the nines in the latest fashion. Long silk and wool frocks, smart buttoned boots, and large-brimmed hats with feathers and flowers gave the impression they were going to a fancy tea or ball even rather than spending an afternoon shopping.

I turned the corner and was surrounded by racks of evening gowns. In the embrace of the best gowns on offer at any department store in London, or perhaps the world—save Paris, of course—I nearly swooned with delight. Luxurious silk, fine wool, and waves of gabardine. The fabrics caressed my fingertips as I admired each dress in its turn.

"Excuse me, miss." The pinched tone made me turn around.

I was face to face with an imposing woman wearing a hat the size of a breadbox, its lampshade brim shading her dark eyes.

"Pray direct me to the evening bags." She held up her own beaded number.

Of course, I knew the evening bags were in the far corner with the gloves and other accessories. I shrugged. "I'm afraid I don't work here," I said in my best cockney accent.

She huffed and walked away.

Crikey. Mistaken for a shop girl. I shook my head. *I'm sorry, Blinker. But modest isn't going to cut it.* I glanced into a full-length mirror next to the clothes rack. The face I saw looking back at me was the spitting image of my Uncle Frank. Features a tad too strong to be considered feminine. It was going to take more than a Harrod's gown to turn me into a passable lady. *Ah, well, with so few available female operatives, as far as the War Office is concerned, beggars can't be choosers.*

My fingers lingered on a buttery deep purple velvet tube-sheath with a beaded bodice. *Sooo soft.* I couldn't stop petting the fabric. I took the dress off the rack and held it up. *How lovely.* I had butterflies just thinking about trying it on. I pressed it against my torso and admired it in the looking glass. Yes, this would do quite nicely. Now, if only I could find a hat and gloves to match. I gushed about hats like other women gushed about babies. A lovely black felt and fur number called out to me from the shelf. I caressed the feather jutting out from its silk band. *Why not?* I plucked it up and tapped it onto my head. A glance in the mirror gave me my answer. My countenance was too severe to be made more so by wearing mourning black. I looked like a boy playing dress-up with his mother's hat.

A salesgirl approached me, finally. She gave me a pitying look as if I were a stray cat that had wandered in off the street.

"What do women wear at Royal Ascot?" I ventured.

"Royal Ascot isn't until June." She looked at the dress I'd selected and tutted her tongue. "And that's too dark. Ladies always wear light colors and big hats, the bigger the better." She waved her hand in front of her face like she smelled something foul. "Planning ahead, are we?" She looked me up and down and shook her head.

"I've been invited to an Ascot-themed house party." I met her gaze. *And I have only three days to transform myself into a graceful, sophisticated lady.*

"Oh, my. Lord Rosebrooke's annual charity house party." She caressed my sleeve. "Those poor war orphans. Why didn't you say?" Her countenance brightened as she took me to a rack of white frilly dresses. "One of these would be perfect." She sighed wistfully as if her life's ambition was to attend such a house party. At least from then on, she was more than helpful.

I couldn't part with the purple sheath, so I added rather than substitute. I'd need to dress for several dinners and luncheons and who knew what else. After spending far too long among the hats, I settled on a gorgeous lavender flat-topped Merry Widow of gold lace, silk pile velvet, and fur, along with an adorable forest-green tam for outdoor activities, and a plain camel tricornered hat for everyday wear.

As the clerk tallied the bill, my cheeks warmed. If the War Office didn't cover the expense, I was out two months' pay. *Sigh*. It was worth it to get back out in the field as a proper British agent on her first independent case... independent of both Fredrick Fredricks and unwanted chaperones. I gleefully tucked the smallest parcel under my arm and carried the other bags in both hands. Maneuvering through the crowds of shoppers was considerably more difficult with baggage. On my way past the men's department, I nearly collided with a burly man who was equally laden with parcels. I stepped out of his way and leaned up against a display case to catch my breath.

I couldn't believe my eyes. *Speak of the devil and he shall appear*. In the men's department, none other than Fredrick Fredricks was admiring himself in a full-length mirror. He tugged at the bottom of a very snazzy turquoise waistcoat. As usual, he was clad in jodhpurs, tall black boots, and a billowy white shirt. His dark curls fell around his shoulders. He twisted this way and that, appreciating the snug-fitting waistcoat. I had to admit, I quite appreciated it too.

I ducked behind an overstuffed chair in a sitting area near the men's dressing rooms. Sliding into the chair, I sat my parcels on the floor and picked up a magazine from a side table. The latest issue of *Men's Wear Review*. I buried my nose in its pages, peeking up over the edge now and then to keep an eye on Fredricks. In fact, it was difficult to keep my eyes off him. With his broad shoulders and muscular form, he cut an impressive figure.

When he glanced around, I held the magazine in front of my

face. For all he knew, I could be just another wealthy lady with too much time on her hands waiting for her dandy of a husband as he tried on evening kit. I stared at an advertisement, wondering if it was safe to peek. *What in the world?* The advert claimed a new medical procedure could reverse aging and restore vitality—the grafting of chimpanzee... *Oh, dear.* Chimpanzee parts onto men. Monkey glands? Whatever will they think of next? And they say women are vain. I scoffed. *The anti-vivisectionists would have a field day.*

I remembered my assignment... and Fredricks. Peeking up over the magazine, I glanced around. Where was he? I dropped the magazine in my lap, sat up straighter, and surveyed the men's department. *Blast it all.* He'd done it again.

Fredricks had vanished.

5

THE STAKE-OUT

I spent the rest of the afternoon at Angel's Fancy Dress Shop on Shaftesbury Avenue. I felt right at home in a shop that had *Misfits* written on the windows above the entrance. When I was a schoolgirl, my mother used to bring me to Angel's to shop for school plays, and I absolutely loved moving among the costumes. It was like a wonderful world of make-believe. So many lovely disguises, so little time. After two hours picking out the perfect outfits, I was too burdened with parcels to stop at the library. With considerable effort, I maneuvered my packages onto the Northwick Terrace omnibus.

My stomach growled, reminding me that I'd been too busy shopping to stop for lunch or shop for provisions. A cup of tea and a stale biscuit at home would have to do. I grimaced. If I didn't eat more, my new gown would hang off my skinny frame like a flag at half-mast. As the bus approached the Wellington Arch, an idea popped into my head. What better place to take a late luncheon than in Piccadilly? If possible, across the street from the Animal Defense Society. A proper stake-out and lunch combination. Jolly good idea, old bean—as Clifford would say.

I reached up and pulled the cord. After the bus stopped, with packages bouncing this way and that, I made my way out and onto Piccadilly. At least it had stopped raining. Still, the winter sky was as gray and as unenticing as an invitation to tea from a stingy old aunt. Clamping my laden arms to my sides, I hurried up the pavement toward 170 Piccadilly and the Animal Defense Society offices.

Piccadilly was a wide avenue with motorcars and carriages speeding past in both directions. Crossing it would be a challenge. Up ahead, I spotted Fortnum & Mason's large brick building. *Should I splurge?* Lunch would probably cost me a week's wages. But I could get there without crossing over the thoroughfare. With a bit of luck, the tearoom windows faced back toward Duke Street, and I could watch the Animal Defense Society office while eating. My stomach grumbled in agreement.

The expense would be purely in the line of duty, mind you.

As I passed 170 Piccadilly, I hesitated. The entrance to the Animal Defense Society was unassuming. The wooden door sported a brass knocker and glass transom. Windows on either side of the door displayed on one side a schedule of events and on the other an anti-vivisectionist poster that read: *Stop the Cruelty, End Vivisection Now.* The image of a dog on an operating table made me flinch and look away. Head down, I continued past.

Stepping into Duke Street, I carefully avoided the puddles. Almost to the other side of the street, a motorcar splashed me with dirty water. Curses. I glanced down at my skirt. It was wet and muddy all up one side. Cold and clammy, the fabric stuck to my legs. My hands full, I couldn't brush it off or peel it off my skin. There was nothing worse than wet clingy clothes on a cold damp day.

By the time I reached Fortnum's, I was shivering. That decided it. Whatever the cost, I was going to get some fortification. Preferably something warm. Both hands full, my skirt dripping, I stood in front of the grand entrance until finally the doorman opened a door for me, shaking his head all the while. I made a beeline for the reception desk. The receptionist told me the women's lavatory was on the first floor. She clucked her tongue as she pointed to the lift. One of my leather boots was soaked through and my feet sloshed as I walked. I couldn't take tea in one of the finest tearooms in London covered in mud and sloshing around like a street urchin.

Once inside the ladies' room, I dropped my parcels and puffed out a great sigh of relief. Now to fix my clothes. There was nothing for it but to change into one of my new outfits. But which one? I couldn't very well put on my new evening gown to take afternoon tea. That left only purchases from Angel's Fancy Dress Shop.

So be it. As a dress rehearsal of sorts, I dragged my parcels into one of the stalls, stripped off my wet clothes and my boots, and opened the box from Angel's. I slipped my legs into the new trousers, slid my arms into the new white dress shirt and buttoned it up, and then tugged on the new wool vest. Waiting until another woman using the facilities left the room, I folded my wet clothes and placed them into the box. Once the coast was clear, I exited the cubicle and took up a position in front of the mirror. I removed my favorite wig and placed my new fedora atop my shorn hair. An occupational hazard. I'd had to shave off my auburn locks for my very first assignment and had kept it shaved ever since. Much easier to put on a wig that way.

Luckily, I'd bought more spirit gum at Angel's. My heart skipped a beat as I removed the new mustache from its case. I dabbed a bit of glue on its underside and then carefully applied it to my upper lip. I continued with the rest of the goatee, piecing it together around my lips and onto my chin. I added a pair of wire-rimmed spectacles—made of clear glass, of course—and then stood back and admired my reflection. Pleased, I tugged on the bottom of the waistcoat. Yes. This would do nicely.

Unless... it occurred to me that most young men my age were in uniform. I hoped one of those suffragettes didn't give me a white feather for cowardice. Still, I had to get in with the medical set. I patted my mustache once more for good measure. I could pass for one of those bright young things on the campus of Cambridge or the University College London medical school. At least that was my plan.

If only I'd bought some new shoes. I cringed as I pulled on my wet boots. Hopefully no one would look at my feet. I rummaged in my handbag, removing essentials, and tucking them into my pockets. Wallet, pencil, notebook. Unless the lads at uni had changed since I went to school, I wouldn't be needing my spy lipstick. And I'd left Mata Hari's pearl-handled pistol at home. When I'd left for work early this morning, I had no idea I'd be on a special assignment by this afternoon.

On my way to the tearoom, I checked my parcels at the cloakroom. Unburdened by packages or skirts, I attempted long manly strides across the tearoom to a table by an east-facing window. I peeked out each window along the east side until I found the best view of the Animal Defense Society. I could only see the pavement in front of the entrance, but well enough to get a view of anyone coming or going from the shop.

I took a seat at the small table by the best window. Snapping my napkin open and placing it on my lap, I surveyed the tearoom. As expected, most of the diners were parties of women, well turned-out women. And not just because it was a tearoom. With the bloody war, most of the young men were off fighting. Feeling a bit guilty, about to enjoy a fancy tea while so many others went without, I studied the menu. By now, even the best restaurants were feeling the effects of war rations. Even so, the menu offered

an assortment of delightful treats. Several varieties of black tea,
some from China and others from India. An assortment of finger
sandwiches including cucumber, egg, and smoked fish. Even a
couple of warm dishes. Welsh rarebit, one of my favorites. And
kedgeree, not one of my favorites. My mouth watered just reading
about the offerings. Still chilled from my encounter with the
motorcar, I ordered a pot of Darjeeling and the Welsh rarebit. The
waitress had turned to go when I called her back.

"And the Victoria sponge for my pudding course." I did need to
fill out that evening dress.

The waitress smiled and nodded. "Very good, sir."

I went back to looking out the window. A woman shaking out
an umbrella entered the Animal Defense Society. Too bad I didn't
have binoculars. From this distance, I couldn't see her face. But she
was wearing a beautiful burgundy coat with a lovely fur collar.

My food arrived and I tucked into the cheesy toasty rarebit.
Delicious. I washed it down with the wonderfully fragrant Darjeel-
ing. *Ahhh.* The warm meal did wonders to boost my sodden spirits.
Between bites, I stared out the window at the entrance to the
Animal Defense Society. Not much activity.

"Excuse me, sir," said the man at the next table. He was
wearing a gray suit and eyeglasses much like my own.

I glanced around. Was he addressing me?

"I noticed you're watching the ADS." He pointed toward the
window.

ADS. Right. Animal Defense Society.

Good heavens. Was I that obvious?

The man got up from his table and came over to mine. He held
out his hand. "Dr. Thomas Cutter."

I stood up and took his hand with a firm grip. "Ah... er..." I
searched out the window for help. "Frank Hightower," I read off a

sign above the entrance to Frank Hightower and Sons, Barristers. "Medical student at the University of London."

"Ah." He chuckled. "A fellow medical man." He pointed at the chair across from me. "May I?"

I nodded and we both sat down at the table.

"So, Mr. Hightower, are you a friend or foe?" He raised his brows.

"Friend or foe?" How could I be either? I'd just met the man. Careful to tuck in my pinky finger, I sipped my tea in as manly a fashion as I could manage.

"Of the Animal Defense Society?" He removed a package of Kenilworth cigarettes from his breast pocket. "Do you mind?"

I did mind. And not because I couldn't abide the foul smell of cigarette smoke. But because Archie smoked Kenilworths. A pang of longing—or was it guilt—stabbed at my heart. "Go ahead."

He held out the pack.

I shook my head. "No, thanks."

He lit up.

"Which do you recommend?" I pushed my plate away. So much for finishing my fancy lunch. "I've never heard of this animal society." Hopefully, my sacrifice would be worthwhile. Dr. Thomas Cutter seemed invested in the Animal Defense Society. Now to find out why. "Are you a member?"

He waved the idea away. "Those barmy ladies are a thorn in my side. Convincing people animals aren't necessary for science. Would they rather we experiment on people?" He jabbed the air with his cigarette.

"So, not a member, then." I tilted my head to better assess Dr. Cutter. *A vivisectionist named Cutter. How appropriate.* "Just spying on the opposition?" Tea at Fortnum's was probably not what Captain Hall had in mind when he told me to do my research. But

I might be able to justify expensing my luncheon after all. I smiled to myself.

"Spying, heavens, no." He shook his head. "Nothing so unseemly."

I furrowed my brows. *And what's unseemly about spying?* "Beg your pardon."

"I'm on rotation with other research scientists who hand out literature rebutting their baseless claims." He pulled a stack of leaflets from a satchel.

"Baseless claims?" I wanted my notebook and pencil, which were tucked away in my parcel in the cloakroom. Not that I could take notes without arousing suspicions.

"We trade in facts and not superstition." He waved the leaflets at me. "As a medical man yourself, you must appreciate our position."

"Yes, as a medical man, I do." I leaned forward. "Tell me, Dr. Cutter, how does one go about joining your group?" Wouldn't Captain Hall be impressed if I infiltrated *both* the vivisectionists and the anti-vivisectionists? Then he'd come around about the usefulness of disguises.

"We meet every Wednesday afternoon just around the corner at the Old Coffee House on Beak Street." He withdrew a card from his jacket pocket and a pencil from his satchel and proceeded to write on the back of the card. He handed it to me. "There, all the details."

Friday afternoon. Could I manage to pop in before heading out to Lord Rosebrooke's house party? I took the card and tucked it into my own jacket pocket. "Much obliged."

"Until Friday, then." He stood up and held out his hand again.

"Until then." Again, I shook it with as firm a grip as I could muster.

I waited until Dr. Cutter had left the tearoom to depart. After collecting my parcels, I made my way back outside to the bus stop, where I caught the number ten to Northwick Terrace.

Apart from bumping another passenger with my parcels, there was only one other mishap on the bus. I sat minding my own business while a young woman standing nearby glared at me all the way across town. Before departing the bus, she shot me a look. "Some gentleman you are!" she hissed at me on the way past. For the life of me, I had no idea what I'd done wrong. Perhaps navigating the world as a man was more complicated than I'd thought.

After struggling to get my packages inside the entrance to my building, I trudged into the lift and strained to keep hold of them until I reached my floor. Once inside my flat, I dropped my parcels by the door, attended to a few necessities, and then headed for the kitchen.

My luncheon having been interrupted by Dr. Cutter, I was still peckish. Tea and stale ginger biscuits would have to see me through. Waiting for the kettle to boil, I changed and unpacked my parcels. I laid my extravagant new frock on the bed and admired it. My pulse quickened as I hung my new disguises in the wardrobe. Nothing like a new persona to lift the spirits.

I pulled the small case from under my bed and knelt next to the bed while I sat the case on top. I lovingly unlatched the lid and opened the case. *Ahhh.* What a thing of beauty. My collection of facial hair. Various mustaches from thin pencil sorts to great bushy crumb catchers. The smell of spirit glue was intoxicating. Gently, I laid my new goatee in an empty compartment. I couldn't wait to use it again.

Sitting at the kitchen table munching a stale biscuit, I spread the contents of the folder out in front of me. There were two pages on Lizzy Lind, another three on the activities of the anti-vivisectionists, a page on their adversaries the vivisectionists, one on my cover as Lady Tabitha, and an envelope marked "Top Secret."

Ooooh, how exciting. I fetched a penknife to split the seam on the envelope. I was too tired to save the best for last. Perhaps Kitty Lane's penchant for starting with dessert had rubbed off on me. If the tea didn't revive me, no doubt the secrets would.

A top-secret military facility called Porton Down located outside London in Wiltshire used primarily for research and development of chemical weapons. *Blimey.* My heart sank. My ex-husband had died of mustard gas exposure. And after volunteering at Charing Cross Hospital for the last three years, I'd seen enough gas exposure to know it was the worst of the worst. If there was such a thing as a just war—and as much as I loved my country, I was beginning to doubt it—chemical weapons couldn't be part of it.

A small folded card was attached to the brief. An identification card. *Oh, my word.* I unclipped it. When I opened it, another folded note fell out onto the table. Staring down at the card, I burst out laughing. Rear Admiral Percival Arbuthnot. An identification card for Rear Admiral Percival Arbuthnot. I nearly squealed in delight.

On one side the card read:

This is to certify that Rear Admiral Percival Arbuthnot is an officer in Grand Fleet Squadron.

It was signed by the Admiral of the Fleet, John somebody-or-other. The penmanship was so atrocious that I couldn't make out the surname.

To my utter astonishment, on the other side of the card was a photograph of me. In profile, my prominent nose and stalwart chin were every bit the admiral. I touched the photograph and giggled. Where on earth did the War Office get this photograph? I'd worn my Rear Admiral Arbuthnot disguise in New York aboard Thomas Edison's yacht. And I may have slipped it on in Cairo to get into a men-only hunting club. Obviously, on one of those occasions someone had taken my photograph. I had a sneaking suspicion who. Lieutenant Archie Somersby, whose clearance level was much higher than mine. And, who, on occasion, showed up unannounced on my assignments. By "on occasion" I mean *every* time. Almost as if he were following me. Not that I minded seeing his beautiful face or kissing his lovely lips or brushing that one wayward lock of chestnut hair from his perfect forehead.

But why? Why did he always show up? Was he checking up on me? Spy spying on spy. Unfortunately, I knew why. Seeing me as an untrained lowly file clerk, Captain Hall had never trusted me.

Did the captain trust me now? Why the change of heart? As my grandfather used to say, "Don't look a gift horse in the mouth." Of course, he was a farmer and knew better. And hopefully this assignment was no gift. I'd earned it. And about time, too.

I opened the note that had fallen out of the identification card.

They're expecting you tomorrow, Wednesday, at 08.00, Admiral.
Root out the mole. Be careful.

It was signed Captain Hall. In small print at the bottom, it said:

Captain Douglas will pick you up at 06.00.

I scowled.

Did I really need a chaperone? And why so blooming early? I reread the note. *I'll be...* Captain Hall was actually ordering me to infiltrate a secret military base in disguise. Mr. "No Silly Get-ups" had changed his tune. My mind awhirl, I sat staring at the identification card and the note. After six assignments, Captain Hall finally took me seriously. Although not enough to let me go out solo.

No matter. A new assignment. Not related to Fredrick Fredricks. Exciting!

The kitchen seemed brighter, as if a screen had been lifted from my vision and for the first time the room before me appeared crystal clear. The windowsill and appliances may be covered in a thin layer of dust, but beyond the grime lay my purpose. A smile played on my lips. Forget about provisions and housework. I was a proper British Intelligence agent about to embark on a top-secret espionage mission for the War Office. My chest expanded to the point of bursting a button off my blouse. I closed my eyes and breathed in the sweet smell of triumph.

Tomorrow.

I exhaled.

Tomorrow, I become Rear Admiral Arbuthnot. Then on Friday, Lady Tabitha.

My first real assignment as a British agent.

6

PORTON DOWN

A knock interrupted my transformation. I glanced at my watch. Five in the blooming morning. I threw on my dressing gown and dashed out of my bedroom and to the door of my flat. On the way, I nearly tripped over the pile of dust sheets in the middle of my living room. I hadn't even bothered to open the curtains since I'd been back. The dark and dreary place felt like a mausoleum.

I opened the door. Clifford looked sharp in his dress uniform.

"Good lord." Clifford blushed. "You're... you're not dressed." He stood staring at my shorn head, his mouth working but his brain obviously lagging behind.

"That's what you get for being early." I looked down at my dressing gown. What was the problem? It covered nearly my entire body. Surely he'd seen a lady in a dressing gown.

"You chastise me for being late." He tapped his watch. "And now you complain when I'm early." He shook his head. "Women are so damned changeable."

"Better early than late." I patted his arm. "You think women are changeable? Just you wait."

He knitted his brows and gave me a curious look.

"Come along." I escorted him to the living room. "It will be a few minutes until I'm ready." I pulled a dust sheet off one of the upholstered chairs and gestured for him to sit.

"And why do women always take an eternity to get dressed?" He dropped into the chair, crossed his long legs, and pulled his pipe from his jacket pocket.

I wasn't just dressing. I was metamorphosing. I ignored the question.

One finger at a time, he pulled off his gloves and then bunched them up and swatted his leg. "I say, are you moving flats?"

"No. Would you like a cup of tea?" I asked, hoping to placate him.

"I'd love a coffee." He brushed imaginary lint from his knee. "If it's no trouble."

It was trouble. I was hoping he'd decline altogether. "I'm afraid it's tea or water. That's all I've got."

"Tea it is!" He gave his knee another swat.

I hurried to the kitchen and put on the kettle. I still had to dress and apply my facial hair. Admiral Arbuthnot couldn't be rushed.

While I waited for the kettle to boil, I scurried about gathering the tea, strainer, and cup. As soon as it started to steam, I poured the hot water over the tea. I didn't have time to let it steep, so I delivered it weak and watery and possibly only lukewarm.

With a smile, Clifford took the cup and saucer from my hands.

"Let it steep," I said as I skittered from the room.

I could barely keep seated. My nerves were live electric wires, sparking with excess energy. Fidgeting wasn't enough. I wanted to leap up and pace about the room. I forced myself to sit at my dressing table. Taking several deep breaths, I arranged my paraphernalia: facial hair, spirit glue, eyebrows, wig. The small spirit glue brush in hand, I painted the back of my beard, pressed it onto my chin, and closed my eyes.

From the next room, Clifford nattered on about some army expedition or other. Usually, I found his stories dreadful and boring, but this morning they were just the ticket for calming my nerves. It wasn't what he said, but the familiar rhythms and tones of his voice. With an audible exhalation, I continued my preparations.

A few minutes later, I stood before my full-length mirror as Rear Admiral Arbuthnot. White cap and uniform decorated with the gold cords and insignias of my rank, brown mustache and beard with matching bushy brows, and shiny black boots stuffed with newspaper in the toes to make them fit. I smoothed a lock of hair poking out from my cap and smiled at my reflection. I made a rather handsome chap.

When I emerged from my bedroom, Clifford was pacing the living room, glancing at his watch. Usually, he couldn't be bothered by anything so inconvenient as being on time. Why was he in such a rush today? Probably in anticipation of our tour of top-secret Porton Down.

He turned to face me. "Good lord." His face paled. With a sour look on his face, he took a few steps closer. "Fiona, old bean, is that really you?"

"Who is this *old bean* Fiona?" I said in my deepest voice and then twitched my mustache.

"I say." He burst out laughing. "You make a jolly good bloke."

"Same to you." I gathered up my spy paraphernalia: magnifying glass, notebook and pencil, small torch. I picked up my spy lipstick, thought better of it, and tucked it back into my handbag, which I left on the side table. One by one, I stuffed the items into my various pockets. Another advantage to men's clothing. Pockets.

Clifford was still laughing.

I narrowed my bushy brows. It wasn't *that* funny. "Come on." I tugged at his sleeve. "Or we'll be late."

***

Even in Clifford's new motorcar, it took forever to get out of the city.

"Fiona, old thing." Hands on the steering wheel, Clifford glanced over at me. He'd been talking nonstop since we left North-wick Terrace. "We make such a good team, don't you think?"

I nodded. "Like Ham and Bud." The comedy duo from the moving pictures.

"I was thinking more Romeo and Juliet, that sort of thing." He blushed.

"Right." I suppressed a laugh. "And look how well that turned out."

The next few minutes we passed in silence. By the time we'd turned toward Wiltshire, Clifford was back at it. Telling stories about adventures in Africa and India and in France on the front lines. Finally, the compound was in view. About time. Clifford had talked my ear off, and my mustache was drooping.

The military research facility was surrounded by a tall barbed-wire fence. On either side of the entrance stood soldiers with long rifles. Clifford pulled up to the gate. One of the soldiers came to the window and asked to see our identification. A rush of adren-aline coursed through my veins as I pulled my identification card from my breast pocket. The moment of truth. I held my breath and stared straight ahead as the soldier examined my identification. What a relief when he waved us in. Giddy with excitement, I sat on my hands to keep still as we approached the compound. The wire fence extended in both directions as far as the eye could see.

Trees lined the drive, no doubt designed to serve as camou-flage. Within a few minutes, a test field appeared and then a bunch of squat brick buildings with large windows. I craned my neck to get a better view. How peculiar. Most of the buildings had windows only on one side. Past the compound, in another field, men wearing hideous gas masks and covered head to toe in brown canvas suits ran up and down a ditch. They looked like something from a horror play. I didn't want to know. Just thinking about the effects of mustard gas turned my stomach. I'd seen too many men succumb to the horrible pain and scarring. I hoped my countrymen were engaged in defensive maneuvers and not developing ghastly inhumane gaseous weapons.

"I've heard so many whispers about this place." Clifford parked near the tallest building, which I took to be administration. "I can't wait to learn Old Blighty's best-kept secrets." He rubbed his hands together.

What was Captain Hall thinking, assigning Clifford to drive? The biggest blabbermouth in the entire British Empire had been allowed to enter our top-secret research facility. If the public didn't know what went on inside these gates, they would once Clifford opened his mouth.

"I don't need to remind you to keep these secrets." Of course, I *did* need to remind him.

He put his finger to his lips. "I'm the soul of discretion."

"The soul of confession, more like." I straightened my cap and patted my beard. "Shall we?"

He jumped out and ran around the car. But I'd already opened my door and stepped out. I couldn't have my driver going around opening doors for me. I wasn't a king. He held out his hand. I shook my head. It would be a miracle if he didn't blow my cover before we finished the tour.

"Keep your eyes open and your mouth shut." I led the way. I outranked him. He was a mere captain while I was an admiral.

As we approached the administration building, the door opened, and a young soldier greeted us. "Private Birdwhistle, at your service." He couldn't have been more than eighteen. *Poor lad.*

"I've been assigned to escort you, sirs." He stood erect and saluted. "I'm to give you a tour of all the safe areas on this side of the base."

"Are the unsafe areas on the other side?" I asked.

He put his hand to his mouth to cover a smile. "The base is nearly seven thousand acres."

"Are you laughing at me, Private Birdwhistle?" I tugged at the finger of my glove and then thought better of removing it.

"No." He cleared his throat. "No, sir." The mirth in his eyes hadn't completely subsided.

I glanced down at my person. Were my trousers on backwards? I touched my mustache.

"If you'll follow me, sirs." Private Birdwhistle gestured for us to step inside. "I'll give you a tour of the center of operations."

"How is your security?" I might as well get right to the point. My mission was to find a breach, a mole, an anti-vivisectionist plant, someone interfering with military experiments.

"Top-notch, sir." He smiled. "I can show you, if you like."

I grunted a manly "Yes."

Private Birdwhistle explained that the Royal Engineers Experimental Station was "brand-spanking-new," but already had quadrupled in size since they'd opened in 1916. "Our primary focus is chemical weapons such as chlorine, phosgene, and mustard gas." He waved his hands as we passed a row of beakers and test-tubes.

I sucked in air.

"Are you alright, Fi, er, Admiral?" Clifford asked.

I nodded. No. I wasn't alright. I was a widow due to mustard gas. My husband of only four years had died in my arms at Charing Cross Hospital. Of course, by then he had already divorced me and married his secretary. Aside from the gruesome end, I resented not getting the chance to kill the cheater myself.

Private Birdwhistle led us to the next room, where several men worked with microscopes and specimen jars. The organs floating inside were ghastly. And the smell of disinfectant mixed with misery was overwhelming. Along one wall were cages occupied by chimpanzees. Sad chimpanzees.

"I say." Clifford took out his pipe and admired the creatures. "We hunted apes in Africa."

"Apes?" I shook my head. "Really?" No doubt his partner was the great South African huntsman and all-round rotter, Fredrick Fredricks.

"I'm sorry, sir," Private Birdwhistle said. "No smoking. Flammable chemicals and all." He waved his arms at the high countertops laden with beakers and test-tubes.

"Oh, right." Blushing, Clifford stuffed his pipe back into his breast pocket.

"Why all the monkeys?" I surveyed the room, but my gaze fell on one particularly agitated chimp whose lively dark eyes reminded me of Mr. Knox. I studied the monkey, trying to determine why. Was it the spark in his eyes or the fact that Mr. Knox behaved like an ape?

"Dr. Vorknoy is developing a treatment to make us stronger, men and beast alike." Private Birdwhistle pointed toward the man hunched over a microscope. "Dr. Vorknoy, sorry to interrupt, but I have some VIPs from the War Office."

What Dr. Vorknoy lacked in hair, he made up for in bushy eyebrows and mustache. In his forties, he was an intense little man wearing a high starched collar under his lab coat. "Sergei Vorknoy, pleased to meet you." His accent was Russian with a touch of French. I surmised that he had spent time in France.

We introduced ourselves and shook hands. I gave him my manly best. The private moved from foot to foot as if he were about to bolt. "Perhaps you could tell the admiral a bit about your research?"

The doctor gave us a patronizing smile. "Of course. My xeno-transplantation involves the implantation onto a human recipient of live cells and tissues from a nonhuman animal source."

"I say." Clifford chuckled. "Can you repeat that in plain English?"

"We transplant the testicles of chimpanzees onto men to give them more vitality. Horses too." He pointed to the microscope he'd been bent over a minute ago. "Care to have a look?" So, this was the man who claimed he could provide the fountain of youth. For men, of course. And horses, also presumably male.

"Good lord." Clifford's face turned the scarlet color of a tomato. "Good gracious, no."

"I will." I bent over the eyepiece. Pinkish-purple circles filled with darker purple dots. "Slices of this rigamarole will make men, er, us stronger."

"That *rigamarole*," Dr. Vorknoy flashed a smug smile, "is highly select testis tissue that not only makes men stronger, but also more vital."

I stood up and looked him in the eyes. "A stronger class of soldier?" I asked, forcing a smile. "Is that it?"

"My work is not limited to soldiers." The doctor shook his head. "This treatment can make men of forty feel twenty again."

"Indeed." I wondered if the doctor had tried the treatment on himself. "Who is lining up for monkey glands?"

"Fi... er, Admiral... I say," Clifford sputtered, giving me a disapproving look.

"Only the most respected gentlemen in England and France." Dr. Vorknoy waved his hands as if conducting a symphony. "Lords, earls, dukes, and princes."

"I see." I surveyed the cages, wondering what the monkeys had to say about their sacrifices. "And the horses? Military animals?" I figured if the anti-vivisectionists were infiltrating Porton Down to stop this monkey business, they would be primarily concerned with the nonhuman donors and nonhuman recipients and not the silly men trying to regain their youth.

"Actually, no." The doctor glanced over at Private Birdwhistle. "Mostly racehorses."

I was beginning to sense a theme. A wealthy theme. The men who requested the good doctor's services were from a certain class, namely those who could afford it. Judging by the diamond-studded ring on the doctor's finger, I'd say he was making a killing.

"Monkey glands are good business, then?" I tugged at my glove and then thought better of it. My hands were large for a woman, still, best not take any chances.

The doctor jerked his head as if I'd hit him with a cricket bat. "Well, the procedure is very time consuming and requires expensive and nonrenewable resources."

"You mean chimpanzees?" I glanced over at the pathetic beasts. *Nonrenewable resources.* I wasn't anti-vivisection, but I wasn't a monster either.

"Excuse me, doctor." A woman in her twenties wearing a WAAC uniform held out a clipboard. "The suppliers need your signature on this invoice." She blushed and didn't meet his gaze.

"Thank you, Dorothy." Dr. Vorknoy patted her arm and then took the clipboard and signed.

I watched the exchange with interest, given my own marriage was ruined by my former husband's wandering hands where an attractive young secretary was concerned. The WAAC took the clipboard and nearly fled the room, the scent of jasmine perfume trailing her out. The doctor watched her leave. "The procedure is costly." He turned back to me. "It's labor intensive to capture the beasts."

"And expensive to transport them." A young man wearing wire-rimmed spectacles and a long white lab coat joined us in front of the cages. "From Africa."

"This is Henry Hobbs." The doctor gestured toward the young man. "He's my research assistant." Looking down his nose at us—a feat since Clifford was a foot taller—he waved a hand in our direction. "These men are from the War Office."

"Captain Clifford Douglas." Clifford held out his hand and the assistant gave it a hearty shake. "Reminds me, once my pal Fredricks and I were hunting along the Congo River when we came upon a shrewdness of apes." His eyes lit up. "It was the darndest thing—"

A shrewdness of apes, my bushy beard. "I'm sure the good doctor and Mr. Hobbs don't want to hear your hunting stories." I gave him a sideways glance.

"Unfortunately," Henry Hobbs shrugged, "they're only good for a few treatments each." He turned back to his test-tubes.

"Seems rather a waste." I peered over his shoulder at his experiment.

"Not at all." Mr. Hobbs poured yellow liquid from a test-tube into a beaker. "After we're done with them, the army uses them to test new chemical weapons and gas masks and such."

"Out of the frying pan into the fire," my grandmother would say.

"Along with goats, dogs, and birds." Private Birdwhistle was wringing his hands. "The unsung heroes of the war."

Dr. Vorknoy scowled at him and then went back to his experiment.

"Where do you get the animals?" I'd learned from past interrogations that standing just a bit too close could elicit an unguarded response.

The doctor spun around. "Do you mind? I have work to do."

I took a step back. Surly fellow, wasn't he?

"I can answer your questions." Henry Hobbs looked up from his test-tubes. "We have various suppliers. Farms, research facilities, even hospitals."

"Jäger brings most of the chimps," Private Birdwhistle said.

Dr. Vorknoy looked up from his work and glared at him. "Move along now." He waved his hand as if he could sweep us out of the room. "We have work to do."

"Perhaps we could see the other experiments?" I headed for the door, dreading what we would find on the other side. The sad monkeys were bad enough.

Private Birdwhistle scurried to overtake me. "Of course, Admiral." He opened the door and gestured us out. "Just down here, we have the chemical warfare laboratory."

My stomach did a flip. After what I'd witnessed at Charing Cross, I was appalled that anyone would use chemical warfare, especially my own countrymen. "Tell me more about how the chimps are procured."

"Mr. Jäger and his team capture them in British East Africa and bring them by boat." Private Birdwhistle bit his lip. "Some don't survive the trip."

"I visited Kalandula Falls a few years ago." Clifford hastened his pace to catch up to the private. "Before the war. We were on an expedition—"

I tugged at his sleeve.

He looked down at me, and I shook my head.

"Right." He had that hangdog look of his.

I gave his arm a consoling pat and then glanced over at the private, who thankfully didn't seem to notice.

"And the other animals?"

"Mostly local farms." The private led us to a door at the end of the hallway. "The War Office pays them but not well. My father's a farmer."

"Salt of the earth." No wonder we're rationing meat.

The private knocked and then opened the door. "This is the chemical lab." He held the door open for us.

The harsh smell of burning garlic filled my nostrils. My hand flew to cover my nose. I knew that smell. Mustard gas. That sharp odor lingered in victims' clothing. My eyes stung.

In the center of the room, two men were busy fitting a third with a gas mask.

"Gentlemen, sorry to interrupt," Private Birdwhistle said. "These men are VIPs from the War Office."

The men stopped fussing with the mask. And the wearer pulled it off, ruffling his wavy chestnut hair.

Oh, my sainted aunt. I lowered my hand to cover my mouth.

Was it the water in my eyes or could I be hallucinating?

Sitting in the center of the room, staring up at me, was Lieutenant Archie Somersby. My Lieutenant Archie Somersby. The Archie who had proposed to me... and then walked out on me. Like a black widow spider, heat crawled up my neck.

What on earth was *he* doing here?

7

THE DELIVERY

My heart was pounding. The trip to Porton Down had been more than I bargained for. I'd never expected to see Archie here. The room was stuffy, and I had to force myself to breathe. What if he recognized me? The walls felt like they were closing in on me.

In uniform, sitting in the center of the windowless laboratory, Archie was being fitted for a gas mask. *Why?* Did he work at Porton Down? He'd never told me if he did. Of course, his entire life was classified, so that shouldn't be a surprise. Frozen, he stared up at me as if paralyzed by a gorgon. Curses. He recognized me. I touched my beard. It was still attached. It was one thing to fool people who'd never met me and quite another to trick my almost fiancé. I cleared my throat as if to speak. The Admiral Arbuthnot disguise might camouflage my appearance, but there was only so much I could do to lower my voice.

Archie continued staring at me, and I averted my eyes and feigned interest in the giant sewing machine in the corner of the room. I quickly crossed the room. As I passed by Archie's chair, the scent of juniper and citrus hit me like an army tank. I inhaled deeply. Big mistake. The heady scent was as potent as a kiss and nearly knocked me over.

After exchanging awkward pleasantries with Archie, Clifford came to my side. At least he hadn't blown my cover... yet. "I say, old bean," Clifford whispered. "If you don't shake his hand, he'll think you rude."

"If I do," I hissed under my breath, "he'll blow my cover."

He bent closer and took my elbow. "Should I tell him you're out of sorts?"

"Men don't get out of sorts." I wriggled away. "Distract him while I come up with a plan." If there was one thing at which Clifford excelled, it was small talk. He could talk the hind legs off a donkey. Clifford didn't budge. "He won't bite."

What a thought. I shook the image out of my head. My mind was racing. Instead of formulating a plan to get out of this sticky wicket, I replayed every romantic scene with Archie over the past six months. I could feel his presence behind me. And the scent of him was inescapable. *If I melt into a puddle, can I disappear down the drain?* Why did he have to be so handsome? It was all I could do to resist whirling around and brushing that devilish lock of hair from his forehead. *Concentrate, Fiona.*

Last time I'd seen Archie—yes, when he proposed—miffed at my response, he'd walked out without a backward glance. If I wasn't such a rubbish skier, I would have gone after him. I hadn't said no, mind you. I'd just suggested he ask me again after the war's end. How could he expect me to marry him during this chaos and uncertainty? I supposed the war had led many couples to tie the knot precisely because of the uncertainty. But for me, not knowing whether I'd see him again or he'd be blown to bits didn't inspire romance. It was bloody terrifying. I glanced back.

Archie had twisted around in his chair and was still staring at me. My cheeks burned and I looked away again.

"Do I know you?" he asked. His voice penetrated my clothing like a winter gale.

Clifford chuckled, and I stomped on his foot.

"Ouch!" He stuck out his lower lip like a scolded schoolboy.

I bit my lip, unsure whether in my present agitated state I could conjure my tenor voice.

Archie stood up. "Admiral Arbuthnot, was it?" He flashed a crooked smile, but it didn't reach his eyes. "We've met before." He strode over and stood next to me. "Good to see you again," he said a little too loudly.

I elbowed Clifford. "Why don't you volunteer to try that new gas mask?" I shooed him away. Sulking, he obliged and approached the two lab technicians who had been working with Archie.

For a few awkward seconds, Archie just stood there blinking at me. He leaned closer. "What in God's name are you doing here?" he hissed through clenched teeth.

So, he did recognize me. Drat. "What gave me away?" I'd thought my disguise one of my best.

"The first time I kissed you, you were wearing that silly mustache, remember?" He smirked.

Trouble was, I did remember... all too well. I stroked my mustache. Far from tacky, it was one of my best pieces.

"What are you doing here?" The way he glared at me, you'd think we weren't on the same side, let alone practically engaged.

"I could ask you the same." I swallowed hard. My only consolation was that for once, Lieutenant Archie Somersby wasn't one step ahead of me. He was asking me what I was doing instead of telling me. For once, Captain Hall hadn't informed him of my mission. And as usual, the captain hadn't informed me of his either.

"I'm testing gas masks," he said stiffly.

"When did you get back?" As far as I'd known, he was still in Italy. Obviously, seeing me wasn't his top priority upon returning to London.

"A while." He refused to look me in the eye. "Why don't you get on with your mission, and I'll get on with mine." He ran a hand through his wavy hair.

A while. How long is a while? My heart sank. He hadn't bothered to contact me. My palms were sweating, and I wanted to bolt.

"Strictly professional, remember?" Finally, he looked at me. His eyes were hard as steel.

"Let me explain—" My lips trembled as I tried to get the words out.

"Still traveling with *him*, I see." He jerked his thumb toward Clifford.

"Who?" I glanced around. "Clifford?" At the sound of his name, Clifford looked up.

"I could hardly believe it." Archie shook his head.

"Believe what?" He knew full well that Captain Hall always sent Clifford as my chaperone, wanted or not. So, what was his problem with Clifford?

"This is neither the time nor the place." He turned on his heels and left me sputtering in his wake. At the door he turned back and glanced from Clifford to me and back. "Good luck to you."

What was he on about? Why was he so angry? I hadn't said no, I'd just asked to wait. Was it so unreasonable to want to wait until after this bloody war ended? I closed my eyes. I couldn't think of marriage now. I hadn't been divorced or widowed for even a year. It was too soon. I sucked in a jagged breath. *Get a grip, Fiona. You're a British agent, for heaven's sake, not a lovesick schoolgirl.* The pain in my chest tested my resolve. Why couldn't I have said yes like a sensible person? *I've ruined everything.*

Raised voices coming from the hallway jolted me out of my mourning. The two men who had been fitting Archie with the gas mask went to investigate. With Clifford in tow, I followed them out into the narrow hall. There, Private Birdwhistle looked on while Henry Hobbs argued with a man built like a Shetland pony, short and stocky with a red cap clamped atop his long brown mane. On a strap of his coveralls, he wore the navy and gold pin issued to civilians working on war service. The man stood behind a cart laden with cages. Inside the cages were more chimpanzees. The man gesticulated as he spoke in a loud booming voice. "Tell Dr. Vorknoy he'd better pay up or—"

"Or what?" Mr. Hobbs scoffed. "You'll go to the police?"

The man's square face turned red. "Or he'll be sorry."

"Is that a threat, Jäger?" Mr. Hobbs lunged at the man. "How about *I* go to the police?"

Mr. Jäger, the man who supplies the monkeys.

In a huff, Mr. Jäger tossed an invoice at Mr. Hobbs and marched down the hall and slammed the door on his way out. Gobsmacked, I watched as the invoice floated to the floor.

"I say." Clifford stood next to me, chewing on the stem of his unlit pipe. "What was that all about?"

"I don't know," I whispered. "Something dodgy is going on at Porton Down."

Obviously, Dr. Vorknoy owed Mr. Jäger money and hadn't paid for his latest deliveries. And Mr. Hobbs had something on Mr. Jäger and was threatening to go to the police. And what of Mr. Jäger's threat? *He'll be sorry, how?* Clearly, Mr. Jäger wasn't working with the animal activists—unless he was deep under cover as a hunter. How about Mr. Hobbs? Was he working with the anti-vivisectionists? Could he be the mole? He *was* eager to tell me about Dr. Vorknoy's experiments and certainly more forthcoming than the doctor. Had I detected a critical note in his tone when he'd mentioned that retired chimps were subjected to chemical weapon tests?

"Is everything alright, Mr. Hobbs?" I said as I approached him.

Clipboard in hand, he counted his new inventory, checking off various boxes as he went. I leaned in to get a look at the clipboard. From what I could see, it was an intake form with basic information about the animals.

"Just peachy," he said, his voice dripping with sarcasm. "That man is a menace." He gritted his teeth. "To man *and* beast."

Did Private Birdwhistle just crack a smile? What did he find amusing?

I made a mental note. Mr. Hobbs called his supplier a menace to beasts. I observed him carefully to get a bead on his attitude toward said beasts. He was in such a foul temper, stewing and steaming, he barely glanced at the poor creatures as he filled out his forms.

Clifford bent down and peeked into one of the cages. "Who's a pretty girl?" he cooed at the monkey.

I shook my head. "How do you know it's a girl?" I examined the chimp to see if its sex was obvious from his vantage point.

"Just look at those eyes." Clifford poked his finger through the bars of the cage. "Good girl." Good heavens. The way the man fussed over animals, it was a wonder he could go around killing them like he did.

"Sir," Private Birdwhistle said. "You shouldn't—"

"Ouch!" Holding his finger, Clifford reared back and hit the wall behind us. "The rotten cur bit me."

"You do have a way with the ladies." I tried to lighten the mood.

The private gave a little snort.

Clifford scowled and put his finger in his mouth. *Egads.* Downright unhygienic. If Mr. Hobbs hadn't been there, I would have insisted Clifford go wash the bloody thing rather than suck on it. Instead, being a manly man, I looked away and bit my tongue.

"Private, be a good fellow and deliver these cages to Dr. Vorknoy." Mr. Hobbs thrust the clipboard at him.

The private tightened his lips but took the clipboard and pushed the cart down the hall toward the doctor's laboratory.

"Isn't your tour over yet?" Mr. Hobbs stuck his pencil behind one ear.

"I say," Clifford huffed. "There's no reason to be rude."

"With all due respect, *sirs*, we're doing crucial research here and don't have time to babysit the upper brass just because they need a bit of entertainment on a Wednesday morning." He flashed a fake smile. "Now, if you'll excuse me." He turned and disappeared back into the lab.

"Why, the nerve." Clifford clamped his teeth around the stem of his pipe. "That's no way to talk to a lady."

"What lady?" I too found the behavior appalling but what could we do? Clifford probably thought he had to defend my honor or some old-fashioned romantic notion about the so-called "weaker sex." I was tempted to order him to hold out his finger so I could show him a thing or two. "I don't see any lady... unless you count your monkey girlfriend." Even she had been removed from the scene.

"I have half a mind to report him," Clifford puffed.

"Horsefeathers." I tugged at his sleeve. "Come on. Let's investigate."

Clifford and I had been left quite alone. Questionable security at Britain's top- secret military facility if you asked me. But it would give us a chance to explore, off the leash, so to speak.

As we continued down the hallway, I peeked through the windows in each room along the way. When the door had no window, I gingerly tried the doorknob. If the door was unlocked, I opened it a crack and stole a look inside. So far, every room was either occupied or locked, and I didn't think it a good idea to let anyone catch us wandering unescorted or we'd no doubt be escorted off the property.

"Fancy a drink?" Clifford tagged along as I searched the building. "Or a bite to eat?"

"After we finish here." My stomach grumbled, obviously in agreement with Clifford. We couldn't let this opportunity go to waste. Glancing both ways, I continued down the hallway.

The next room was dark. I put my face to the glass, shaded my eyes, and peered through the door lite. Rows of glass cabinets held brown and green bottles of all shapes and sizes. Put me in mind of the drugs dispensary at Charing Cross Hospital. I suspected these bottles contained more lethal potions. My first alter-ego, Dr. Vogel, an expert in poisons, could have a field day. If only the door wasn't locked.

At the end of the hall, a door stood ajar. I peeked inside. An office with a desk and filing cabinets. The room was vacant except for the lingering scent of jasmine perfume. Dorothy. This must be her office.

"Stand guard." I patted Clifford's arm.

"And what should I do if someone comes?" He was as whiny as a feverish child.

"Stall them with your witty conversation." I smiled sweetly. "Play to your strengths."

"I say," he said softly, blushing. Jolly pleased with himself, he tugged on the bottom of his jacket and stood at attention near the door.

I headed for Dorothy's desk, which I might add was nice and tidy. I nodded my approval. Next to her typewriter sat a stack of invoices. I picked up the one on top. An invoice marked paid for live animals, including that latest shipment of chimps. I committed the page to memory and quickly made my way through the stack, page by page. Each invoice had a familiar seal at the top. The royal seal used by the War Office with its lion and unicorn and banner. "God and my right" in French. I'd always wondered why the British War Office had a French seal.

Fredrick Fredricks once asked me: "Is an act right because God loves it or does God love it because it is right?" Whatever the answer, I'd often wondered about the "my" in the royal seal. Surely even the king couldn't count his right on par with God's.

I was three pages into the stack when I heard Clifford clear his throat. I stopped shuffling papers and listened. High heels clacked in the distance.

"Lovely morning, isn't it?" he called out.

It was decidedly *not* a lovely morning. I quickly returned the papers to their proper places and straightened the stack. I raced across the room toward the door, glancing around the room as I went. I didn't know what I was looking for, but perhaps something would jump out at me. Hopefully not a live animal.

I joined Clifford at the threshold.

A tad disheveled, Dorothy straightened her skirt and tucked in stray hairs. When she saw me, she quickened her pace.

"There you are, Dorothy." My voice cracked. "Please thank Private Birdwhistle for us." I concentrated on steadying my tone.

"You're leaving already?" She looked past me into her office. Her lipstick was smudged. What had she been up to? "Where's Birdy? He's not supposed to leave guests unattended."

I shrugged and adjusted my cap. "And bid adieu to Dr. Vorknoy."

At the mention of the doctor's name, she flushed. "Adieu," she repeated.

Adieu. Oh, my word. I nearly choked on my goodbyes. The

image of the invoices flashed before my mind's eye. Some dodgy business going on here.

Dieu. The royal insignia.

Dieu et mon droit. God and my right.

The inscription beneath the royal seal. And yet, the inscription on those invoices said "*Diue et mon droit.*" *Diue* and not *Dieu*.

Obviously, the invoices were fakes… and the forger needed spelling lessons.

Dodgy business indeed.

8

THE MEETING

By the time Clifford and I got back to the Old Admiralty, it was nearly noon. The overcast sky had gone from a hazy gray to an oppressive white, and a chilly breeze assaulted my cheeks as we walked from the motorcar to the entrance. I wiped my watering eyes with the back of my hands. I thought of Archie's steely gaze, and it wasn't only the wind that made me cry.

Clifford chattered on about what he planned to eat for lunch at the canteen. Ignoring him, I mentally rehearsed what I planned to say to Captain Hall. Under the pretext of giving him a report on my findings at Porton Down, I would pump him for information about Archie. When had he gotten back? What did he mean by a while? Yesterday? A week ago? If Archie was back in London, was Kitty back, too? If so, why hadn't I heard from her either?

Clifford held the door open for me and I slipped inside. The relative warmth of the foyer was a welcome change. And so were the high ceilings and marble columns. Much nicer than Porton Down. Unfortunately, once I adjusted to the temperature, I'd be cold again. With war rations we never seemed to have enough coal to adequately heat the building. But some heat was better than none.

"What about you?" Clifford looked at me expectantly.

"What about me?" I shook the chill off.

"What will you have at the canteen?" He narrowed his eyes. "Haven't you been listening?"

"Of course I have, Clifford dear," I lied. "Save me a seat and I'll meet you there in a few minutes." I had to satisfy my curiosity first... right after a much-awaited stop at the ladies' lavatory. I'd been holding on rather than use the men's room at Porton Down.

Clifford nodded and trotted off toward the canteen.

Although there were gents' lavs on every floor, in the whole of the Admiralty, there was only one ladies' lav, and it was in the basement. I hurried down the stairs and burst into the lav. Two Girl Guides stopped their chitchat and stared at me. I pushed past them.

"Mister, this is the ladies'," one said.

I mumbled apologies as I ducked into a stall.

"You can't be in here," the other chimed in.

"I'll be out in a jiff." I latched the door.

"We're going to report you." The bathroom door slammed shut and I was left in peace. Thank goodness.

Climbing the grand wooden staircase to Captain Hall's top-floor office, my heart was pounding, and not only from exertion. I stopped in front of his office door, tugged on my jacket, and adjusted my hat. Patting my facial hair, I stepped inside.

"May I help you, sir?" Captain Hall's secretary didn't recognize me.

"I'm here to see Captain Hall." I glanced around the office. The burgundy carpet, wooden paneling, and spacious luxury gave it an air of security.

"Do you have an appointment?" she asked.

"No, but I have an important report from the field." I didn't know whether to reveal my true identity. I had no reason to hide it from her.

"I'm afraid Captain Hall is out for lunch at the moment." She gave an apologetic smile. "Might you come back in an hour?"

"Righto." I nodded and took my leave. If I couldn't satisfy my curiosity about Archie, I might as well attend to my stomach.

The canteen was a cavernous space with a high ceiling and wooden beams. It smelled of boiled cabbage and baked lard and was buzzing with military men and a few women and Girl Guides. Or should I say, the men were buzzing around the girls. A chalkboard announced today's special, fish and potato pie, cabbage soup, and suet pudding. For excitement, the canteen staff had recently moved bean soup and treacle pudding to Wednesdays. Today, they had made an exception.

At least I could look forward to a bit of fish in the gluey pastry and mutton fat in the pudding. "Save the wheat, defend the fleet" meant the pastry could be made of sawdust or who knew what. As Clifford liked to remind me, it was a damn sight better than the bully beef and rock-hard biscuits they ate in the trenches.

Since officers had their own dining room next door, Clifford and I were the only officers in the main hall. He was chatting up the lads sitting at his table. Always chipper. Good old Clifford. When he spotted me, he smiled and patted a chair next to his.

I fetched my lunch, such as it was, and then joined him. He was in the middle of a story about our adventures with Mata Hari in Paris last autumn—emphasis on *story*. Only half listening, without bothering to remove my winter coat, I tucked into the thick pastry and bits of fish, washing down every bite with a swig of strong tea.

As Clifford nattered on about the Grand Hotel, I couldn't help but think of Archie. For it was there in Paris that he'd first kissed me. I'd been disguised as Harold the helpful bellboy, and he'd been my contact from British Intelligence. *Sigh*. Even then, I couldn't fool Archie. He'd known it was me from the first. The trickster didn't let on. He'd let me think... *Oh, Archie. How can I repair the damage I've done?*

I pushed my plate into the center of the table. My appetite had flown. I drained my teacup to quench the desperation rising in my throat. If only I knew what was going on. What had I done? Surely Archie couldn't be so angry at me just because I didn't want to discuss marriage until after the bloody war.

Clifford tapped me on the shoulder. "A penny for your thoughts."

"They're not worth a penny."

"I was just going to introduce you to the lads." He gestured across the table and then rattled off their names. He turned back to me. "And this is my dear friend, Fi, er, Admiral." He blushed.

"Arbuthnot," I said, coming to his rescue. If I was such a dear friend, the lads must be wondering why he'd forgotten my name.

"You're slumming it too," one of the soldiers said, popping an entire biscuit in his mouth. "More birds in here than the officers' mess." He chuckled and his friends joined in. "Have you seen that blonde in records?" He whistled. "She's a dish."

Glancing at my watch, I took that as my cue to leave. Half past twelve. Hopefully Captain Hall had returned from lunch. If not, I'd escape the lads' lewd comments and wait in peace with my thoughts for company.

Captain Hall's secretary instructed me to wait. She pointed to three chairs lined up against the far wall. Mentally refining my nonchalant inquiry into the exact date of Archie's return to London, I took a seat. "Strictly professional." I'd never said that. I'd merely told him to ask again after the war. By the time Captain Hall returned from lunch, I'd chewed on that bone until my jaw was sore.

"Sorry to keep you waiting, Admiral." The captain narrowed his eyes and stared at me. He clapped his hands together with a great guffaw. "Astonishing." He held out his hand. "Admiral Arbuthnot, I presume."

I stood up and shook his hand. "At your service, sir."

"By God, you're good." His face broke into a grin. "Really good." I'd never seen him so amused. Shaking his head, he led me into his office. He sat behind his desk, and I sat in the chair across from it. He held out a small case to me. "Cigar?" he said with a chuckle.

"No, thank you." That's where I drew the line in proving my manliness.

"What did you discover at Porton Down?" He snipped the end of a cigar with a special cutting apparatus. "Did you find our mole?"

"I'm not sure." I removed my cap. "But there's something fishy going on over there."

The captain's eyelashes fluttered like a hummingbird's wings. No wonder the men called him "Blinker."

"A Dr. Vorknoy is experimenting on chimpanzees. He procures the animals from a fellow named Jäger. There's no love lost between them. In fact, a Mr. Henry Hobbs, the doctor's assistant, had words with Mr. Jäger, whereupon Jäger threatened him." I troubled the insignia on my cap. "The paid invoices for the animals were forged." I fiddled with my hatband. "On War Office stationery."

"I see." Captain Hall's countenance had gone from sunny to cloudy in a matter of seconds. He snubbed out his cigar in an ashtray. "Any sign of anti-vivisectionist infiltration?"

"Not that I could confirm, but I suspect Mr. Hobbs could be our man."

"Do you think he's behind the forged documents?"

"I don't know yet, sir." I shook my head. "My suspicions are just based on vague feelings at this point."

"Women's intuition?" He cracked a smile. "Good work, Figg. Keep after him."

"Yes, sir." I curled the end of my mustache around my index finger. "Might I ask you, sir, when was Lieutenant Somersby recalled from Italy?"

"We pulled him out at the same time we recalled you." He glanced down at a calendar on his desk. "What was that, about two weeks ago?"

"Ten days, sir." I bit my lip. Archie had left Italy when I did, but he didn't bother to tell me or contact me once he got back. "What about Kitty?"

"My niece." He was blinking out regular morse code. "Yes, Kitty is still in Italy putting the finishing touches on Operation Fugazi." He tilted his head. "Why do you ask?"

Operation Fugazi was Archie and Kitty's clandestine assignment, above my security level and below my tolerance for deceit. It involved that horrible Mr. Mussolini and his well-paid espionage work for MI5.

"Curiosity." Truth be told, I missed the girl. At this moment, I didn't know how I felt about Archie. Just the mention of his name pierced a hole in my heart.

"Lieutenant Somersby told me you were invaluable to the success of the Italian mission." Captain Hall tapped his pencil on his desk.

My assignment in Italy was to follow Fredricks. Only by accident had I become involved in Operation Fugazi. How was I invaluable? I did solve the murder of Mr. Mussolini's double. But I couldn't bring myself to turn the killer in. Poor child. Instead, Fredricks had taken the rap. *Thank you, Fredricks.*

Captain Hall cleared his throat. "On his recommendation I put you up for the service award."

"Archie recommended me?" Now I was blinking. Until this morning—when he'd given me the cold shoulder—I hadn't seen Archie since Italy. He must have recommended me before I refused, er, postponed, his proposal.

"Kitty will finish up in the next couple of weeks." The captain waved his pencil. "By then, you should have found the mole."

"Yes, sir." I tried to keep a stiff upper lip.

"Find out what you can at Lord Rosebrooke's house party this weekend." Deep in thought, still blinking, Captain Hall sighed. "His daughter Lady Sybil and that Lizzy Lind character are in cahoots on this animal mischief. You need to get to the bottom of it, Miss Figg."

"Yes, sir." *Good heavens. The house party!* I still had to finish shopping and pack. Friday was right around the corner, and Lady Tabitha Kentworthy had better be ready to hobnob with London's posh set.

"Captain Douglas will escort you for the weekend." He waved his hand. "He will have the expected donation for the War Orphan Fund."

"Clifford!" *Oh, bother.* I did not need an escort, especially not busybody Clifford.

"Yes, Captain Douglas." He leveled his gaze. "Is there a problem?"

"No, sir." Such was my lot. I was stuck with him.

"If there's nothing else, Miss Figg." He waved again as if shooing a pesky insect.

"No, sir." The captain couldn't answer the question burning my heart. Why had Archie given up on me? I trudged back downstairs, marched across Room 40, and went straight to my desk. When I passed his workstation, Mr. Dilly Knox did a double take. I didn't acknowledge him but quickened my pace. I felt his presence behind me. *Sigh.* I was not in the mood for his high jinks.

"Go away," I said without turning around. "Leave me alone."

He caught up to me. "Is that you, Miss Figg?"

Blast. I hadn't bothered lowering my voice. I whirled around. "Rear Admiral Arbuthnot," I said in my best tenor. "I outrank you, so go away."

Mr. Knox burst out laughing. His round face reddened with amusement. "Admiral... *Rear* Admiral." He could barely get the words out. "*Rear* Admiral." He gasped for breath. "Why, Miss Figg, you make an exceptionally handsome man." He winked at me. Cheeky cad.

"I'm not in the mood." I continued to my desk, dropped into my chair, and unbuttoned my winter coat.

"Maybe later?" He chuckled and cracked his knuckles.

Sigh.

"Was your beloved Fredricks fooled by this get-up?" Pointing at my uniform, he looked me up and down.

I narrowed my eyes. "Fredricks?" Why was he asking about Fredricks?

"What did he have to say for himself?" Mr. Knox sat on the corner of my desk. "Secret meetings at Big Ben."

Good heavens. I'd completely forgotten about the telegram and Fredricks.

"I was half-tempted to go myself." He raised an eyebrow.

I gaped at him. Curses. How could I have forgotten? I glanced at my watch. It was almost one. Would Fredricks wait for me?

"Spill it. What happened?"

I jumped up from my desk and hurried out of the room. Mr. Knox pursued me as far as the door. "Where are you going?"

"Classified," I called back as I crossed the threshold.

Fifteen minutes later, I was standing under Big Ben surveying the plaza, on the lookout for Fredricks. For all I knew, he was in disguise. And what if he didn't recognize me in mine? I couldn't believe I'd forgotten to meet him. Wallowing in self-pity and indulging lovesickness was not beneficial to espionage. I needed to learn to better control my emotions and not let them interfere with my work. I paced up and down in front of the clocktower. By the time the clock struck two, I was shivering. My teeth chattered as I walked around the tower one last time before giving up and heading to the bus stop.

I'd missed my chance at Fredricks. And who knew when he'd surface again?

9

THE VISITOR

After a quick stop at my flat to change clothes and adjust my facial hair, I headed out again. Any excuse to get out of my depressing digs. I'd missed Fredricks, but I wasn't about to miss the vivisectionists' meeting. Dr. Cutter had told me they met every Wednesday afternoon at the Old Coffee House on Beak Street. I checked the bus schedule and planned my route to Beak Street.

What name had I given him? *Crikey.* Keeping track of my aliases was going to be difficult. I scrunched up my face, trying to remember. Give me any document and I could take a mental photograph and recall it perfectly. My own flights of fancy were quite another matter. I'd nicked it from a sign across the street from Fortnum's. I closed my eyes and conjured the letters on that sign.

Aha. Yes. Frank Hightower and Sons, Barristers. I'd told Dr. Cutter that I was Frank Hightower, a medical student at the University of London. I'd have to be sure to tell him that I was just beginning my studies, otherwise, he might wonder why I knew nothing about medicine—unless you counted the lessons on poisons before my first assignment as Dr. Vogel, a toxicology expert.

To my surprise, the Old Coffee House wasn't a coffee house at all, but a public house. Most of the clientele were coppers, many of them women. The Old Bill, a training center for police, was across the street. And recently, so I learned, they'd started a program for women police officers. I glanced around the pub. The ceiling was painted red, and the walls were covered in sketches of royals holding court. Strange juxtaposition with the rowdy coppers drinking beer. The pub was dark, making it difficult to spot Dr. Cutter and his vivisectionists.

As my eyes adjusted to the dimly lit pub, I saw a man waving at me from a corner table. *Aha.* Dr. Cutter. I joined the group. Around the table sat seven men, all wearing dark woolen suits and ties. I'd interrupted the medical men in the middle of a heated conversation. My arrival didn't stop their passionate speeches in support of vivisection, or their disparaging remarks about the Animal Defense Society.

"If those women had their way, we'd still be in the dark ages," Dr. Cutter said. The other men nodded in agreement. "They just don't understand the progress we've made thanks to experiments on animals. There is no other way to learn about the human body. Cadavers can't tell us anything about medicines to cure the living. Only animal experimentation can do that."

They continued in this vein for the next hour when none other than Dr. Vorknoy joined them. Dr. Cutter introduced him as a pioneer in animal experimentation. I stared down at my hands, hoping to heaven he didn't recognize me from Porton Down. Dr. Vorknoy gave a very long and boring speech that came down to him repeating how brilliant and successful he was. Even the other doctors seemed put out by it. After they'd finished and the group was breaking up, Dr. Vorknoy approached me.

"Don't I know you?" he asked.

"No, sir, I don't believe we've met." I didn't meet his gaze.

"You look exactly like an admiral I met this morning." He shook his head. "Uncanny."

"Perhaps you mean my brother, Rear Admiral Percival Arbuthnot."

"That's it!" He slapped me on the shoulder. "But isn't your name Hightower?"

"Half-brother. We share a mother." I dug myself deeper into a hole.

"You're a medical man." He lowered his voice. "Explain the importance of our work and keep him out of my way." He slapped me again, only this time harder.

I nodded and then glanced around for an escape route. What a relief to get out of that pub and out into the brisk air. I was glad to be away from Dr. Vorknoy and his associates, but apart from planning a protest with speeches in front of the Animal Defense Society and arranging to hand out leaflets, apart from Dr. Vorknoy's threats, the vivisectionists seemed harmless enough—except to their animal subjects, of course. I left the meeting with a new appreciation for the importance of animals to human survival, but not much to advance my mission.

My facial hair was itching like the dickens. I couldn't wait to get home and remove it.

* * *

Sitting at my dressing table, I carefully peeled off my mustache. "Ouch." My skin was red and angry underneath. An allergy to spirit gum was deuced inconvenient. When I finished removing my facial hair, my face looked like a perfectly cooked roast beef. My stomach growled, reminding me I hadn't eaten since, well, since lunch. I bemoaned my empty cupboards but didn't feel like going back out to the greengrocer. Out of biscuits and milk, plain black tea would have to do. Soon I'd run out of that. Then the only sustenance left would be the bottle of Scotch whiskey Andrew left when he moved out—and in with Nancy. Empty flat. Empty heart. Thank goodness for work.

A nice warm bath would lift my spirits and hopefully distract me from the hunger pangs. While the bath was running, I hung Rear Admiral Arbuthnot in the back of my wardrobe. I smiled to myself. My little assortment of disguises gave me goose bumps. And this assignment was perfect for incognito espionage. I could continue my snooping at Porton Down as the rear admiral. Medical student Frank Hightower could attend more vivisectionists' meetings. And then there was Lady Tabitha Kentworthy. I fingered the buttery velvet of my new gown. Friday would be here before I knew it.

I might be doomed to a loveless life eating stale biscuits, but I'd never be bored. Since I'd become a spy, my life had been one adventure after another—always with the admonition from my boss, "No silly get-ups." So now I planned to make the most of Captain Hall's blessing to use "silly get-ups." He'd seemed rather impressed with Rear Admiral Arbuthnot. I brushed my hand across my porcupine hair. Maybe Blinker was coming around to see the value in a brilliant disguise.

After adding a few drops of rose bath oil, I turned off the tap and climbed into the bathtub. Sinking slowly into the warm water, I closed my eyes. *Ahhhhh.* Nothing like a warm bath after a chilly day. *Sigh.* The beauty of the bath was that it calmed my nerves and settled my mind. The trouble was when my nerves were calm and my mind settled, my imagination ran wild. And when my imagination ran wild, it inevitably ran headlong into Archie. Curse him. Recommending me for an award and then snubbing me. What in heaven's name happened? Had he met someone else? I'd just seen him in Italy. He couldn't have had the time. Scrubbing my burning chin, I managed to take my mind off the handsome Lieutenant Somersby. As my grandfather always said, "One nail takes out the other."

I forcibly turned my thoughts to my assignment. I had yet to infiltrate the Animal Defense Society, but I had attended the vivisectionists' meeting at the Old Coffee House, where I'd learned only that women police officers now outnumbered men. Of course, with most able-bodied men away fighting, that was true in most walks of life. I was lucky my line of work allowed me access to both the worlds of men and of women. And this assignment was especially full of both. After my bath, I'd make a list of my personae and where they belonged. Frank Hightower to Dr. Cutter. Rear Admiral Arbuthnot at Porton Down, where I had discovered some monkey business with the invoices. I hadn't found the mole. But I had some suspicions. Day after tomorrow, I'd create Lady Tabitha Kentworthy.

If I was to become Lady Tabitha, I needed to study my backstory. Lady Tabitha. Great-grandniece of Baron Strathbogie of Atholl. I'd glanced at the page on Lady Tabitha. To test myself, I closed my eyes and tried to reconstruct it from memory. Conjuring the paper in my mind's eye, the letters and words appeared as if I held the sheet in my hands—although since I was in the bath, it was handy that I didn't.

Lady T's history went as far back as the fourteenth century when John Kentworthy was taken prisoner during the English invasion of Scotland. He was hanged in London on gallows thirty feet higher than normal to signify his high status. His body was burnt, and his head fixed on London Bridge. *How horrible.* I reared up out of the bathtub, splashing as I went. Grabbing a towel from the rack, I dried myself and wrapped my shorn head in another smaller towel.

I slipped my feet into my slippers and padded my way into the bedroom where I threw on my robe and cinched the waist. Conjuring the file again, I continued studying Lady Tabitha's backstory. Lady T's branch of the family had lived in London for the last century, no doubt avoiding that section of London Bridge. Her parents died in a boating accident when she was eight and she was raised by a spinster aunt. And although she'd been out in society for the last decade, she was at risk of following in her aunt's footsteps. I knew how she felt. I'd been married, but it had been years since... I padded into the kitchen, put on the kettle, and then sat at the table with the folder that contained my assignment and cover. I read the page on Lady Tabitha to confirm I'd reconstructed it accurately. Of course I had.

A loud thud from the hallway interrupted my concentration. Someone was at my door. Why didn't they just knock? I wasn't expecting anyone.

I adjusted my robe and went to the door. Opening it a crack, I peeked out.

"Fiona." The voice was strained.

I opened the door.

His head hanging, Fredricks slumped against the doorframe, panting. "Ma chérie." He looked up at me with dark pleading eyes. *What in the world?* "You're a vision of loveliness."

As usual, he was wearing an oversized tweed riding jacket, khaki jodhpurs, and knee-high black boots. All that was missing was his slouch hat. With his long black hair pulled back into a ponytail, and the white frills of his shirt sleeves poking out of his jacket, he put me in mind of D'Artagnan from *The Three Musketeers*.

I tightened my robe. "What are you doing here?" I'd never seen him so disheveled.

"When you didn't come..." His voice trailed off. "Where were you?" He sucked in air.

"I'm not at your beck and call." I didn't tell him I'd been so preoccupied with Archie that I'd forgotten. "And you're a German spy, remember."

"You're a British spy and I don't hold that against you." He gave me a weak smile. "Aren't you going to invite me in?" Grasping the doorframe, he looked past me, and I glanced around to see what he was looking at. When I did, the towel on my head came loose and fell around my shoulders.

"Why should I?" I squinted at him.

"Because you've missed me." He tightened his grip on the doorframe, and I was face to face with his panther insignia pinky ring.

"Don't be cheeky." I rewrapped the towel around my hair, or lack thereof. "Why are you here? What do you want with me?"

"I thought you'd never ask." His voice was hoarse. "Want with you?" He smiled. "Everything. I want everything." Holding his right side, he stumbled backwards.

"What in heaven's name is wrong with you?" I looked him up and down. *Oh, my sainted aunt.* Droplets of blood dotted the carpet. And a streak of red ran up the right side of his jodhpurs.

"You're hurt." I stepped closer and gingerly opened his jacket. "Good heavens." His lacey white shirt was soaked red.

"Shot, I'm afraid." He shrugged and gave me a baleful look.

"Shot!" My pulse quickened. "You need a doctor."

"No doctors." He waved a hand at me. "No authorities. German spy, remember?"

"Who shot—"

"I'd love to tell you the whole sordid tale." He cut me off. "Right after I regain consciousness." The color had drained from his face.

I took his left arm, careful to avoid the blood streaking down his right. "Let's get you inside."

"Thank you, ma cherie." He leaned against me. "You're a sweet angel."

"And you're a cheeky devil." I helped him inside and then kicked the door closed behind us. "Try not to drip on my carpet." I led him into my bedroom. What else could I do? I could wash the bedding. The same couldn't be said for my upholstery.

"At your command, I would stop my heart from beating." He took a step and winced. "If I could."

"No need for drama." His arm around my shoulder, I sagged under his considerable weight. "Getting shot is quite enough drama." Was it my imagination or was his grip a bit tighter—and lower—than necessary? The pressure of his hand on my upper ribs reminded me that I was wearing only a thin silk robe.

His breath was quick and warm on my neck. The scent of sandalwood and danger wrapped me in its heady embrace. By the time we reached my bed, we were both panting. Whether from exertion or the proximity of our bodies I couldn't say. I deposited him on the bed. He dropped onto the mattress with a moan. He reached out, took my hand, and pressed it to his lips. "Fiona, ma chérie." He leaned back and rested against the pillows, taking my hand with him. "Seeing you like this is more lethal than any bullet." He gazed up at me. "Your beauty is a dagger through my heart." His eyes pulled at me with such intensity that I jerked my hand away and took a step back. My hand tingled with the lingering sensation of his touch.

"Fiona, are you alright?" He sat up. "You've gone white as an Arabian oryx."

"I suppose that makes you a jackal." I squared my shoulders. I was not about to become prey for the great South African huntsman. When I crossed my arms over my chest, the skin of my forearms met the skin of my... torso. My cheeks caught fire. My robe had come open. I shut my robe and retied the sash tight around my waist.

"All good things." Fredricks lay back against the pillows again. He grinned and then groaned.

I didn't know whether to kiss him or kick him. I opted for helping him out of his jacket and shirt to assess the damage. His smooth muscular chest was deuced distracting. I leaned over to get a closer look at the wound. He took hold of the corner of the towel around my hair and unwound it. "I like your hair short."

"Nonexistent, more like." I snatched the towel away from him. "Now I know you're pulling my leg."

"And a very nice leg it is." He looked me up and down and grinned. If he weren't injured, I would have pummeled him with a pillow.

"Use this and apply pressure to the wound." I handed him the towel—one of my favorites. "I'll go get some supplies. You stay put." When I turned to go, he grabbed the end of the sash and pulled it loose. "Behave, or I'll shoot you myself."

"I don't doubt it." He chuckled and then winced. "You've done it before." That wasn't quite true. In the Viennese Alps, he'd convinced me that I'd shot him so he could make his escape in an ambulance. Tricky devil. In fact, if I hadn't seen the bullet hole with my own eyes, I might have suspected this was another one of his ploys.

The blood seeping through my favorite towel encouraged me to hurry. Fredricks was putting on a good face—quite a handsome face, truth be told—but he was losing a lot of blood. I knew from volunteering at Charing Cross Hospital that his injury was serious.

I dashed about the flat gathering supplies: more towels, needle and thread, and Andrew's bottle of Scotch whiskey. When I returned to the bedroom, Fredricks was splayed out on the bed, motionless. I rushed to the bedside and sat my burden on the nightstand. "Fredricks?" Holding my breath, I put two fingers on his neck and felt for a pulse. He was alive. Thank goodness. I exhaled. "Fredricks?" No answer. He was unconscious. I poked his shoulder to make sure he wasn't faking it. Not a peep.

Now what? He was a big man and moving him would take all my strength. I gritted my teeth and, mindful of his wound, pulled his arm to roll him on his good side. With great effort and much grunting on my part, I got him turned onto his left side and then stuffed pillows and towels behind him to keep him there.

As fast as I could, I fetched the chair at my dressing table and dragged it over to the bedside. My bedroom was not an ideal operating chamber, but it would have to do. Biting my lip, I doused the wound in whiskey. If that didn't wake him, nothing would. It had to sting like the dickens. I dipped the needle into the bottle and covered it with alcohol. My shaking hands made it difficult to thread the needle. I hoped he didn't mind pink thread. It was the first one I had grabbed.

I dried the area around the wound with a fresh towel. Luckily, the bullet had only grazed his side. Unluckily, I was going to have to stitch him up. Pinching the wound shut, I took a deep breath, and made the first stitch. I'd never stitched a man before. How different could it be from stitching a pair of trousers? For one thing, trousers didn't moan and flail about. Halfway through, Fredricks let out a yelp.

"Quit complaining." I let the needle fall and took up the whiskey. "Drink this." I held the bottle to his lips. "I've heard it's a decent analgesic." Being a near teetotaler myself, I wouldn't know.

His lips parted slightly, and he obeyed. I dabbed beads of sweat from his forehead and offered him another drink. Once he had settled, I took up the needle again. Only a few more stitches.

Another deep breath and I pierced his skin for the fifth time. By my count, only three left to go.

"Fiona, ma chérie." He groaned. "You know how much I adore," he sucked in air, "and admire you," he said through his teeth.

"Hush." I couldn't let him distract me. "You're delirious."

"Your proximity *makes* me delirious."

I stabbed him again.

He grimaced. "Be careful, ma chérie."

"Hold still then." I was being as careful as I could under the circumstances. A beautiful half-dressed man on my bed. A needle in my hand. Blood spreading across my duvet.

"Not with me." He winced. "With that bastard at Porton Down."

He knew about Porton Down? "What bastard?"

Dr. Vorknoy? Henry Hobbs? Mr. Jäger? Archie?

"Who?" I touched his arm. "What do you mean?" I leaned in closer. "Fredricks?"

No response. He was unconscious again.

10

BREAKFAST IN BED

Throughout the night, I got up hourly to check on my patient. He was restless and delirious, but alive. Between visits to the bedroom, I camped out on the Queen Anne camelback sofa I'd inherited from my grandparents. I spent the night sneezing from all the dust. Needless to say, I didn't get much sleep. By dawn, I was completely knackered and had decided to cancel my appointments for the day. At a decent hour, I planned to call Clifford and beg off our lunch date. And I would call the War Office and tell Captain Hall that I was sick and had best stay in bed.

Of course, my bed was occupied. And by a German spy, no less. But I wasn't about to tell Captain Hall. First, I wanted to find out what Fredricks was up to, how he got shot, and by whom. For all I knew, someone from the War Office had shot him. Heck. It might have been Archie. Fredricks insisted Archie was a double agent and Archie, well, he hated Fredricks. Just last month in Italy, Archie shot at Fredricks and might have killed him too if I hadn't pushed him out of the way, catching a whiff of the bullet myself in the process. Why I'd taken a bullet for Fredricks I'd never know.

My plan was to get Fredricks in shape to interrogate him and then find out what he knew about Porton Down. Before he'd lost consciousness last night, he'd tried to warn me about someone at Porton Down. When he woke up, I aimed to learn everything he knew. And if he tried to get coy with me, I'd rub salt in his wound. Literally. Provided I had any salt.

I checked on Fredricks. He was sound asleep, his broad chest heaving up and down. Still alive. Good. Tiptoeing to my wardrobe, I slowly opened its door and retrieved a loose-fitting day dress. I glanced over at my patient. On second thoughts, today I would wear something a bit nicer. I exchanged the plain dress for a tailored green wool one with a pretty, black velvet waistband. Careful not to wake Fredricks, I crossed the room to my dressing table and collected my favorite strawberry-blonde bob from my wig rack.

I stood for a moment and watched Fredricks sleep. Seeing him lying there, his raven locks falling over his bare shoulders, his full lips parted, and his tanned cheeks pink with sleep, he looked more like a romantic poet than an enemy spy. Even poets must eat. And my empty pantry couldn't sustain a hibernating bear, let alone a strapping huntsman on the mend.

Retreating to the loo, I attended to an abbreviated version of my toilette and put on my clothes. To mark the occasion of having Fredricks completely at my disposal, I added a bit of rouge, a brush of eye kohl, and a swipe of lipstick. I even dabbed rosewater on my wrists and behind my ears. Enough vanity. I had to get to the market and back before Fredricks awoke. I threw on my coat, hat, and the only footwear ready to hand, Rear Admiral Arbuthnot's boots. I could feel my heart beating as I descended the stairs. Why I was so excited about a trip to the greengrocer was beyond me.

At the corner market, I picked up a can of peaches, a jar of marmalade, and a pint of milk. Unfortunately, with oranges in short supply, the marmalade was made of carrots. Carrots, potatoes, and a futile longing for fresh fruit and vegetables were the only things not in short supply. Next stop the bakery. Thanks to the Bread Order last year, the only bread available was day-old war bread. Oh, what I wouldn't give for a nice croissant or even a slice of regular white bread. They did have a lovely cake sold in dense slices made with raisins and currents. By lovely, I meant square.

I had just reached the entrance to my building when I remembered coffee. I didn't drink the foul beverage, but no doubt Fredricks did. I dashed back to the grocer and bought a packet of soluble coffee powder. I'd never tried the stuff but had heard it was popular in the trenches. I did know how to boil water, which is all the skill the brew required.

Balancing packages on my knee, I struggled to retrieve yesterday's post from its cubby in the foyer. I dropped the mail into one of my shopping bags. After slogging my purchases in and out of the lift, I labored to hold onto the packages and dig the key out of my handbag. Trying not to make too much noise proved difficult. Especially when my parcels fell to the floor with a thud. I unlocked my door, scooped up the parcels, and headed for the kitchen to deposit my bounty. While there, I put the kettle on to boil. Then I went to check on my patient.

Quietly I peeked into the bedroom. *Oh, no!* My heart sank. The bed was empty. Fredricks was gone. I should have known better than to leave him unattended. The blackguard had disappeared on me so many times before. With his injury, he couldn't have got far. Now what? Should I go out looking for him? I didn't know where to start. Unless he left a trail of blood, I had no chance of finding him. He was the expert tracker, not me.

I dropped onto my bed with a great sigh. *Curses.* I shouldn't have left his side. I should have tied him to the bedpost. Who knew when he'd show up again? I put my head in my hands. Lack of sleep and loss of my prisoner weighed on me. Alright, not a prisoner, but still.

I had him incapacitated and at my mercy. Or so I thought. *Blast him.* When I got my hands on him again, I planned to—

"There you are." His voice startled me. "I wondered where you got to."

"What are you doing up?" I wiped my eyes and smoothed my wig. "You'll reopen your wound."

Fredricks stood in the doorway, one of my bath towels wrapped around his waist, cutting a fine figure of a man. Fascination drew me to him like a moth to a flame. I tried to avert my gaze but couldn't. For my own self-preservation, I must restrain my overactive imagination—although the small bath towel left very little to the imagination. Even his legs were tanned and muscular. And his feet. His feet were beautiful.

Fiona. Get a grip. For crying out loud. The man's a rogue, not to mention your enemy.

"I missed you." His smile widened.

"Yes. Well." I cleared my throat. "I went to get some groceries." At least I had a good breakfast to look forward to. Still, I doubted food would quell the peculiar hunger in my belly at present.

"Brilliant!" He joined me at the bedside. "I'm famished." When he sat down next to me, the heat of his freshly bathed body caused me to jolt off the bed. Had he used my rosewater? Cheeky cad.

The kettle whistled. Just in the nick of time, too. "I'll make us some tea. Unless you prefer coffee?"

"What I *prefer*," he said with a sly smile, "is just out of my reach, I'm afraid." His hand brushed against my hip, and I jumped back. "More's the pity." He lay back on the bed. "Coffee will have to do."

I scurried away. When I was out of sight of the bedroom, I leaned against the wall to catch my breath. I put a palm to my forehead. Downright feverish. I'd survived a close call. Too close. The huntsman was moving in. And I was his prey. I didn't know how much longer I could resist. I had to interrogate him and then get him healed up as soon as possible. The longer he stayed, the more my virtue was in danger. I had been married, of course. But I hadn't... ahem... in a long time. A very long time.

In the kitchen, I took out my best china: the set my mother had given me as a wedding present. I laid two placemats on the dining room table and added silverware from another wedding present. When everything was just right at the table, I placed slices of fruit cake on a plate and war bread in the toaster. I even found a tiny silver spoon for the carrot marmalade. No amount of dressing up would make it a true substitute for thick-cut orange. But it was all we had. I prepared a cup of tea for me and coffee for him and then stood back, admiring the table. Rubbing my hands together, I went to fetch Fredricks.

When I stepped into the bedroom, he gave me a sheepish look. Wrapped in my bathrobe, he lay back against the pillows, holding his side. My robe barely covered his torso. The sleeves hit him at the elbow. Luckily, he'd covered the lower portion of his body with a blanket.

"I told you." I went to the bedside. "You should have stayed in bed." I pulled back the robe to reveal the wound. Sure enough, it was seeping. I shook my head. "Stay put!" I hurried to the lavatory to fetch a towel and a gauze wrap.

When I came back, his mischievous dark eyes danced as he watched me rewrap his wound. I pulled the gauze extra tight, and he yelped. Served him right. Now our beverages would be luke-warm. Nothing worse than lukewarm tea.

"Get dressed." I straightened my frock. "Some breakfast and you'll be right as rain."

"I'm afraid my clothes are soiled with blood." He pointed to the stack of neatly piled clothing sitting on the floor next to the lavatory door. "Perhaps I should take your advice and stay in bed." He tilted his head with a question in his eyes.

My answer was to turn on my heels and head back to the kitchen. So much for my lovely table. I tucked my post under my arm and arranged our breakfast onto two trays, which I delivered one by one to the bedroom. "Don't get used to this kingly treatment." I sat his tray on the nightstand and mine on the dressing table along with my mail. "Do you have everything you need?" I waited for his reaction, hoping he was pleased.

"As long as you are here, ma chérie." He took a slice of cake. "Yes. Yes, I do." He tucked into the cake and coffee with gusto. "Please join me." He waved his hand toward the dressing table. "I hate to eat alone."

I happily obeyed. Twisting around in my dressing chair, I managed to get a comfortable angle from which to enjoy my toast and tepid tea while keeping an eye on Fredricks. Watching him devour his breakfast was more satisfying than polishing off my own.

When I'd finished my toast, I picked up my spoon and stirred my tea and contemplated how to bring up Porton Down. Fredricks knew something, but what? I couldn't risk telling him more than what he already knew. Now, how to turn the breakfast conversation to Britain's secret military testing facility. *Have you heard about the new chemical warfare they're trying out on goats out at Porton?* My lashes fluttering as fast as Blinker's, I studied Fredricks. What was he really up to and how did he get shot?

"You still haven't told me who shot you." I sipped my tea. "And that warning you gave me right before you passed out... a bast—er —danger to me." Had he been at Porton Down? Had he seen me there? Did he know about my mission? The blackguard was always one step ahead of me. I narrowed my gaze. This time, I planned to turn the tables. He was, after all, incapacitated in my

bed. I'd never get a better opportunity to take advantage of him...
professionally.

"Your countrymen insist on hunting me down like a dog." He
shook his head. "No doubt you would consider the man who shot
me a patriot." He winced. "As for Porton Down. It is a dangerous
place full of dangerous men committing every manner of atrocity."

"If you mean mustard gas, may I remind you that the Germans
invented it and used it first." I sat my teacup back onto my saucer
with a rattle.

"That, ma chérie, is a juvenile rationalization befitting a child."
He waved his hand. "No matter who invented the heinous chemicals, it is morally reprehensible to use them."

"I wholeheartedly agree." I thought of poor Andrew gasping
for breath, his beautiful face deformed from the wretched stuff.

"That is why we should work together—" He raised his arm
and then retracted it again with a yelp, the color draining from his
ruddy cheeks.

"Enough." I held up my hand. "You need rest." Fredricks was
always going on about how we should work together to stop the
war. Not only was the idea ludicrous—what could the two of us do
to stop a Great War that had been raging for years?—but also, we
were on opposite sides, for pity's sake.

He held his side and closed his eyes. "Perhaps you're right." His
voice was weak.

I bit my lip. Should I bring a doctor? Fredricks had asked me
not to, but what if he died? A pang of guilt stung my heart. I'd be to
blame.

"Don't worry, ma chérie." He flashed a smile. "I'm as hale as an
ox," he said, as if reading my mind. "You won't be rid of me any
time soon."

To distract myself, I took another sip of tea and sifted through
my meager post. One pink envelope stood out among the adverts

and notices. I could tell from the flowery cursive handwriting that it was from Kitty Lane, my erstwhile espionage partner and Captain Hall's adopted "niece." Unbeknownst to me, he'd assigned Kitty to work with me on the New York mission, as if I needed a helper. An enigma, Kitty was as delicate and silly as any finishing-school girl and yet a fierce foot-fighting spy with a knowledge of forensics.

As I tore open the envelope, I got a whiff of lavender perfume. *Crikey*. Had the girl spritzed the stationery?

> *Dear Aunt Fiona,*
>
> *We've almost completed our task and I can't wait to get back to London and see you and Poppy. Please tell Poppy-poo that I love her and miss her and can't wait to cuddle her and kiss her adorable little nose.*

By *task* she meant our last assignment in the Dolomites of Northern Italy. Or should I say *her* assignment. Kitty's security clearance was obviously higher than mine. She had stayed behind to finish briefing Mr. Mussolini on his work for British Intelligence, MI5—a plan I thoroughly disdained. Why our government was paying a man like that was beyond me. And I only knew the half of it. I hated to think...

By *Poppy* she meant her spoiled Pekingese, currently under the care of favorite "uncle," Clifford. And while I did not disdain the little creature, I did find her manners questionable. As to kissing the dog's nose, I found the image disgusting. Furthermore, I didn't approve of the girl's run-on sentence. She would do well to spend more time on grammar and less time flirting.

Archie talks about you constantly. It's like the grand inquisition.
He's asking me how you feel about him. If you ever mention him.
If he has a chance with you. He's as bad as a lovesick schoolgirl.

By *Archie*, she meant my... *my what*? My *almost* fiancé? My pulse quickened. *Archie.* That lock of chestnut hair falling over his forehead. His crooked smile. Those sea-green eyes. That smooth... I stopped myself from sending my fantasies in a direction they had no business going. Especially since he wasn't speaking to me. Why hadn't I just said yes? I glanced over at Fredricks and then went back to Kitty's letter.

Truly, it gets so tiresome. To make him stop, I told him that you
and Uncle Clifford eloped yesterday and got married in a secret
ceremony in Surrey.
Until soon.
All my love, Kitty

"What!" I sat my teacup down with a bit too much force. A brittle sound told me I'd cracked the saucer. "Blasted girl. How could she?"

"Let me guess." Fredricks smirked. "The irrepressible Miss Kitty Lane."

I scowled at him. Irrepressible indeed.

"What does your darling niece have to say for herself?" Sipping his coffee, Fredricks leaned back into the pillows.

"She's not my niece, wretched girl." Kitty called me "Aunt Fiona" except when she was in a pique and then she'd remind me that I wasn't really her aunt.

"Now, now." Fredricks tilted his head. "Kitty is a very clever young woman and a worthy adversary." He raised his eyebrows. "Second only to you, of course, ma chérie."

Worthy adversary my tepid tea.

Fredricks wriggled his fingers at me. "Let Uncle Fredrick see what's upsetting you so," he said in a mocking voice.

I shook my head but read the letter aloud, nonetheless.

"Eloped. Secret wedding in Surrey." Fredricks howled with laughter.

I could strangle the rotter... and the wretched girl too. No wonder Archie was angry with me. I stood up and paced the length of the room. Archie didn't believe it, did he? He couldn't. He wouldn't. He knew how I felt about him. I took another lap around the bedroom. How *did* I feel about him? We'd seen each other only a handful of times, always on assignment, occasionally undercover and in disguise, a stolen kiss in a stairwell, a farewell embrace held a bit too long, accidentally brushing hands as we worked. But did I love him?

Our last reunions had made me question everything I knew about him. In New York, he'd killed a man in cold blood. A German spy. And on orders from the War Office. But still. In Northern Italy, he'd been involved in some rather shady business with that Mussolini character that left me queasy. Confident in our shared sense of duty, lately, I was forced to ask, duty to whom or what? King and country? Truth and justice? Peace and freedom? Or duty for its own sake? And more to the point, at what cost?

Archie talks about you constantly. He's as bad as a lovesick school-girl. I couldn't imagine Archie as a lovesick schoolgirl. Still, learning he had thought of me gave me a pang. Thought of me *past tense* thanks to Kitty's sick prank.

"Sit down, Fiona." Fredricks moved over and patted the bed next to him. "You're making me queasy."

"Sorry." I dropped onto the bed next to him.

"Lieutenant Somersby is a fool if he believes you've eloped

with that ninny Clifford." Fredricks took my hand. "Anyway, he doesn't deserve you."

I pulled my hand away. "And you do?"

"Lieutenant Archie Somersby is not what he seems." Fredricks shook his head. "He's a dangerous man." He tried to take my hand again, but I stood up and moved out of his reach. "I wish you'd believe me."

"Why should I?" He'd deceived me too many times for me to ever trust him.

"Because I'm in love with you, ma chérie." His voice was unusually soft and baleful.

Horsefeathers. His romantic charade was getting old. He couldn't love me, for heaven's sake. The idea was absurd. And even if he did... I wiped tears from my eyes with the backs of my hands. "So much the worse for you." I turned to face him and squared my shoulders. "I'm in love with Archie."

11

THE ANIMAL DEFENSE SOCIETY

Between Kitty's letter and the strong tea, I was quite revived and ready to start my mission. Resolved not to let Fredricks interfere with my work, I left him stewing in my bedroom and steeled myself to begin my assignment. Today, I would infiltrate the Animal Defense Society as ordered. I couldn't have Captain Hall thinking I stayed in bed all day. I'd call him back and tell him I was fit for duty. I wasn't about to muck up my very first solo assignment. No. I must make this mission a great success and prove to Captain Hall that his faith in me was not misplaced. And if Archie didn't know me well enough to know that I'd never elope with Clifford, then so be it.

Locking the bathroom door, I ran a hot bath. I did my best cogitating in the bath. I opened a new bar of rose-scented soap and added a few drops of rosewater to the tub. As I soaked, my mind returned to Fredricks's warning. Why was he always insisting that Archie was a double agent and dangerous? True, Archie had tried to frame him in New York and had shot at him in Italy. But surely Archie was no more dangerous than any other patriotic soldier with a sidearm. And what of Fredricks himself? Him calling

Archie dangerous was the Camembert calling the Manchego "cheese."

Fredricks was a renowned German spy and suspected poisoner. Why should I believe a word he said? The cad was toying with me. Getting me confused. Testing my loyalties. I scrubbed the backs of my arms with a sponge. He wouldn't get the best of me. I scrubbed harder. No. I'd show him. My forearms were as red as lobsters by the time I finished.

As I completed my toilette, I planned my wardrobe. What would Lady Tabitha Kentworthy wear for a day in town? I had just the thing. A smart forest-green serge with a sweet collar of chamois-colored satin with matching belt and trim atop quaint gathered pockets. Unfortunately, Lady Tabitha probably didn't wear practical Oxfords. I would have to break out my button-up boots—they *were* adorable, if not exactly comfortable. And for a hat, always the most difficult choice, my brown velvet cloche or perhaps my wide-brimmed boater trimmed with roses. Better yet, my veiled cadet-blue halo. Yes. That would add an air of mystery. And soften my angular face.

By the time I emerged from the bathtub, I was giddy with delight. I couldn't wait to perform the transformation from plain old Fiona Figg, file clerk and erstwhile spy, to Lady Tabitha Kentworthy, wealthy woman of the world and protector of beasts. Trouble was that my clothes were in the wardrobe and the wardrobe was in my bedroom and so was Fredricks. I wrapped a towel securely around my torso and another around my head. I peeked in the bedroom to assess the situation and plan my route to the wardrobe.

Fredricks was sound asleep. With his ruddy cheeks pink with slumber, his ebony curls flowing over the pillow, his bare arms stretched above his head, his long lashes caressing his lower lids, and his full lips looking utterly kissable, he was the picture of masculine beauty. I stood admiring him for a few seconds before tiptoeing to my wardrobe to fetch Lady Tabitha. Carefully, I opened the wardrobe door, stopping abruptly when it creaked. My heart skipped a beat and I glanced back at Fredricks. He hadn't moved. With a sigh of relief, I soundlessly retrieved the day dress, halo hat, and buttoned boots, and then made a hasty retreat.

"No need to rush on my account." The voice stopped me in my tracks.

I glanced around. Hands clasped behind his head, muscular arms forming two perfect triangles to frame his glorious locks, his dark eyes heavy with sleep, he smiled over at me.

"A vision of loveliness." He sighed. "If only I could wake up to such a vision every morning, I'd die a happy man."

"If you don't stop flirting, you may get the chance, and soon." I pulled a face and then darted out of the room.

"Another cup of coffee in bed?" he called after me. "Or perhaps tea for two?"

Cheeky rogue.

I ducked back into the loo and assembled Lady Tabitha, adding a good dose of face powder, rouge, and eye kohl. *Blast.* I'd forgotten to get my wig. Staring back at me in the mirror was an exaggerated mask of an actress preparing for her stage debut. After I'd finished dressing, I hurried to the kitchen to prepare a quick cuppa. As I put the kettle on, I noticed the file folder and its contents spread out on the counter. I gathered up the papers and slid them back into the folder.

Now where to hide it? I couldn't have Fredricks reading classified documents from the War Office and learning about my clandestine mission. I looked around the kitchen. Where could I put the folder that no one would look for it? I opened the oven and placed the folder on the top rack. He'd never look there.

Pleased with my hiding place, I finished making my cup of tea and also prepared a ghastly cup of coffee for Fredricks, placed them on a tray and took them through to the bedroom. I sat the tray down on the nightstand.

"Thank you, ma chérie." Fredricks caught my wrist. "You smell divine, my sweet peach." He inhaled deeply. "And you're too altogether good to me."

"Yes, I am." I pulled away. But not in time to avoid the warm tingling of his touch that traveled up my arm and caused my neck to burn and a fire to ignite in my cheeks. I retreated to the dressing table with my cup. Between sips of tea, I adjusted my favorite blonde bob and fastened it with pins to what little hair I had left.

"Having tea with the queen, are we?" Fredricks asked with a wink. "Or are you meeting your beloved Lieutenant Somersby?" He smirked.

"None of your business." I tugged on a pair of ivory-colored gloves. "I'll be back in a few hours. While I'm gone, get some rest so we can get you back on your feet." And out of my flat.

He tilted his head. "Tired of me of already?" He patted a spot on the bed. "Perhaps I can find a way to repay your kindness and earn my keep," he said with a wink.

I rolled my eyes. Insufferable man.

How could I keep Fredricks from fleeing? How could I keep him here? I couldn't very well lock him up. As I stepped out of the bedroom, I spotted the pile of clothes stacked neatly next to the lavatory door. Fredricks's clothes. I smiled to myself. He couldn't very well go out into the streets naked. I glanced back and when I was sure he couldn't see me, I hastened to scoop up his clothes. On the way to Piccadilly, I'd drop them off at the laundry. They needed laundering. And what better way to keep Fredricks captive?

My assignment papers well-hidden and Fredricks rendered without the means to escape, I left the flat confident I would finally get the best of the bounder.

* * *

I exited the bus a few streets from the Animal Defense Society lest someone see me. A proper Lady wouldn't be caught dead on a city bus. Or in a laundry, where I dropped off Fredricks's soiled clothes. Luckily, the overcast skies hadn't burst into rain yet and my brisk walk to Piccadilly warmed me up. In fact, when I reached the building, I dabbed beads of perspiration from my brow. I stood for a moment under the awning to catch my breath and adopt the persona of Lady Tabitha Kentworthy. Closing my eyes, I inhaled deeply just as Mrs. Benson, my acting teacher at North London Collegiate School for Girls, had taught me to do before a performance. *And to think, my father said my acting studies wouldn't pay off.*

Mustering an aristocratic air, I opened the door and stepped inside. As I did, a bell tinkled. I surveyed the empty reception area. The small room was dark and dank. The walls were adorned with hideous illustrations of animals on operating tables, a long table held various stacks of flyers and pamphlets, and in the back of the room was a desk sporting a telephone, a typewriter, and one wooden box marked "in" and another marked "out."

An attractive matronly woman in her late thirties or at most forty bustled in from a back entrance. "May I help you?" She was all pleasantry and smiles.

"Lady Tabitha Kentworthy," I said, putting on a posh accent.

"Happy to meet you." She held out a pudgy hand. "Lizzy Lind, co-founder of the Animal Defense Society." Lizzy Lind had kind eyes and the lovely demeanor of someone eternally cheerful. Her chestnut hair was piled on her head like a great bird's nest. And she wore a gorgeous claret-colored satin blouse with a high collar and a ruffle down the front. Across the collar hung a gold chain with fantastical dragons on either side. Her fitted jacket and matching skirt were a deep purple wool that made for a bright contrast with her shirt in a most amiable fashion. I'd never thought of putting red and purple together. Jolly clever.

I gave her hand a little shake. "I'm interested in joining the Animal Defense Society."

"You've come to the right place." She went to the desk and sat down behind the typewriter. "We ask for a donation of your choice, which you may put in this envelope." She handed me a small brown envelope. "While I take down your details."

My details. Good heavens. What was Lady Tabitha's address? Certainly not my own humble residence in Northwick Terrace. "Perhaps you could tell me a bit about the society first?" As I fished in my bag for a donation, I racked my brain for a suitable residence for a Lady living in London, and an excuse for not giving out too many details, for example a fictious street number. How much would a posh lady donate?

"Of course." Lizzy Lind looked up from the typewriter. "My pleasure." She launched into the evils of vivisection and animal cruelty. It was all too gruesome for words. I wished I hadn't asked. When she stopped to take a breath, I ventured another question. I made a great show of depositing a week's wages into the brown envelope and sliding it onto the desk. "Have you heard of this monkey glands doctor?" I tugged off my gloves one finger at a time. "I saw an advert in a magazine. Ghastly business."

Her eyes lit up. "Indeed." She stood up and came around the desk. "Dr. Vorknoy is his name. I've met him. Vile man. What he does to those poor chimpanzees." She shook her head and clucked her tongue. "I have no objection to vivisection provided the vivisectionists experiment on themselves." She gave me a sly smile.

"Indeed." I couldn't help but smile in return. These anti-vivisectionists had a point. Even if we needed animal experimentation to better understand ourselves, there was no reason to be cruel. Animals should be given the same pain relief as humans.

The doorbell tinkled and I turned to see a sandy-haired boy and his father enter the reception area. The boy's eyes were red and puffy. His father pushed him at us. "Timmy, tell the nice ladies."

The boy bit his lip and looked up at his father and then over at us. "They want to take Star and get him killed fighting over there in France."

"Star?" Lizzy asked. "Is that your horse?"

The boy nodded. His father patted him on the head.

Lizzy turned to me. "The War Office commandeers horses from farmers and lords alike, even beloved pets and prize racehorses are sent to the trenches." She opened the top drawer of the desk and took out a piece of stationery. She smiled at the boy. "Let's write a letter to the War Office, shall we? Timmy, is it?"

"Yes, ma'am. Then I can keep Star?" The boy's eyes lit up as he wiped his nose on his sleeve.

"We shall see." Lizzy slipped the stationery into the typewriter. "Better yet." She yanked the paper out again, took up a pencil, and handed it to the boy. "Can you write?"

He nodded again.

"Perfect." She slid the stationery across the desk. "It will be more persuasive coming from your own hand." She coached the boy as he scrawled crooked letters across the page.

"Will it work?" the father asked. "Timmy's not eaten so much as a pasty since they sent the order." He ruffled the boy's hair.

"Let's hope so." Lizzy folded the letter and tucked it into an envelope. "For Star's sake as much as Timmy's."

"Come on, boy." The father took his son's hand. "Thank the nice ladies and then we'll be off home." He looked up at me. "We've come from Devon, we did."

"All the way from Devon to save your horse?" I blurted out.

"It's Star, ma'am," the boy said. "My best friend."

"We must stand by our friends." I gave him a bright smile. "You're a courageous young man." If only all friends were as loyal. I waved to the boy as they left.

On the way out the door, a well-dressed woman nearly knocked them over on her way in. "Lizzy, have you heard?" She was breathless and flushed. "They've arrested Birdy."

"Whatever for?" Lizzy came to the woman's side. "Was he one of those arrested at the rally?" she asked under her breath, glancing over at me.

"Not at the rally." The woman shook her head. "Poor Mrs. Birdwhistle is beside herself."

Birdwhistle? As in Private Birdwhistle from Porton Down?

"Let's talk about it later." Lizzy patted the woman's arm. "Nina, let me introduce you to Lady Tabitha Kentworthy." The woman gave a little smile, but it didn't reach her eyes. "She's joining the society."

I held out my hand. "Pleasure to meet you."

"Nina is the Duchess of Hamilton," Lizzy said with a hint of pride. "We founded the society."

Curls escaping in all directions, the Duchess of Hamilton had a great pile of fair hair atop her head and a long string of pearls wrapped around her throat and décolletage. Her face was fresh and lovely without a drop of make-up.

"May I ask, is this Birdy a friend of yours?" I tried my best nonchalant tone. "Is he—or she—in trouble?"

"My cook's son." The duchess glanced at Lizzy. "He's in the king's army, but he... ah, helps us from time to time."

I bet he does. Private Birdwhistle must be the anti-vivisectionist mole at Porton Down. "Why was he arrested, if I may ask?" I couldn't wait to tell Captain Hall.

"Something about a fist fight with a fellow named Mr. Jäger."

Lady Nina was wringing her hands. "Poor cook. That boy will be the death of her."

"Now, now, Nina." Lizzy put her arm around her friend's shoulders. "Let's get you a cup of tea." She gave me a sidelong glance. "I'm sure Lady Tabitha has better things to do than listen to gossip about your staff."

"Birdy is a good boy." Lady Nina removed a handkerchief from the pocket of her coat. "The least we could do is post his bail." She troubled the corner of her hanky.

"If you'll excuse us." Lizzy turned to me. "I'm so sorry we don't have more time." She put her hand on my sleeve. "But do come again, Lady Tabitha." She opened the front door for me. "We would love to see you more involved in the defense of the animals."

"Thank you." I took the not-so-subtle hint. "I will."

Next stop the War Office to give Captain Hall an update on my progress. I planned to omit any mention of Fredrick Fredricks, at least for now. I couldn't wait to tell him that I'd found the mole. Who would have suspected it was that nice boy, Private Birdwhistle?

Captain Hall was out for the day. His secretary told me to return tomorrow. I'd have to wait for my moment of glory. I got back on the bus, hopped off to fetch Fredricks's clean laundry, and continued home. I hoped the scoundrel was still there.

When I opened the door to my flat, the smell of fresh-baked bread and roasted meat wrapped me in a cloud of mouth-watering goodness. Fredricks had opened the curtains and light flooded in, accentuating the dust motes dancing in the sunbeams.

"Hello." I removed my coat and hat and hung them on the rack by the door. "I'm home." As I neared the kitchen, the aromas of garlic and rosemary grew stronger. My stomach grumbled. "Fredricks?"

He was cooking and singing, too. Mozart's *Don Giovanni* if I wasn't mistaken. *What in the world?* Wearing my polka-dotted pinny over his ruffled white shirt and jodhpurs—*Wait. Where did he get those clothes?*—Fredricks stood at the stove, stirring a pot, belting out the aria. His voice wasn't half bad.

"Fiona, ma chérie." He smiled. "I told you I'd earn my keep."

"Shouldn't you be in bed?" I tugged off my gloves.

"Later." He winked. *Cheeky cad.*

"I didn't know you cooked." I surveyed the stovetop, trying to determine what was in the pot.

"There's much you don't know about me." He pointed toward my meager spice rack. "Pass me the black pepper."

"What are you making?" I inhaled the promise of a delicious meal and a tasty pudding. "And more to the point, where did you get the ingredients?" My larder wasn't well stocked. In fact, it was empty. "Furthermore, *how* did you get them?" Not only were such delicacies rationed or nonexistent but also, he was supposedly bedridden—not to mention, without clothes. I sat the package from the laundry on a chair.

"I have my ways." He grinned as he continued to stir the pot. "I can't tell you all my secrets." He held out the wooden spoon to me. "What do you think?"

I opened my mouth and he put the spoon to my lips. *Scrummy.* A rich red sauce. Reminded me of my grandmother's cooking on the farm. "Ummm." I licked my lips.

With his index finger, he gently wiped a bit of sauce off the corner of my mouth. "Salty enough?" His voice was low and hoarse.

"Plenty salty." I held his gaze as I licked the sauce off his finger.

He wrapped me in his arms and pulled me close. "Ma chérie." His breath on my neck made me shiver. Worse yet, his lips on my neck sent an electric current down my spine. "*Je t'adore,*" he whispered in my ear.

My knees went weak.

Then I saw it. My file folder. Marked Top Secret. Sitting in the middle of the table. I pulled out of his embrace. *Curses.* Of course. He'd found the folder in the oven.

The tug-o-war between my desire and my duty had never been stronger. A pang of guilt thumped my heart. Not to mention my would-be fiancé, Archie Somersby. I was only human, after all. And by any standards Fredrick Fredricks was a devilishly attractive man.

"You snoop!" I snatched up the folder. "How dare you go through my things!"

"Would you have me burn down your flat?" He tilted his head. "The oven is a strange place to keep your papers."

"Top-secret papers," I corrected him.

"May I suggest the ice box next time?" He smirked. "Revenge is very good eaten cold, as the vulgar say."

"I'd like to eat you cold." Clutching the folder to my chest, I scowled at him.

"I'd like that, too." His grin broadened.

My cheeks burned. "I didn't mean..." I dropped into a chair. No doubt he'd read the file. Now he knew my assignment. And if he knew it, so did the enemy. "How did you get those clothes?" I'd taken his only clothes. Did he leave the flat naked and go shopping? My head was spinning. The scent of garlic mixed with Fredricks's sandalwood cologne was overwhelming. I fanned myself with the file folder. "And the food?"

"I told you." He tilted his head. "I have my ways."

Oh, how I wanted to jump up and wipe that grin off his beautiful face.

He uncorked a bottle of wine, poured out two glasses, and then sat down next to me. He brushed a lock of wig hair from my forehead. "You look exhausted, ma chérie." He slid one of the glasses toward me.

He was right. I was exhausted. One night on a deuced uncomfortable sofa will do that.

"Have some wine." He took my hand. "And some food." He kissed my palm. "And then take a nice catnap."

"How much do you know?" I withdrew my hand and glared at him.

"That depends—"

"Answer me," I demanded. "Who shot you? Why are you here? What are you doing in London? Did you read my file?"

"Alright. Alright. Slow down." Taking his wine glass with him, he stood up and went back to the stove. After stirring the sauce, he turned to me. "I'm not sure," he said, counting on his fingers. "You're the only person I can trust. Using my powers of persuasion. Of course." He raised his eyebrows. "Happy now?" He took a sip of wine.

"No." I sighed. "What do you mean you're not sure? You didn't see the person who shot you?"

"A sniper. Best I could tell, it came from somewhere on the rooftop of the Palace of Westminster." He shrugged. "Someone who knew I'd be there, waiting for you under the clocktower."

Someone who'd read the telegram. Someone from the War Office. Surely not one of the codebreakers. Mr. Dilly Knox's weapon of choice was a pointed barb, not a sniper's rifle. "Someone adept with a rifle."

"Military, no doubt." He shook his head. "MI5, perhaps?"

"MI5?" When we were in Italy, Archie's assignment was tangled up with MI5. How exactly, I didn't know. All Archie said when I asked was *classified*. "Why would MI5 want you dead?" I knew for a fact that the War Office wanted him alive. Captain Hall had told me on several occasions Fredricks was more valuable to us alive, if we knew where he was and could follow his every move.

"My powers of persuasion are considerable." He raised his eyebrows. "And your government doesn't like the idea of an agent promoting peace over war."

"That's not true." *Is it*?

"Suit yourself." He went back to the stove and his sauce.

I toyed with the edge of the file folder, trying to remember its exact contents. Of course he'd read it. Any spy worth his salt would have done the same. What had Fredricks seen? I closed my eyes and conjured one page at a time. My cover as Lady Tabitha and the invitation to Lord Rosebrooke's Ascot-themed house party this weekend. Rear Admiral Arbuthnot's mission at Porton Down—to root out the animal defense mole who was interfering with military operations. Finally, to infiltrate the Animal Defense Society, and report on the activities of Lizzy Lind, suspected German spy and agitator.

"Do you know Miss Lizzy Lind?" What harm could it do to ask? He'd already seen the file. I took a sip of wine—I wasn't a connoisseur by any means, but this was the tastiest wine. Light with just a hint of sweet fruit.

"Emilie Augusta Louise Lizzy Lind af Hageby." Still concentrating on his cooking, Fredricks waved his hand over the simmering pot. "Swedish feminist, animal rights advocate, cofounder of the Animal Defense Society who also founded field hospitals for wounded war animals, and all-around pleasant woman." He wiped his hands on my apron. "Dinner is ready, if you'd be so kind as to set the table." He held up his glass. "To us. Our first proper meal together."

I held up my glass. "To my first proper homecooked meal since the war began."

"To many more." He clinked my glass.

"To many more," I said, referring to homecooked meals, not necessarily with him.

Forgoing my everyday plates, I went to the sideboard where I kept my mother's fine china. I put out my best woolen place mats, silverware, and floral china plates. As I stood back admiring the table, Fredricks sliced a pork roast and served it with spaghetti and roasted Brussel sprouts. What a treat. The only other time I'd eaten pasta was on assignment in Italy.

"How ever did you procure such delicacies?" My mouth watered and I rubbed my hands together in anticipation.

Fredricks tutted his tongue at me. "A man must have some mysteries."

"Yours could fill a library." The man was full of surprises.

Fredricks pulled out a chair for me and I sat down to the feast. Barely able to wait for him to lift his fork—as my mother taught me—I tucked into the meal. The pork was moist and tender, the pasta perfectly cooked, and the rich tomato sauce was heavenly. Audible moans of ecstasy escaped my lips despite myself. Fredricks might be a scoundrel and a cad, but he was a magician in the kitchen.

"Tell me more about Lizzy Lind." I took another bite of pasta. *Scrummy.* "How do you know her?" Fredricks would know if she were a German spy. Perhaps they were working together. Not that he'd tell me.

"I met her a few years back during the Brown Dog affair," he said between bites. "Posing as a medical student, she'd infiltrated the University of London and wrote about one particularly grue-some illegal vivisection by Dr. William Bayliss. Although Bayliss won in court, Miss Lind prevailed in the court of public opinion."

"Is she a German spy?" I locked my gaze on him.

His eyes went wide, and he nearly choked on a bite of pork. "That's one of the things I admire about you, ma chérie. You don't mince words." He dabbed at his mouth with his napkin. "No. Your precious War Office couldn't be more wrong. Unless advocating for peace makes one an enemy spy."

"Agitating more like." I didn't take my eyes off him. Did I know him well enough to detect when he was lying?

"Yes, well." He chuckled. "Some of us agitate and others advo-cate. Two sides of the same coin."

"So, you're working together? You and Lizzy Lind?" I held my knife in mid-air lest cutting my meat I miss a wince or a blink.

"Only insofar as we're all working together for peace." He took a sip of wine. "She's a member of the International Committee of Women for Permanent Peace and the author of many fine anti-war pamphlets. I have the highest regard for Miss Lind."

The way he said it made me uneasy. "And what is your business with her?"

"Since you've shown me the error of my ways..." He grinned. "I employ less direct means of *persuasion* than I did in the past." He drained his glass. "Now I travel the world fanning the flames of justice already ignited by others." His countenance turned deadly serious, and he looked right through me. "In London, if Miss Lind is the match, I am the petrol."

A shiver ran up my spine. "What do you mean?" Was he planning an attack of some kind? "What are you planning? A bombing?" He'd planted bombs on British ships in the past.

"No, you've reformed me on that score." He shook his head. "Anyway, the art of persuasion is more powerful than any bomb." He refilled his glass from the bottle and topped off mine too.

"Me? I've reformed you?" He always gave me more credit than my due. Since I'd met him, my life's ambition had been to catch him in the act and discover his dastardly plans in time to prevent him carrying them out. A tiny part of me felt disappointed. Chasing a wordsmith was not nearly as exciting as chasing an assassin.

By the end of our pudding course—a lovely dish of fresh strawberries and whipped cream—we'd finished the bottle of wine. "Where did you get these luscious berries?" The berries and cream were the perfect end to a delightful meal. I couldn't remember the last time I'd had berries and cream. Probably back on my grandfather's farm when I was a child. My grandmother would make meringues and serve them with fresh strawberries and whipped cream. Heavenly.

"Speaking of luscious." Fredricks stood up and offered me his hand. "Why don't we retire to the sitting room where we can converse in comfort?"

I took his hand. Not until I stood up did I feel the full effects of the wine. I teetered and took hold of his arm for balance. I couldn't help but laugh. Even my dusty living room seemed amusing with its mismatched furniture and biscuit crumbs dotting the floor.

Fredricks steadied me and led me to the evil sofa where I'd spent the last sleepless night. He sat me down and then slid in next to me. I leaned my head on his shoulder, inhaling the scent of sandalwood and garlic. I *thought* the meal had satiated my appetite. The proximity of Fredricks had awakened dormant appetites all the fiercer for their reappearance after so long. Was it the wine? I hadn't felt like this since my honeymoon. My desire was fierce like a wild animal. When I buried my face in his neck, he quivered. He lifted my chin and kissed my lips. Intoxicating. I felt my body melting into the warmth of his. I giggled. "You smell good."

"So do you, my sweet peach." He gazed down at me. "Let's get you to bed."

"Yes," I whispered.

He led me to the bedroom. I stood teetering as he helped me out of Lady Tabitha, slowly, one layer at a time. When I was down to my smalls, he stopped and held me out at arm's length. "You are exquisite." His voice was hoarse.

"So are you." I hiccupped.

He led me to the bed and sat me down. "Sleep well, ma chérie."

Still wobbly, I sat there like a zombie, unable to say or do anything.

He bent down, took hold of my ankles, and gently swung my legs up onto the bed with one arm while supporting my head with the other. He laid me back and then pulled the quilt up to my chin.

"Good night, my love." He kissed my forehead and then turned to go.

"Wait... aren't you..." I wasn't sure what I was asking. But a longing deep inside me wanted him to stay. "Aren't we..."

"It's my turn for the sofa," he said softly.

"You're too big." My voice sounded like it had come from across the room.

"And you're tight." He raised his eyebrows. "Too much wine."

"Don't go." When I tried to roll over, my arm slipped and hung off the bed. "Don't go," I said into my pillow.

"I wish I could." He sighed. "But a gentleman never takes advantage of a lady."

"I'm not a lady." Was I slurring my words?

"But I'm a gentleman." He straightened his jacket. "And if we do... I want us both to be dead sober."

"Dead?" I raised my head.

"Sober." He blew me a kiss and left the room.

13

THE ASCOT HOUSE PARTY

Aaaagghh. My head ached something awful. I pressed my hands against my ears to quell the explosion. My mouth was dry and pasty. What was wrong with me? I must have come down with a dreadful cold, or perhaps that horrible Spanish influenza from America. I sat up on my elbows. The room tilted and I fell back against the pillow. I was in my bedroom in my bed, but how did I get here? And why was I wearing only my lace vest and knickers instead of my pajamas?

"Good morning, ma chérie," a cheerful voice boomed from the doorway.

"What's so good about it?" I pried one eye open and looked at him.

Fully dressed in his usual costume of Duxbak jodhpurs, canvas hunting jacket, and tall black boots with wet sheepdog locks hanging loose around his shoulders, he looked every bit the great South African hunter. Given the state of my head, not to mention my stomach, I suspected he'd set a trap for me last night. Unfortunately, no matter how hard I tried, I couldn't remember anything except the smell of roasted pork, which was decidedly not welcome at this moment.

Carrying a tray, Fredricks came to the bedside. "I brought you a cup of strong tea with sugar."

"I'm afraid I've come down with something." I groaned. "I'm feeling quite unwell."

"It's called a hangover." He chuckled as he placed the cup and saucer on the nightstand. "Would you prefer a bit of the hair of the dog?" He sat on the edge of the bed, which only made me more nauseated. "I could make you a coffee come-up."

"No hair. No dog. No come-up." I buried my head in the pillow. "Just shoot me, please." I was afraid to ask what happened last night. If anything had, then I deserved to be shot. A pang of guilt followed by a kick of regret hit me in the gut. I rolled over and hugged myself.

"Have you forgotten about Lord Rosebrooke's Friday-to-Monday?" He put his hand on my shoulder. "Drink this." He poured a packet of aspirin powder into a small glass of water and handed it to me.

Good heavens. The country house party. I was in no shape to socialize. It would take monumental effort to get out of bed, let alone make myself presentable. I drained the glass. The bitter taste matched my bitter mood.

"Lady Tabitha is expected at Mentmore Castle by teatime." His deep voice was soft and soothing. "Peace, bread, and land await." He got up and threw open the curtains. *Cruel man.*

I buried my eyes in the crook of my elbow and wished I could just stay in bed all day listening to the sound of his voice. But duty called. I sat up and leaned against the pillow, waiting for the room to stop spinning. My hand shook as I retrieved the teacup from the nightstand. Slowly, I forced myself to take a sip. Swallowing my pride along with the tea, I ventured to address the elephant in the room. "What happened last night?" I grimaced. "Did we..."

"You were perfectly charming." He grinned like the cat who ate the canary.

"That's what I'm afraid of." My lips trembled. *How could I have?* I was in love with Archie. *Wasn't I?* Confound it. Why wouldn't the floor hold still, for heaven's sake? What a mess.

A knock at the door startled me. Fredricks and I looked at each other.

"Expecting company?" he asked.

I glanced at the clock on the nightstand. *Oh, my sainted aunt.* Noon. I'd slept all morning. "Why didn't you wake me?"

Noon. Clifford. Argh. For once, I wished bloody Clifford hadn't been on time. I made myself finish the tea and then gingerly swung my feet out of bed. "Go stall your old pal Clifford while I get ready." What else could I do? I'd have to swear Clifford to silence. Impossible. He was a notorious blabbermouth. No doubt all of London would soon know I'd been living in sin and with the enemy. For all of two days, mind you. And only one of them truly sinful. My teeth chattered and I pulled on my dressing gown. As I did, a whiff of sandalwood caressed my nose. Was there no escaping the man? A bit of the hair of the dog indeed.

An hour—and several doses of bicarbonate—later, I was packed and ready to go. When I emerged from my bedroom, I found Clifford and Fredricks happily exchanging hunting stories. Or, more accurately, Clifford regaling Fredricks with animated reminders of their adventures together in Africa. Clifford clearly worshipped him. It was all I could do to pull him away from the great hunter so we could be on our way. Still nattering on about some Cape water buffalo, he picked up my suitcase. Fredricks saw us to the door. Only when I tugged on Clifford's sleeve did he finally exit the flat.

"Don't do anything I wouldn't do," Fredricks called after us. Since there was nothing Fredricks wouldn't do, that was an entirely toothless imperative.

To my surprise and relief, Clifford never asked why Fredricks was in my flat. Indeed, he acted as if it were perfectly normal to find Fredricks living at my place. Instead, he continued the water buffalo story and then moved on to another about an aggressive rhinoceros. When I woke up, the animal in question was a pregnant hyena and the car had stopped in front of an enormous wrought-iron gate.

"Are we there?" I rubbed my eyes.

"I say, why doesn't he open the damn thing?" Clifford got out of the car to talk to an attendant standing at attention on the other side of the gate. When he returned, his face was pale. "We have to go to the other gate." He shook his head. "Lord Rosebrooke locked the gates when his son went off to war and won't open them again until the boy returns." He sighed. "Sadly, his son will never return. Rum do. He was killed in Palestine last year."

I patted his arm. "No one remains untouched, not even Lord Rosebrooke." Fredricks and I might be on opposite sides, but we did agree on one thing: this bloody war had to end.

The grounds of Mentmore Castle were lush and verdant even in early February. In the distance, a forest dusted in early white snowdrops created the effect of a winter wonderland. The house itself was enormous, of course, but not ostentatious. To the contrary, it was made of brick and stone and surrounded by wooden stables.

"Look," I said as we passed a pasture where a heavily pregnant horse grazed. "What a beauty."

"Lord Rosebrooke is an avid horse breeder." Clifford waved his hand in both directions. "He has some of the best racehorses in the country. And an indoor arena and his own racetrack."

That explained the Ascot theme. I thought of poor little Timmy, faced with giving up his beloved horse, and wondered if Lord Rosebrooke was expected to do the same. The war touched everyone, but short of death, not always equally.

I'd never been to a country house party, let alone one with its own arena and racetrack. The closer we got to the entrance, the more butterflies buzzed in my stomach... or was that the lingering effect of too much wine? There was a reason I didn't usually drink much. When I asked Fredricks whether we... he didn't exactly give me a straight answer. I cringed. At least not being able to have children eliminated one worry. Being barren may have cost me my marriage to Andrew, but at least I wouldn't be sharing a pasture with one of Lord Rosebrooke's pregnant fillies.

"Good gracious." I pointed to a nearby treetop. "Who is that?"

A woman wearing a bright purple frock sat on a branch shouting through a bullhorn.

"Good lord, will you look at her." Clifford slowed the car to a snail's pace and stared up at the oversized purple bird. "Why that's Lord Rosebrooke's daughter, Lady Sybil." He turned back to me. "You really should read the society pages, old bean."

"Does Lady Sybil make it a habit to sit in trees?" I gawked up at her.

"Lady Sybil is a complete nutter." He cranked his neck to get a better look. "She lets the gypsies camp on the estate." He chuckled. "Sometimes she even joins their caravan. Can you imagine?"

"How curious." If all toffs were like Lady Sybil, the weekend was going to be even more amusing than I'd imagined.

No sooner had Clifford stopped the car than a swarm of footmen arrived to park the car, transport our luggage, and direct us inside. From the treetop, Lady Sybil shouted instructions. One of the footmen left us with the butler, who delivered us to the music room. Its floor-to-ceiling windows looked out onto a beautifully manicured garden with more stables and pastures in the distance. The bright and cheery room was alive with chatter from various ladies and gentlemen taking tea. On a long sideboard, various cold-cuts, perfectly triangular egg sandwiches, and assorted biscuits adorned silver platters. Additional footmen delivered cups of hot coffee and milky tea.

As surprising as the luxurious spread was the abundance of footmen. Most of the young men were off fighting. I glanced around. Yes, well. With neatly trimmed gray beards and crow's feet, these footmen were not exactly in their prime. Still. Many older men went to serve their country too. Whichever man who didn't, risked the suffragettes serving him up a white feather, despite their attestations of pacifism.

Sitting in striped satin chairs and open-backed divans, lords and ladies sipped tea and nibbled on sandwiches. Clifford joined the ladies and immediately launched into one of his stories. I surveyed the room, taking it all in. To my surprise, I knew two of the guests. Dressed in an expensive-looking tailored morning suit, blending in with the finery on display in the music room, Dr. Vorknoy stood near the sideboard chatting with two other men, one of whom was his assistant, Mr. Henry Hobbs. Clearly not all the guests were peers.

I reminded myself that the doctor knew me as Frank Hightower, and both he and his assistant knew me as Rear Admiral Arbuthnot. Hopefully they would not recognize me as Lady Tabitha Kentworthy. They knew Clifford as Captain Clifford Douglas. He need only play himself. There was no reason for them to suspect him. Why couldn't he escort a beautiful lady to a posh country house party?

Perking up my ears, I moved to the sideboard and took up a plate. As I surveyed the buffet, I eavesdropped. All in the line of duty, mind you. The scent of jasmine floated atop the smell of egg sandwiches. I sniffed. It was coming from the direction of the doctor. Interesting. I suspected it was not his own perfume.

The doctor and his assistant were discussing a patient named Champion and his upcoming operation. Ghastly. Out of the corner of my eye, I spotted Dorothy from Porton Down. She was beckoning to the doctor from the doorway. Odd. Why was the doctor's secretary—or was she his nurse—at a posh house party? Glancing around as if looking for someone, the doctor shooed her away. What was that all about?

Tap. Tap. Tap.

I turned to see Lady Sybil tapping on the window. With her were Lizzy Lind and Nina, Duchess of Hamilton. From outside the window, standing in a flower bed, they waved at the party. The shopgirl was right. All three were wearing frilly white dresses and large hats adorned with flowers and feathers. I glanced down at my all-too-green dress. Lady Sybil pulled a face and then darted out of view. The other ladies followed her. A minute later, flushed with laughter, the three women appeared in the music room. To the person, in turn, each of the guests fawned over Lady Sybil. For all her eccentricities—or perhaps because of them—she was wildly popular. In turn, she happily exchanged pleasantries with her guests, until she reached Dr. Vorknoy. Without a word, she turned on her heel and snubbed him. My mouth dropped open, and so did his.

Lady Sybil held her hands out to me. "And you must be Lady Tabitha," she gushed. "So lovely to finally meet you. I've heard so much about you and your father."

My father? I scanned my memory for mention of a father in my briefing files. I thought the whole point of Lady Tabitha Kentworthy was no one knew her. "Likewise." I couldn't think of anything else to say, so I squeezed her hands and smiled.

"Everyone knows *my* father." She leaned closer and whispered, "He's napping now but will join us for dinner." She turned to Clifford, who had torn himself away from the other ladies and joined us. "And this must be the handsome Captain Douglas."

"I say." Clifford blushed and sputtered.

I resisted rolling my eyes at him.

Everyone was chatting and drinking when a young lady appeared in the doorway. A very pretty but disheveled young lady wearing a riding costume. She had the rosy glow that comes from physical activity.

"My sister Margaret, but everyone calls her Peggy." Lady Sybil got up and kissed her sister on the cheek. "Did you have a good ride?" Her tone was sarcastic.

"Very good," Peggy purred.

After another hour of mingling and gushing, Lady Sybil invited her guests to take in the grounds or a restful interlude in their rooms before the dinner gong, which she warned would ring promptly at ten minutes before eight. "Tonight, we'll take a buffet. Tomorrow will be a proper dinner."

Arm in arm, Lizzy Lind and the duchess resolved to take a turn around the garden. I asked if I might join them. Their enthusiasm seemed genuine. No doubt, they were happy to have another recruit for the Animal Defense Society. My attempts to shake Clifford, however, were in vain. That was, until he spotted Lady Sybil struggling to remove a twig from the heel of her shoe. Unable to resist a woman in need, Clifford flew to her side and offered his assistance. While he was engaged with Lady Sybil's twig, I made my escape.

As soon as our trio was out of sight of the grand house, Lizzy stopped and stamped her slippered foot. "What is that horrible man doing here? Why ever would Sybil invite him?"

The duchess glanced at me and then back at her friend.

"Apparently, one of her father's friends is having him perform that wretched operation on a prized stallion."

Lizzy gasped. "We must stop him!"

"And how do you propose we do that?" The duchess sounded almost annoyed. "We're house guests, not revolutionaries."

"You mean the doctor?" I asked innocently. "Dr. Vorknoy, the monkey gland man?"

"What he does to those poor chimpanzees should be criminal." Lizzy's face was red. "If this friend wants the operation done so badly, why doesn't he have the good doctor remove his lordly glands and transplant them onto his horse... or better yet, onto the doctor." Lizzy wiped tears of rage from her eyes with the backs of her hands. "The doctor is happy to take their money. Not only is he a torturer of innocent creatures, but he's also a charlatan."

"Indeed," I agreed.

"If only we could dispose of the man as easily as he disposes of his laboratory animals." Lizzy's nostrils flared. "We must intervene for the sake of the chimpanzees, not to mention the poor horse."

"I'm surprised the horse wasn't requisitioned by the War Office," I offered.

"The rich have ways of circumventing the laws," Nina said in a matter-of-fact tone.

"Rumor has it the best of Lord Rosebrooke's stock has disappeared." Lizzy threw up her hands. "Poof. Vanished into thin air."

"How so?" I asked.

"Apparently," Nina said, examining her finely polished fingernail, "the day after the War Office requested the beasts, they were stolen, or so says Lord Rosebrooke's groom."

"What a coincidence." Lizzy raised her eyebrows.

"Indeed," I agreed again.

Nina took a few steps and put our trio in motion once again. The tour of the garden was not only delightful, but also informative. I'd learned that Dr. Vorknoy and company were here to perform an operation, and Lord R's requisitioned horses had conveniently disappeared.

That evening passed pleasantly with stimulating conversation and an excellent dinner followed by card games and jigsaw puzzles. Lady Sybil stayed out of the trees. And by bedtime, Lizzy and Nina and I were thick as thieves.

The next morning, after breakfast, the party assembled for a tour of the stables followed by a horse parade in the arena. Lord Rosebrooke wanted to show off his prize racehorses, the ones the War Office hadn't requisitioned... yet.

The stables were vast and extremely clean for animal habitats. A tweed-clad, lanky, bearded groom wearing a green plaid cap gave us a tour of the stable closest to the house. His head bobbing as he went, he hunched a bit, no doubt due to his considerable height.

Four horses occupied four stalls, each munching away on hay. A young lad brushed a beautiful bay. Every time he hit a particular spot on its hind end, it stomped its hoof. As we passed a pretty gray horse, he stopped eating and turned to regard us. He nuzzled the hands of anyone willing to offer one. Once he was satisfied there were no treats to be had, he went back to munching hay. Another lad hung a bell-shaped golden-brown lump by a rope on a nail so the horse could lick it.

"What's that?" I pointed at the brown lump.

"Jaggery, miss." The lad let the animal chew off a bit and then moved the jaggery to the next stall.

"And what's jaggery?" I called after him.

"Sugar, miss." He poked his head out of the stall. "Gives 'orses a bit of extra energy, it does."

With sugar rationing, I was surprised horses got any at all. "I wouldn't mind a bit for my tea."

"Tastes like molasses, it does." The lad chipped off a piece and held it out to me.

I shook my head. "You have it."

He smiled and popped it into his mouth.

After the stable tour, the groom led us to the arena for the horse parade. The indoor arena was an impressive affair with a cavernous barn-like structure and an enormous arched ceiling with curved wooden beams. Stadium seats lined one side of the dirt track. An entire garrison could practice maneuvers inside, out of the rain and cold. Lord Rosebrooke used it for exercising his precious horses and putting them on display for his guests.

At one end of the structure, a gigantic sliding wooden door allowed animals to enter. At the other, the morning light shone through a large window, giving the arena the feel of a great outdoor cathedral. Instead of incense, the air was heavy with the smell of horses and hay. Dust motes danced in the sunrays, creating a gauzy ambience. Beaming, Lord Rosebrooke and his daughter Sybil greeted their guests, obviously proud of their herd. The lord was older than I'd expected. His hair was silver, and he walked with a cane. Apparently, he never removed his mourning suit even though his wife had died years ago.

A footman showed us to our seats. After a commotion at the grand entrance, the lanky groom appeared, leading a gorgeous bay into the arena. Using a riding stick and voice commands, he had the horse kneel so a jockey dressed in the Rosebrooke silks could mount. On my grandfather's farm, if you wanted to ride a horse, you had to climb aboard. This one was trained to kneel like a camel. After taking several laps at increasing speed, the jockey stopped the horse in front of the audience and then tapped it with the stick. The beast knelt again so the diminutive man could dismount. Both the man and the horse took a bow. The groom led the horse from the arena. The next in line was a chestnut filly with a dark brown mane. She was polished to a shine and her mane was braided with ribbons. The beautiful creature pranced around the arena and then ran a course of ever higher jumps over white fences that had been arranged along one side of the track.

After the horse parade, the guests stood up, clapping and cheering in admiration. At the end of the show, Dr. Vorknoy stepped into the arena and the groom delivered a gray horse to the center of the arena. Smiling and waving, nurse Dorothy stood alongside the horse. Mr. Henry Hobbs joined the doctor, who described his "miracle cure" for aging "guaranteed" to make this seven-year-old run like a two-year-old. Thankfully, he didn't go into details about the operation. But he did promise that within a month of the operation, we'd all be invited back to witness the result, when "Champion will be back in the race." *So that's Champion.* A photographer was on hand to document the day. And he would be back when the result was put on display next month. When the doctor announced that the operation would take place this afternoon, the small crowd gasped in horror or delight, depending on their attitudes toward animal welfare.

A noise outside the window caught my attention. In the distance I spotted a man pushing a large wheeled cage. He wore a red cap. Could it be Mr. Jäger delivering the sacrificial chimpanzee? Lizzy Lind whispered something to the duchess, who nodded.

I wished I knew what they were planning. I sensed that Lizzy would stop at nothing to prevent the exploitation of the poor beasts.

14

THE DINNER GUEST

After the horse parade, the men in the party went bird hunting. With considerable help, still in his mourning suit, Lord Rosebrooke joined the party. I half expected Lizzy Lind and the duchess to throw themselves in front of the rifles. To my great surprise, the duchess joined the hunt. And she and Lizzy indulged in cold-cuts and roast beef along with the rest of us. They even wore fur collars and carried stylish leather bags. Ironically, the doctor did not hunt, calling the sport barbaric. Obviously, experimenting on animals was seen as a separate moral issue from eating them, wearing them, or chasing them. The platform of the Animal Defense Society was baffling. I reminded myself that my job was not to explain their behavior but to root out a possible mole-saboteur among them.

Despite the blue skies, I did not join the hunting party. I did, however, take advantage of the sunshine to walk in the garden. The winter garden was especially lovely with snowdrops, irises, cyclamens, and daphne flowers in ivory, white, purple, and pink. Behind the flowerbed, a row of evergreen box bushes stood neatly trimmed. And beyond the hedgerow, along the side of the closest stable were hollies and junipers. The air was fresh and cool but the sun on my face warmed me through.

As I neared the stable, I heard voices. Men's voices. Angry men's voices. I moved closer to make out what they were saying. Standing at the corner of the barn, I held my breath and perked up my ears.

"Replacing his nads with a chimp's is bloody daft and a waste of shrapnel."

"It's not replacing, it's adding, and it's his lordship's money, not yours."

"Champ'll be lucky to not end up on the wrong side of the grass."

"If you don't stay out of it, you'll be lucky not to end up on the wrong side of the grass."

"Oh, yeah?"

"Yeah."

A scuffling sound sent me back toward the house. When I reached the winter garden, I turned round to regard the stables. From that vantage, I saw the silhouette of one of the men. Judging by his diminutive size, I'd bet it was the jockey. Obviously, Lizzy Lind and the duchess weren't the only ones suspicious of the monkey doctor. Was the jockey's interlocutor the groom or Mr. Hobbs? If only I could get a good look.

A shadow made me jump. Dorothy appeared in the doorway. Forehead furrowed, she headed straight toward me. "Can I help you?" she asked in an accusing tone.

"No. No." I waved her away. "I'm just taking a stroll."

She nodded and then went back to the stable door and stood there like a sentry.

After one more turn around the winter garden, I made my way back to the house. And just in time for luncheon, too. Most of the party had taken lunch as a picnic out on the grounds where the men were hunting. Lady Sybil stayed behind with Lizzy and me, along with the doctor and a woman I'd not met yet. The doctor introduced the woman as his wife, Oksana. Oksana Vorknoy was taller than the doctor with silky black hair and an even silkier voice. Her accent was stronger than his. A long silver cigarette holder between her teeth, she puffed out smoke rings. As she slipped her long fingers into mine, I got a whiff of flirtatious languor with a hint of orange blossom. The doctor and his wife retired to their room "to rest."

Lady Sybil, Lizzy and I sipped tea, nibbled on biscuits, and worked on the jigsaw puzzle, which was big enough to warrant its own table in the music room. The puzzle box called it "Pastime Puzzle Hunting Hounds" and had a picture of what the finished puzzle should look like—hunters on horseback following hounds, along with various animals including a bear and an owl. I read the back of the box. Over 100 pieces of hand-cut wood. At the rate they were going on it, they would need several more house parties to finish.

Taking a break from the puzzle, I went to my room to freshen up. One lavatory was shared by the bedrooms on either side of it. I shared mine with the Vorknoys. Although the walls were thick and sturdy, from the loo I heard a crash. The sound of glass shattering. My breath caught and I hurried to wash my hands. I'd opened the door and was about to exit into the hallway when Oksana Vorknoy stormed out of their bedroom with the doctor in pursuit. I quickly shut the door all but a crack.

"Either she goes, or I do." She hurled her cigarette holder at the doctor's head. "You won't make a fool out of me."

I peered out into the hall.

"Darling, wait." The doctor held his hand to the cheek where the cigarette holder had hit him. "It's over. I swear."

There was nothing I hated more than an unfaithful husband.

"Then get rid of her," Oksana said, without looking back. "Now."

"But I need her for the procedure—"

"Now!" Oksana stomped off down the hall.

After the doctor retreated into his bedroom, I made my escape from the loo. I wondered how many marriages had ended at country house parties.

When I returned to the music room, the duchess was with Lizzy and Lady Sybil at the jigsaw. Heads together, they whispered like conspirators as they moved pieces around the table.

"You left the hunt." I joined them.

"I got my exercise, that's all I went for." She tilted her head. "You didn't think I went to kill something!"

"Heavens, no." I blinked.

"The men will be back soon." She shrugged. "Their bags are full."

Lizzy shook her head. "They've satiated their bloodlust... for now."

"Speaking of bloodlust," the duchess said. "Birdy made bail and is back home."

"That's a relief." Lizzy tutted her tongue. "Poor boy."

"Birdy?" Lady Sybil asked.

"My cook's son." The duchess patted Lady Sybil's arm as if consoling her. "The boy is always in trouble."

"He's a good boy." Lizzy came to his defense. "He loves animals and hates fighting. As it should be."

"Yes, well, I'll be in trouble if I don't greet the men and send them up to change for dinner." Lady Sybil waved an elegant hand. "You should do the same." In a cloud of lavender chiffon, she left the music room. The rest of us followed her out.

I wasn't used to all these wardrobe changes. I felt like a stage actress, dressing for the next scene. But I followed orders and returned to my room to prepare for dinner. I changed from my smart day dress into my evening costume, a stylish burgundy satin sheath with a rose-pink scarf and long black gloves. I wished I'd studied Kitty's fashion magazines more carefully. Heaven only knew if I'd got it right. I'd soon find out. Funny. I was far more comfortable dressed as Rear Admiral Arbuthnot or Frank Hightower than I was as a posh lady attending a dinner party.

Before dinner, we met in the drawing room for cocktails and canapés. Unlike the light and airy music room, the drawing room was dark and masculine with heavy drapes and wood paneling. The aging footmen delivered trays of tiny squares of toast topped with chopped olives. A bartender prepared whiskeys and champagne cocktails. After my last experience with wine, I steered clear, preferring to wait until dinner. The men looked sharp in their evening suits. Even Clifford cleaned up nicely. And the women presented a pretty party, dressed in silks, satins, and fine wool gabardines. A fire burned in the hearth, giving the room a cozy cheerful glow. The harshest of features were softened by the flickering of the flames. Thank goodness for me.

Still wearing mourning clothes and smoking a cigar, Lord Rosebrooke sat in a high-backed leather chair, surrounded by several of the male house guests, including Clifford, who tried without success to turn the conversation to his tales of adventure. The other men were more concerned with whether bread shortages would lead to our king being exiled like his cousin Tsar Nicholas in Russia.

Near the fireplace, Lady Sybil engaged in spirited conversation with Henry Hobbs. When she touched his arm, he blushed. An intrigue between the lady of the house and a lowly doctor's assistant? I'd heard rumors of bed-hopping at these posh country weekends. Perhaps Clifford was right. I should read the society pages.

A commotion outside in the foyer turned all heads. A well-dressed man carrying a top hat burst into the drawing room. Hot on his heels was the butler.

"Apologies, sir." Addressing Lord Rosebrooke, the butler stepped in front of the interloper. "I told him to wait in the library, but—"

"No matter, Hastings." Lord Rosebrooke waved away the butler. "Lord Battencourt-Cox is always welcome."

Rather than leave the room, Hastings the butler stood at the ready near the door.

Lord Rosebrooke stood and tugged on the hem of his evening suit. "To what do we owe the pleasure, Albert?"

In his fifties with salt-and-pepper hair and a tremendous handlebar mustache, Lord Battencourt-Cox cut a fine figure of distinguished British aristocracy. His round cheeks reddened as he surveyed the room, all eyes upon him. "Sorry to barge in on your party, old chap." He sighed heavily. "I need to have a word with Dr. Vorknoy."

The doctor came to his side. "How'd you find me?"

"I rang your office yesterday." He shifted from foot to foot. "I debated whether or not to come. But its urgent." His voice broke off. "Is there some place we might..." He turned to Lord Rosebrooke. "Someplace private?"

Lord Rosebrooke nodded to the butler, who led the two men from the room.

I pulled Clifford aside. "What was that all about?"

"Damned if I know." Clifford puffed on his pipe.

An urgent need for monkey glands, perhaps.

Half an hour later, when Hastings returned, he announced dinner and the guests retreated to the dining room. The long banquet table was set with more china and cutlery than I'd seen in all my life. Floral arrangements adorned the center of the table from one end to the other. Each place was set with a gold-trimmed china bowl and saucer, a bread plate, no less than four forks, three spoons, and two knives, along with four crystal goblets of differing sizes. Name cards stood in brass holders in front of each setting. Lady Sybil directed us to our assigned seats, and we settled in. Husbands were separated from their wives, no doubt to encourage conversation and whatever else went on after dark.

The place across from me was unoccupied. I leaned over to get a look at the name card. Of course, I couldn't see it. A footman's arm cut through my line of sight, putting an end to my futile attempts. He ladled clear broth into my bowl.

"How are you enjoying the party, Lady Tabitha?" Dr. Vorknoy asked. He was seated on my other side.

"Very much." I studied Lady Sybil to see which spoon she used and copied her. The broth was light but delicious.

"Did you finish your jigsaw?" The doctor slurped his soup from his spoon.

I shook my head. "What happened with Lord Battencourt-Cox, if I may ask?" He hadn't been invited to stay for dinner.

"He's a patient of mine." The doctor cleared his throat. "He had a complaint."

"A complaint?"

"I misspoke." The doctor laid his spoon across the edge of the soup saucer. "An ailment. A private matter."

"Of course." I sipped my soup. A patient with a private complaint. Monkey glands gone wrong? "How is Champion recovering?" With the help of Mr. Hobbs and Dorothy, he had performed the operation on the creature earlier in the afternoon. Thankfully, the procedure was not part of the weekend's entertainment.

The doctor gushed about the operation's success while I feigned interest. I glanced across the table where Clifford was chatting up Lady Sybil, who smiled politely, no doubt unable to get a word in. Poor woman. I knew just how she felt.

The footmen delivered the fish course. A cold white fish served with hard bread and a light white wine. Also very good. Before I knew it, the footman whisked away the fish course and brought out roasted wild birds served with rice and steamed vegetables. By the time I had finished tasting a bite of everything, I was stuffed. I had only enough room for the pudding course, which I expected would be excellent. Never pass up dessert.

In between bites, I asked the doctor about his practice and training. He was more than happy to discuss his genius and catalog his successes. A light citrus sorbet arrived next. Tangy, slightly sour, and delightfully sweet, it was the perfect cap to an excellent dinner. I laid my tiny dessert spoon alongside the tiny sorbet dish and then leaned back in my chair.

The footman cleared away the sideboard and then made a great show of arriving with a large roast of beef on a platter. *Crikey.* Another course! How many were there? The meat was surrounded by potatoes and other vegetables arranged in an appetizing presentation, provided one was a three-hundred-pound giant. Did these people eat like this every night? There was enough food to serve an army. And to think of our poor Tommies eating tinned beef and stale biscuits. It was shameful. And yet I could hardly wave away the main entrée.

"Apologies, Lady Sybil, your lordship." A familiar tenor echoed through the dining room. All eyes turned to the tardy dinner guest. *Good heavens.* What was *he* doing here? Lieutenant Archie Somersby, that devilish chestnut lock falling over his forehead, looking far too handsome in his evening suit.

"Lord Archibald Kentworthy," Lady Sybil announced. "So glad you could finally join us." She glanced over at me and smiled.

What in blazes? Lord Archibald Kentworthy. Was Archie under-cover, too? Or was he secretly a member of the aristocracy?

More importantly, what relation was he to my cover, Lady Tabitha Kentworthy? Her brother? Her father? *Not hardly.*

No. Surely, not.

Her husband?

15

STRANGE BEDFELLOWS

The large dining room was suddenly too hot. I fanned myself with my napkin.

"Hello, Tabitha dear." Without properly looking at me, Archie leaned over and gave me a peck on the cheek, his familiar citrus scent sending shivers up my spine. "Sorry I'm late." *Her husband!* Cringe. *Wait.* I thought Clifford was posing as my escort. What kind of tart was this Lady Tabitha Kentworthy? I planned to have a chat with Captain Hall when this weekend was over. Blast him anyway. Didn't the captain trust me? Sending Archie to spy on me again. I sat huffing like an angry bull.

Archie strode around the dining table to the empty seat, looking gorgeous in his evening kit but none too pleased as he glared across the table. My cheeks warmed. *Oh, my word. That's why I have a double room on the couples' floor.* My mouth hanging open, I sat gaping at him. He mimicked my face, and I clamped my teeth hard. Just because he hated me was no reason to be rude. Staring straight down at my plate, I grabbed my wine glass and gulped the claret that had been served with the roast course. No sooner had I drained my glass than a footman was on hand to refill it. *He might as well leave the bottle.* My grandfather always said, "The answer is not in the bottom of a glass, so don't bother looking." But trapped at this table across from my erstwhile, now estranged, fiancé, I didn't know where else to look.

"Slow down, Tabitha dear." Archie leaned forward and stage whispered, "Or I'll have to carry you to bed." *Good grief.* Bed. At some point, we'd be expected to share a bedroom. Where did I draw the line of duty with Archie? Time would tell.

Throughout the rest of the dinner, I avoided eye contact with Archie, who seemed to be enjoying my discomfort. When I did glance over at him, he was smirking... when he wasn't flirting with Lady Sybil's younger sister, the beautiful, blue-eyed Lady Peggy. Rather than sulk or brood, I was determined to enjoy the rest of the meal.

The roast course was followed by a salad course, a pudding course, and then a cheese course. An eight-course meal in the middle of a war. Lady Sybil assured us that everything was made with war rations and the cooks were wizards. I had my doubts. Fredricks had showed me the fruits of a thriving black market. He had no qualms about trading with thieves and criminals. My suspicions about the source of the marvelous meal didn't stop me from sampling every course, especially the sweet course, which was an exceptionally light fruit jelly. All in the line of duty, mind you.

After dinner, we retired to the music room for a concert. A friend of Lady Sybil's was a concert pianist and gave us a wonderful private performance. During a break in the music, Archie took me aside and led me out onto the veranda. It was pouring with rain, so we stood under an awning. The evening air was brisk, and I wished I was disguised as Harold the helpful bellboy or Rear Admiral Arbuthnot instead of this sleeveless sheath. I wrapped my arms around my torso and steeled myself for whatever Archie had to say. The last time I'd seen him at

Porton Down, he'd made it clear that he wanted nothing to do with me.

"Captain Hall sent me to warn you." He glanced around. "The plot is more serious than those harmless animal defense ladies."

"Harmless ladies?" Refusing to look at him, instead I stared out into the night. The grounds were illuminated by a heavy full moon hanging low in the sky. "Is that why I got the assignment?"

"The animal thing is a cover for something more deadly." He tapped out a cigarette. "You may be in danger."

Through the rain, in the distance, I saw two figures standing just inside the large barn door. Two men, a cage between them. Their silhouettes sharp in the moonlight, I saw one man hand the other a packet.

Archie took my shoulders. "Did you hear me?"

I looked up into his face. His eyes shone with trepidation. Those beautiful eyes... and lips. I jerked away from him. "Do you see those men?" I pointed toward the stables. "Looks like Mr. Jäger and another man."

"That's Jäger alright." His hand to his brow, he peered into the night. "But who's that with him? And what in the blazes are they doing out there in the middle of the night?"

It wasn't exactly the middle of the night. But it was late enough to wonder why they were at the stables. "Could he be checking on Champion?" Maybe that was the doctor with him. They could be checking on their charges. And the packet was the doctor paying Mr. Jäger for the chimpanzee. But why so late and in the pouring rain, no less?

"Champion?" Archie asked.

I'd forgotten he'd missed the horse parade and announcement about the monkey gland operation. "The lord's friend's racehorse," I said, my teeth chattering.

"Ahhh." Archie lit his cigarette. "The monkey doctors."

Shivering, I nodded.

He took off his evening coat and handed it to me. I shook my head.

"We'd better get back inside before you catch your death," he said, putting his hand on my arm, warming my goose flesh. I put my hand atop his and held fast.

"Oh, Archie. It's all a terrible misunderstanding."

"Now is not the time." He removed his hand. "We have to find the spy before he finds you."

"Me?" Why in heaven's name would a German spy be after me? I was a lowly file clerk occasionally assigned to follow *harmless women*. Unless... Fredrick Fredricks. Could the man who shot him be coming for me, too? But why?

"Whoever it is, he's working with that rotter Fredricks." Archie's eyes hardened. "And if I catch him, I'll kill him."

"I say." Clifford appeared out of nowhere. "There you are. I've been looking for you, old bean."

Speaking of wanting to kill someone.

"I'll leave you with your *better half*." Archie's eyes were as hard as emeralds. "Watch your back. He's dangerous." He blew out a cloud of smoke and then turned and disappeared back into the house.

"Good lord. Who's dangerous?" Clifford huffed. "Surely he doesn't mean me."

"No, dear Clifford." *Sigh*. I patted his arm. "Not you."

* * *

To my surprise, the concert did not conclude the evening's entertainment. Lady Sybil shepherded us into the drawing room for a special performance. Dark fabrics, heavy curtains, and thick oil paintings on the walls made for a cozy scene in front of the fireplace. None other than Mr. Jäger introduced us to Lazarus, his trained chimpanzee. On cue, the furry creature delivered sweets to the ladies and poured whiskeys for the gentlemen. The ladies cooed and the men laughed. All in all, it was a delightful evening. After the show, a few of the party retired to their rooms. Despite the late hour, the rest of us stayed drinking and playing cards. At half past eleven, I hung back in the drawing room sipping sherry and making small talk with the harmless ladies until the last one retired to bed. Dreading bedtime, I watched the men play billiards until the games broke up.

"I bid you goodnight, my friends." Lady Sybil's hint wasn't subtle. "I'm going to bed and so should you."

"After I finish my whiskey." Archie held up his glass.

"You'd think the bloom had gone off the rose." She winked at Archie. "Where one bloom falls, another thrives." With that, she left us.

"Do you think that was an invitation?" Archie chuckled.

"I don't doubt it," I said between my teeth.

"Now, now, Fiona." Archie leveled his gaze. "Just because you won't have me—" He drained his glass and sat it on the sideboard with a bit too much force.

"I never said I wouldn't have you." I troubled my low-slung silk collar. "I want to wait, that's all. I never—"

"Then wait you shall." He left me sputtering my excuses to his receding backside.

Now what? My only choice was to follow him up to my room, our room.

When I arrived, Archie had already stripped off his evening suit. His hat was hanging from the bedpost and his jacket and trousers lay over the back of the dressing chair. Wearing only his smalls, he made a bed on the floor. My cheeks warmed. Except at Charing Cross Hospital, I hadn't seen a man in such a state of disrobe since my marriage. I looked away. What had seemed a spacious bedroom yesterday was feeling rather cramped now. The four-poster bed loomed in the center of the room. The fresh-cut flowers and candelabra on the nightstand made me blush. Yesterday, they'd seemed cheery and thoughtful. Tonight, they seemed dangerously romantic. And the washstand and dressing table only reminded me of Archie's state of undress.

Ignoring me, he continued piling blankets onto the floor. Ridiculous. We were grown adults on a joint mission. Surely we could work together in a civil manner.

I tutted my tongue. "You don't have to sleep on the floor." Trying not to admire his lean torso, I grabbed a corner of the blanket he held in his hands.

"Yes, I do." He tugged on the blanket.

"We can share the bed." I tugged back.

"I don't think so." He wrenched the blanket from my hand, and I fell backwards against the bed.

"Why not?" I righted myself and smoothed my dress. "We're adults." Although after our tug-o-war with the blanket, I wondered.

"*Mister* Douglas wouldn't approve." He'd demoted Clifford from captain to mister. No doubt to suggest I was his Mrs.

"Kitty made up that fantastic yarn about me and Clifford."

He stopped fussing with the blanket and stared at me.

"She made it up." My tone was harsh. "The wretched girl."

"Why ever would she—" His voice broke off and he started laughing. "Oh, my lord." He doubled over with laughter. "She had me going."

"I'm astonished you believed her." I stood, arms akimbo, watching him guffawing. "It really isn't funny."

He wiped tears from his eyes with the backs of his hands.

I shook my head. "Are you quite finished?"

He threw his arms around my waist and pulled me to him. "Fiona, darling, I've missed you." He kissed my neck. Shivers ran up my spine. He kissed my ear. A gasp escaped my lips. He silenced my gasp with a kiss. I melted into his arms. What kind of girl was I? Canoodling with Fredricks back at my flat, and now I was sharing a bedroom with Archie. I was as bad as Lady Tabitha.

Thud.

I pulled out of his embrace. "What was that?" A loud noise came from next door. Dr. Vorknoy's room. It sounded as if someone had fallen to the floor.

"Ignore it." Archie tightened his embrace. If I didn't know better, I could have sworn he was wearing his pistol.

"I heard glass breaking in there earlier." I pushed him away. "The doctor and his wife were fighting."

"Lovers' quarrel." He grabbed my arm. "Happens all the time."

"That sounded like a body hitting the floor." I adjusted my gown, which was threatening to fall off my shoulders. "We should investigate."

He ran his hand through his hair.

"You said yourself there was a dangerous spy lurking about," I reminded him.

He sighed. "Oh, alright." With some effort, he tugged on his trousers and then threw his evening jacket on over his bare chest. "Let's go investigate."

Oh, how I wished we could do otherwise.

I followed him on tiptoe as he marched next door. He knocked on the door. No answer. He pounded. Still no answer. I moved closer and called out, "Dr. Vorknoy?" I listened at the door. "Doctor, are you alright?"

Crash.

The sound of exploding glass shattered the silence. Archie and

I looked at each other. Taking it as his cue, Archie kicked in the door.

"Was that necessary?" I tried the doorknob. It didn't budge. Yes. It had been necessary.

"You wanted to investigate." Archie stepped inside. "Come on."

I followed Archie inside. The room was dark except for a flood of moonlight streaming in through the window. The bedcovers were pulled back and rumpled, obviously slept in. I flipped on the electric light. The room was a mirror image of my own, complete with four-poster bed, washstand, dressing table and chair, wardrobe, and closet. I peeked around the side of the bed.

Good heavens. I gasped.

Lips blue, foaming at the mouth, Dr. Vorknoy lay on his side on the floor next to the bed, a broken lamp within arm's reach. I rushed to his side, bent down, and shook him. "Doctor!" His lifeless eyes stared over at me. I roiled backwards, crawling like a startled crab to get away from the body.

"He's dead."

16

THE INVESTIGATION

No blood. No wounds. No bullet holes. No signs of trauma to the body. But the doctor's face was red and swollen. I forced myself to take a closer look. Down on hands and knees, I leaned in and sniffed. *Garlic.* I didn't recall having any garlicked dishes for dinner. So how to account for the strong smell? I wished Kitty were here with her forensics kit. But she was still in Italy. So, I made a mental note to find out about poisons that smelled of garlic.

"We need to alert Lady Sybil and the staff," I said halfheartedly.

"And we will." Archie surveyed the room. "But not until we get a bead on what happened here."

"It looks like the doctor fell out of bed and took the lamp with him on the way." I bent down to examine the lamp, or what was left of it. *What the devil?* There was a long filament amid the fragments. It was tied to the doctor's wrist and stretched out halfway across the room. "Strange."

Archie came to my side and we both stared down at the dead man. "Is that fishing line around his wrist?"

"Perhaps he was a fisherman." I glanced up at Archie. "Heart attack, or something more sinister?"

"Like murder?" Archie tilted his head.

"A love triangle." I thought of the doctor's wife storming out.

"You go alert Lady Sybil while I search the room." Archie did a 360-degree turn.

"Why don't *you* alert Lady Sybil while *I* search the room?" I wasn't about to leave the scene of a possible murder without investigating first.

"We'll both search the room." Archie shook his head. "You're quite a girl."

"And you're quite a boy." I returned the compliment—if it was one.

Archie gave me a queer look and then cracked a smile. "A real brick."

I tightened my lips. "We'd better hurry." I opened dresser drawers and searched through underclothes while Archie searched the closet. We did a quick inventory of the room. Except for the broken lamp, nothing seemed out of place. I checked the window. It was shut but not locked. It was large enough for someone to crawl through. I opened it and looked out. Next to the window casing, a trellis covered in vines adorned the side of the house all the way from the ground to the second floor. I reached out and tugged on it. A bit rickety, but sturdy enough to support a killer, provided they weren't too heavy.

"Shall we?" Archie asked, gesturing to the door, which I reminded myself had been locked from the inside when we arrived.

"Give me a minute." I dashed back to my room and grabbed a pair of tweezers and two pieces of clean white paper. Returning to the body, I bent down and plucked some carpet fibers off the dead man's lips and folded them into one of the pieces of paper. The carpet was wet where he was lying. The garlic smell again. Not blood. What then? His saliva? Vomit? Bracing myself for the worst, I plucked a few fibers there too and folded them into the second sheet of paper. "There. Now we can go."

We went down to the drawing room and rang the bell for the butler. I wouldn't begin to know where Lady Sybil's bedroom was in this mammoth house. And given the bed-hopping likely going on this weekend, I wouldn't want to show up unannounced at her bedroom. The butler's cheeks went white, and his eyes went wide. "Yes, sir." He scurried off to fetch his mistress.

Soon, the doctor's room was swarming with household staff darting back and forth, wringing their hands, and following orders from Lady Sybil's bullhorn. Before long, the local constable showed up looking sleepy and bedraggled. He put me in mind of Conan Doyle's description of Inspector Lestrade in *A Study in Scarlet* as a "little sallow rat-faced, dark-eyed fellow." I hoped he fared better than the fictional policeman... or the poor dog poisoned by Holmes in the course of his investigation.

During the commotion, I sneaked off to inspect the garden. If someone had climbed up or down the trellis, there could be a broken strut or a footprint in the mud. After changing from my evening gown into a split-legged wool skirt with my ample pockets filled with the necessary tools, I slipped my stockinged feet into Wellington boots and made my way downstairs. Grabbing an umbrella from a stand near the door, I stepped outside.

The rain hadn't let up. It had been pouring for hours and the grounds were soaked. Clicking on my torch, I trod through many a puddle to get to the side of the house. The clouds obscured the full moon, and the wind howled like something out of a gothic novel. I shivered and pulled my arms in tight. It was deuced difficult to hold the umbrella and the torch, especially with this wind. When a gust nearly ripped the brolly from my hand, I gave up and closed it. Immediately, I was drenched. By the time I found the trellis, my soaked coat weighed a ton. I shifted it on my shoulders and shone my torch on the ground beneath the trellis.

Standing water in the flowerbed obscured any chance at footprints. And as far up as I could see through the rain, the trellis seemed intact. Odd. A short rope dangled from a bush near the bottom of the trellis. I snagged it and stuffed it into the pocket of my coat. A piece of rope for tying the horses? I'd learned from experience and from reading Sherlock Holmes, the more the appearance of innocence, the more likely the guilt.

I shone my torch up and down the flowerbed and then nearby on the grass. Puddles and wet grass. Nothing more. *I wonder.* Shivering, I headed across the grass toward the stables. I couldn't get any wetter. I blew at the rainwater dripping from my lashes and off my nose and trudged along through the wet grass until I reached the barn. The large door was open, just as it had been when Mr. Jäger and the other man exchanged a mystery packet. I stepped inside and to my relief got out of the rain. Like a dog, I shook myself. Still dripping, I tiptoed further into the bowels of the barn. Holding my torch aloft, I bit my lip as I surveyed the stalls. The warm spicey scent of horse filled my nostrils. The bay whinnied at me as I passed. What was I looking for? A bottle of poison? Muddy boots? No one's boots could be muddier than mine.

Beyond the stalls I discovered a wooden door. If I recalled correctly, on the tour the groom pointed it out as the tack room. I pushed open the door. Inside the small space smelled of damp leather. It was pitch dark except for the beam of my torch. My pulse quickened as I stepped inside. I held my breath and scanned the area. Saddles stood on wooden frames, bridles, harnesses, and leather reins hung from hooks, jugs of soap and bottles of medicines sat on shelves. Like the rest of the stables, there was a meticulous neatness about the place, which I greatly appreciated.

I examined the bottles and jugs, looking for a possible poison. Several of the bottles had the telltale skull and crossbones insignia. Did any of them smell like garlic? Laying my torch on the shelf, I picked up a bottle marked iodine, uncorked it, and sniffed. A salty metallic smell. Not garlic. I uncorked another bottle marked sulfur, sniffed, and immediately wished I hadn't. The overpowering odor of rotten eggs. Whew. I picked up a bottle marked vinegar but didn't bother smelling it.

"Who goes there?" A voice came out of the darkness followed by the click of a pistol cocking and loud barking.

I gasped. The bottle slipped from my hand and crashed onto the wooden floor. The acrid smell of vinegar exploded into the room, burning my eyes and nostrils.

"I'm warning you." A floorboard creaked. "I'll shoot." The threat was accompanied by a dog growling.

Where did they come from? I hadn't seen anyone in the barn when I'd entered.

"It's me." I finally managed to croak. "Tabitha Kentworthy. I'm a guest of Lady Sybil."

"What are you doing out here, ma'am?" His pistol preceding him, the groom stepped into the light and so did his dog, its teeth bared, and its hackles raised.

"Dr. Vorknoy's dead." I lifted my hands.

"No. Can't be." The groom lowered his gun. *Thank goodness.* The dog, on the other hand, did not lower his hackles.

"When was the last time you saw the doctor?" Gathering up my courage, I took the opportunity to question the man.

"When I took Champion in for the operation." He shook his head. "What happened to him?" He made a hand motion and the dog sat down.

"You tell me." I snatched my torch off the shelf and shone it into his face.

"I mean, how did he die?" He shielded his eyes with his hand.

"We don't know yet." I lowered the torch. "Was the operation successful?" I didn't know what would count as success in such a procedure.

"Champ was curling his top lip." The groom opened his tweed jacket and slid the gun into an inside pocket. "So, he weren't supposed to do the operation." He demonstrated the upper lip curling.

"Why ever not?" What did lip curling have to do with the operation?

"'Orses curl their upper lip when they're colicky, ma'am." He held his stomach like he had a tummy ache. "Shouldn't operate on a colicky 'orse."

"I see." My upper lip was curling from the smell of the vinegar. "The doctor didn't operate?" Why had he told me the operation was a success? I scrutinized the groom's face, wondering if he had something to do with this curling upper lip. How hard would it be to make a horse curl its lip? He easily could have applied something to its nose, vinegar perhaps, to make its lip curl. And then used that as an excuse not to do the surgery. Earlier, I'd overheard him disparaging the doctor in discussion with the jockey. But would he go so far as to kill the doctor to stop the operation going forward?

"Idiot doctor did it anyway." His face reddened and he balled up his fists.

"I see." As Lady Tabitha, I ought not to come on too strong. But as Fiona Figg, British secret agent, I need to know. "Were you here in the barn an hour ago?" I asked, not taking my eyes off his face. "And all evening?"

"Here, yes, ma'am." He looked perplexed. "Why?" He reached down and scratched the dog behind its ear.

"You were here in the barn at midnight?" Rather odd hour to be tending horses.

"I always come to check on the 'orses before bed." He sounded sincere.

"Do you always carry a gun when you do?" I pointed at his sidearm.

"The war's brought out thieves and such, ma'am." He shrugged. "Never know who might be sniffing around the barn breaking bottles." He patted his jacket where he'd put the gun. "Blue and me gots to be prepared." He smiled down at the dog.

"Midnight is rather late, is it not?"

"The master demands proper care of his 'orses, ma'am." He adjusted his cap. "Night or day, don't matter much to them."

"And you were here alone?"

"Course not." He frowned.

So, he had an alibi. Either that or an accomplice. "Who was with you earlier?"

"Only the 'orses." He reached down and patted the dog on the head. "And old Blue, 'ere."

There went his alibi—unless one of the horses could tap out answers with a hoof like Clever Hans.

"Shall I walk you back to the house, ma'am?" He doffed his cap.

"That won't be necessary, thank you all the same." I was hoping to snoop around the barn a bit more. But that would prove impossible with the groom hanging about.

The groom spun around and pulled the gun from his pocket. "Who goes there?"

My hand flew to my mouth. What in heaven's name?

"Shhhh." He put a finger to his lips. The dog perked up its ears and so did I.

A shadow emerged from the tack room and slid along the far wall.

"Stop or I'll shoot!" Nose outstretched, hackles up, but quiet as a fox, Blue led the way and the groom followed, pistol pointed.

I held my breath and followed them with my eyes. They stopped when they reached the far wall. In unison, dog and man turned their heads this way and then that. They must have lost the intruder. Whoever it was could be our killer. Why else would someone be sneaking around the barn at this hour?

A warm hand clamped around my mouth. "Good evening, ma chérie." The whispered breath on my ear made my skin crawl. "Or should I say good morning?" A whiff of sandalwood confirmed his identity.

I bit his hand and he jerked it away with a mock whimper.

"Fredricks," I hissed. "What are you doing here?"

"I missed you," he said, his canines glowing in the dim light.

17

OUT OF THE FRYING PAN INTO THE FIRE

After I explained to the groom that Fredricks was with me, and we were guests of Lady Sybil—not entirely true in Fredricks's case—he took his dog and went back to caring for the horses. The rain had stopped, and the full moon illuminated our way back to the great house. The air smelled clean and fresh and full of promise. Fredricks walked with me across the dewy lawn. In moonlit silhouette, I could see how he got the nickname "Apollo."

"What are you really doing here?" I asked.

"I thought I'd show up as Lord Kentworthy." His baritone lilted with mirth. "But I hear Lieutenant Somersby has beaten me to it."

"He'll beat you, alright." The last time Archie encountered Fredricks, he'd tried to shoot him. If my head hadn't intervened, Fredricks might not be here now. I shuddered, remembering the bullet grazing my temple.

The night's events combined with lack of sleep weighed on me. I could hardly put one foot in front of the other. Fredricks took my hand and tucked it into the crook of his arm. I didn't resist. Instead, I leaned on him as we made our way back to the house.

"Is Lady Sybil expecting you?" I asked.

"Depends on who you mean by *you*." He chuckled. "I'm a man of multiple personae." He put his hand on top of mine. "Not unlike you, ma chérie."

"You seem to have recovered from your gunshot wound." I lightly poked him in the ribs.

"Ouch." He feigned injury. "Thanks to your loving attention."

"I'm beginning to wonder whether you were shot at all."

He stood suddenly and turned to me. "You wound me." He put his hand to his heart. "Would I feign near-death just to get your attention?" His tone was playful.

"Yes. You would."

He winked at me. "You cut me to the quick."

Had I fallen for another one of his ruses? Cursed man. Either that or he had the constitution of Hercules. With the wound I'd stitched, he should still be recuperating. I stopped and looked up into his dark eyes. "You faked the whole bloody thing, didn't you?" And to think, I'd almost slept with him.

A smile played on his lips.

I stomped my foot. "Didn't you?"

He looked me up and down. I must have looked like a drowned rat with my wet clothes clinging to me and my ruined wig dripping down over my ears.

"Temper becomes you, ma chérie." He tilted his head. "A bit of pique brings a rosiness to your lovely cheeks." He brushed a lock of wet wig hair from my face.

I slapped his hand away. "Then I must be in a permanent state of rosiness when I'm around you." I couldn't believe he'd fooled me again. The bounder. To what end? Because I didn't heed his beck and call and meet him at the clocktower? Or so he could get into my bed? I didn't know which was worse. If I hadn't been assigned to follow the rotter, I would happily say goodbye to him forever.

Wait. I'm not assigned to follow him. My current mission was to infiltrate the Animal Defense Society and find out how they planned to sabotage the war efforts. I suspected the doctor's death had something to do with his research at Porton Down and therefore fell under the purview of my investigation—more or less. But I didn't need to kowtow to Fredricks. "I've had enough of your tricks."

"My feelings for you are no trick." He reached for my hand and brought it to his lips. "Unless you count putting me under your spell a trick."

I yanked my hand away. "Go to the devil." I wasn't about to let him manipulate me again. Without looking back, I ran across the grass to the front entrance, not stopping until I arrived. Panting, I heaved the door open and dashed inside. The cad would not get the best of me this time. Lips tight, I hurried up the stairs to my room and slammed the door shut.

"Where have you been?" It was more of an accusation than a question.

Curses. I'd forgotten I was sharing a room with Archie. I brushed a stray wig hair from my face and sniffed. "Inspecting the grounds, if you must know." Men, always asking me to account for myself.

"In the middle of the night with a possible killer on the loose?" He came to my side. "You should be more careful. If anything happened to you..." His voice broke off.

"I can take care of myself." I slouched out of my wet coat and then sat at the dressing table, tugging at my soggy boots. "Right now, I need a warm bath and a hot cup of tea." My teeth chattered as I spoke. Chilled to the bone, my immediate concern was getting warm.

Archie knelt in front of me and helped me get my boots off. I made the mistake of glancing in the mirror. Good heavens, I looked a sight. My bedraggled wig was at an angle over my left ear, my cheeks were red and windburned, and the bit of eye kohl I'd applied before dinner had run in rivulets down my face. My presentation was downright ghoulish. Avoiding Archie's gaze, I made a beeline for the closet and stepped inside. Although I could barely turn around in the tiny space, I had to get these wet clothes off *tout suite*.

"I've been called back to London," Archie said through the closet door.

"Captain Hall called you back?" I asked from the closet.

"I didn't say that." I could hear his footfalls.

Was he being coy? "Who called you back and why?"

"The who is classified." The sound of footfalls stopped. "I suppose I can tell you why. They've found Fredricks."

My heart sank. I hoped he hadn't been *found* leaving my flat. I knew I should have told Captain Hall. When he found out I'd harbored an enemy spy, especially the notorious Fredrick Fredricks, I'd be sacked for sure.

"Fredricks is in London?" My voice cracked. "I wonder what he's up to now." I closed my eyes. What was I doing, perpetuating a lie? *Come on, Fiona, you've got to tell him.* I bit my lip. I couldn't.

As much as I hated Fredricks, I didn't want him killed.

"As you already know, the War Office intercepted a telegram to his contact in London asking to meet him at Big Ben." He knew that I knew about the telegram. Did he also know that *I* was the contact in London who was supposed to meet Fredricks?

I heard a match strike and then smelled foul cigarette smoke. No doubt, on the other side of the door, Archie was smoking and pacing. "The man sent to investigate winged him." Archie scoffed. "Incompetent fool. I would have killed the bastard."

The War Office—or the classified office—sent someone to investigate? A British agent had shot Fredricks. If so, it was a good thing I didn't turn up at Big Ben at noon. "Fredricks was shot?" I feigned ignorance. So, he wasn't faking it? My stomach churned. Archie had been trailing him around the globe for months and when he got another chance, he'd end the chase for good. If Archie saw Fredricks, he'd kill him. I had to warn Fredricks. But how? Blast it all. I had to keep Archie from leaving the room.

I threw on my silk robe and flew out of the closet. "Who shot Fredricks?"

"Classified." He took a drag of his cigarette and blew out a foul-smelling cloud.

"Someone from the War Office?" I asked.

"Not the War Office."

"Not the War Office," I repeated. I didn't think so. Captain Hall always said Fredricks was more use to us alive than dead. Could the *classified* office be MI5? Archie had been involved with MI5 in Italy. When I took up pacing, he stopped.

"I'd best get going." His lips twitched like he wanted to say more. He grabbed his hat off the bedpost where it was hanging. "See you around."

"You're not still angry with me, are you?" I dashed to the door and stood in his way. No doubt Fredricks was still loitering outside. Or chatting up Lady Sybil in the foyer. Or who knew what. I had to stall Archie long enough for Fredricks to make his way to his room. At least that was what I hoped the bounder was doing.

"I could never be angry with you." His tone softened. "Just disappointed. I don't like waiting—"

"Alright." I put my hands on his lapels. "Let's not wait."

"Really?" His face brightened. "You mean it?" He took my hands and threaded his fingers through mine.

I nodded. A pang of guilt thudded in my chest. And something else... that familiar electric current whenever I was around Archie.

"Fiona, darling." He drew me closer and then let go of my

hands and wrapped his arms around my waist. "You're my best girl."

"Don't you mean your *only* girl?" I teased.

He nuzzled my neck. "My one and only girl." His warm breath sent shivers up my spine. He kissed my throat and I sucked in air. "I wish I could stay." He held me out at arm's length. "But duty calls." Archie was a stickler for duty.

On tiptoes, I stretched up and kissed his beautiful lips. He pulled me close again and returned the kiss with such passion I thought I might collapse from the weight of it. The desperation in his kisses was contagious. Breathless, I tore myself away.

How far was I willing to go to protect my enemy? To protect my virtue. To protect my heart.

The room was spinning. The moment of truth was upon me. Exactly what—or who—was I trying to protect? My body had set in motion something my mind couldn't stop. I reached up and touched his cheek. His gaze was soft and magnetic.

We loved each other. *Right?* No one need know. *Right?* So, what did I fear?

"I'm sorry, dearest." Archie tapped on his hat. "I have to go before I can't." His smile was resigned. "We'll talk about this, about us, soon." He gave me a quick kiss.

"But Archie, how will I contact you—"

"Give me that notebook you're always packing around." He wiggled his fingers at me.

I pulled my notebook from my skirt pocket and handed it to him, along with a pencil.

"My phone number." He jotted down his number. "Call me when you get back to town." He kissed me again and then was off.

I dropped my notebook back into my pocket and ran to the window. *Curses. Where is Fredricks?* Archie could meet him on the stairs and dispose of him then and there. Or he could meet him in the grounds and shoot him in cold blood. Dawn was breaking and the horizon glowed orange. The full moon was a mere outline in a blue-gray sky. I surveyed what I could see of the lawn. *Oh, no!* Fredricks. He was leaning against a fencepost, smoking a cigarette. I had to warn him. I opened the window and called out.

Blast. He couldn't hear me.

As soon as Archie rounded the corner of the house on his way to the car park, he would spot Fredricks. I cinched the belt on my robe and threw my leg over the windowsill. The trellis was just over a foot away from my window. If I could get purchase, I could climb down. If the killer had done it, so could I. Gingerly, I placed one foot on the flowerbox just below my window. Sliding down from the sill, I placed the other foot on the flowerbox. My heart pounded as I twisted to face the window and grabbed onto the ledge. Holding with all my might, I swung a foot toward the trellis. The wood slat was sharp against the bottom of my slipper. I scooted my body toward the trellis and with one great heave I hoisted myself onto the bloody thing. The trellis shook with my weight, and I closed my eyes. This was it. I would fall to my death wearing nothing but a flimsy silk robe.

When the trellis stilled, I climbed down, one slow foothold at a time. *What have we here?* Halfway down, I spotted a tuft of green silk fabric on one of the slats. I plucked it off and slipped it into the pocket of my robe. Who had been wearing green? No doubt the killer. My trellis theory confirmed, I had only to match the torn fabric with the article of clothing from which it came.

First things first. I called out to Fredricks again. He sprang off the fencepost and dropped his cigarette. "Fiona? What in heaven's name." He ran over and held up his arms. When I was within reach, he took me round the waist and lifted me down. "Don't tell me." He held a finger to his lips. "You're undercover as a cat burglar." He raised an eyebrow as he looked me up and down, a sly smile playing on his lips.

"If Archie sees you, he'll kill you." I tugged at his sleeve. "You've got to hide."

"You want me to climb up the side of the building?" He chuckled. "Your concern is appreciated, ma chérie. Let him try." He waved his arm. "Lieutenant Somersby has not succeeded yet."

"I'd prefer not to take another bullet for you." I tugged again. "Let's not tempt fate." *Oh, dear.* Out of the corner of my eye, I saw Archie round the corner. I pulled Fredricks into the bushes and flattened myself against the stone. Chuckling, Fredricks did the same. Holding my breath, I put my hand over his mouth and watched as Archie sauntered to his motorcar. He whistled as he went, focused on the path ahead, he never gave a sideways glance. Once his car was out of sight, I pulled Fredricks out of the bushes. He brushed at his jacket and then his jodhpurs. "I could do with a sherry."

"It will be time for breakfast soon." The sun on the horizon reminded me that soon the household would be up. I didn't want to be caught with my trousers down, so to speak. I had to get back inside before the household awoke. But what to do with Fredricks?

"Come on." I took him by the hand and led him into the house and up the stairs to my room. "Get inside."

"I thought you'd never ask." Fredricks grinned.

As I turned the doorknob, a maid scurried past. My cheeks hot, I glanced at her, my eyes saying silently, "This is not what it seems."

"Day, miss." She gave a knowing smile. "Day, sir." She bobbed a quick curtsey and continued down the hall.

What must she think? A married lady wearing nothing but a robe leading a man who was not her husband into her bedroom at dawn. I consoled myself that she'd probably seen worse.

18

SHERLOCK AND WATSON

A hot bath went some distance to reviving me after another late night. I lingered in the clawfoot bathtub, admiring the floral wallpaper and crystal sconces on either side of the framed mirror. No doubt Fredricks was in my room snooping through my things while I bathed. Of course, I no longer needed to worry about sharing the loo with the doctor. And his wife hadn't been back since their argument. But I'd locked the door anyway. As I dressed, I tried to remember if I had anything confidential or top secret in my room. Nothing. *Unless you count my assortment of wigs.* After I finished my toilette, I returned to my room and found Fredricks lounging on my bed reading one of my Sherlock Holmes stories.

"Fascinating fellow, this Holmes." He laid the magazine on the bed. "His powers of deduction border on sorcery." He patted the bed.

I'd learned my lesson about getting too close to the rogue. He was becoming harder to resist by the minute. I shook my head. "I'm late for breakfast."

He bounded off the bed. "I'll accompany you."

My eyes went wide. "You?"

"Why not?" He tugged at the hem of his jacket.

"You shouldn't be here." I ticked off the reasons on my fingers, then added, "Not at the house party. Not in my room. Not with me."

"I'm not." He went to the dressing table and admired himself in the looking glass. "I'm with Scotland Yard." He removed a small tin from his pocket and twisted it open. Rubbing a finger on its contents, he proceeded to wax his mustaches into perfect curls.

"You're what?"

"Detective Inspector Baker Evans." He bowed. "At your service."

"No." What was he playing at?

"I know your penchant for solving murders." He straightened his tie. "Think of it as something we can do together, ma chérie, like your Mr. Holmes and his servant Watson."

"Dr. Watson is not his servant." I glared at him. "And I am not your servant either."

"Of course not." His eyes danced. "But I am yours." He bowed. "You have more experience at this sort of thing." He twisted his pinky ring around his little finger. "You should take the lead, of course."

"Why would an inspector from Scotland Yard be coming out of my bedroom?" I stood with my hands on my hips, waiting for some clever response.

"How about I go out the window, down the trellis, and come back in through the front door?" He tilted his head and grinned.

"Are you having me on?"

"Yes, actually, I am." He laughed. "And it's such fun too."

Tempted to whack him with my handbag, I tightened my lips and restrained myself.

"Don't worry about me." He continued his preening in front of the mirror. "Discretion is my middle name."

"Deception, more like." I considered his scheme. Lady Tabitha Kentworthy could not investigate a murder. But if an inspector from Scotland Yard showed up, he could. And Lady Tabitha could tag along. As much as I hated to admit it, Fredricks's plan might work. "Just don't blow my cover." No doubt Captain Hall would chastise me for "playing detective" again... unless I could prove that the doctor's death was related to whatever funny business was going on at Porton Down. Our mole-saboteur and the doctor's killer could be one and the same. Perhaps I was wrong about Private Birdwhistle being the mole. He wasn't at the house party. So, he couldn't be our killer. Could he? I made a mental note to question Private Birdwhistle as soon as possible.

Fredricks came to my side. "Fiona, ma chérie."

"I'm Lady Tabitha Kentworthy, remember." I regretted gazing up into his soft eyes.

His gaze fixed on mine, he took my hand and kissed it. "Yes, your ladyship."

I pulled my hand away and then rubbed the residual mustache wax into my skin. "Whatever you do, don't let anyone see you leave this room." I hoped that maid's name was also discretion.

"Yes, your ladyship." He bowed and doffed his slouch hat.

"You really need to rethink your costume." I looked him up and down. "I doubt an inspector from Scotland Yard would wear hunting kit."

"You worry about Lady Tabitha, and I'll take care of DI Baker Evans." He winked at me.

Shaking my head and cursing under my breath, I left and headed downstairs to the morning room.

Breakfast was laid out along the sideboard. Lady Sybil sat at the head of one table. Seated on either side of her were Lizzy Lind and Nina, Duchess of Hamilton. I joined them and asked a footman for a cup of strong tea. "Where is everyone?" I wasn't *that* late.

"Mrs. Vorknoy will be back sometime this morning to claim her husband's things." Lady Sybil tutted her tongue. "Such a shame. We've never had anyone die at a house party."

"Does rather put a damper on the weekend," I agreed. "She'll be back? When did she leave?" I had, of course, noticed she wasn't in the doctor's room when we found him dead.

"She left yesterday afternoon and went back into town." Lizzy munched on a piece of toast.

Ah, yes. After the argument. She'd stormed out and went back home. In which case, she couldn't have killed her husband, unless she sneaked back and climbed the trellis. She did have a pretty good motive. Nothing like a faithless husband to inspire homicide.

"Captain Douglas and my father are out shooting birds." Lady Sybil shrugged. "Even a dead body won't keep them from the hunt. And Peggy is out riding *again*." The way she said it, she obviously didn't approve of her sister riding. Why ever not?

"Really." The duchess waved a spoon in the air. "A diversion is one thing but it's hardly appropriate to hunt the day after a man dies in your house."

I wasn't up on the etiquette on how to behave at a posh house party after murder. But I agreed it was a bit callous. I'd have to have a word with Clifford. Then again, maybe he was pumping his lordship for information about the killing. Could Lord Rosebrooke have a motive to murder the doctor? I was eager to find out from Clifford what he learned.

"What of the doctor's assistant and his nurse?" I asked, taking a sip of tea.

"Apparently, the nurse had a fit this morning when she learned the news." Lady Sybil raised a brow. "Perhaps they were more than work associates?"

"Friends, perhaps?" I ventured, suspecting they were lovers.

"Perhaps," Lady Sybil said with a wry smile. "Or riding partners."

Golly. What did she mean by that?

"Speaking of." Lady Sybil winked. "Where is Lord Kentworthy this morning? Sleeping in?"

My cheeks warmed. "He was called back to London, I'm afraid."

I was about to ask after Mr. Hobbs when the butler interrupted our breakfast. "Mr. Hobbs has returned." No sooner had he made the announcement than Mr. Hobbs burst into the room.

Speak of the devil and he shall appear.

"I came as soon as I heard the news." He removed his hat and fiddled with its band. "Poor chap had Bright's disease. Finally got the best of him."

I held my tongue. Disease or not, Dr. Vorknoy had been the victim of foul play.

Lady Sybil paled and looked as if she'd seen a ghost. She gave her head a quick shake and regained her composure. "Sit down, Mr. Hobbs." She gestured to a chair. "Hastings, fetch Mr. Hobbs a cup of coffee, if you please."

Hastings nodded and then disappeared.

"Bright's disease." Lizzy dropped a piece of half-eaten toast back onto her plate. "Your dear mama." She turned to Lady Sybil. "That's what took her, too, is it not?"

"Took my mama when I was only eleven." Lady Sybil nodded. "Papa hasn't been the same since."

I'd noticed he still wore mourning clothes. "If I may ask, what is Bright's disease?"

"Kidney necrosis." Henry Hobbs put his hands on his back as if to demonstrate.

"What are the symptoms of Bright's disease?" I glanced at Lady Sybil, and she averted my gaze. Lizzy Lind gave me the evil eye and the duchess stopped midbite.

"Apoplexy, convulsions, coma." Mr. Hobbs's voice was animated. "Eventually death."

"Please could we—" Lady Sybil stared down at her plate.

"My apologies." I didn't tell her that I was trying to confirm whether the symptoms matched the death scene. It was possible that Dr. Vorknoy succumbed to his illness, went into a fit of convulsions, and knocked over the lamp. But my gut told me otherwise. "So, you weren't here last night when... it happened?"

"Oh, no." Mr. Hobbs waved his hands as if conducting a symphony. "I went back to town after dinner last night. You can ask my wife." The man was so eager to share his alibi, I half expected him to produce his wife on the spot. I made a mental note to have Clifford check out his alibi as soon as possible and corroborate with someone besides Mrs. Hobbs.

I tried to get a look at the lining of his jacket to see if it was torn. I would have to come up with a clever way to get the man to take it off. "Do you know anyone who might wish the doctor harm?" There was no gentle way to ask that question.

"Harm?" Henry Hobbs gave a start. "You don't believe... He died of natural causes. Surely you can't—"

"Murder!" The duchess coughed, choking on a bit of toast. "You can't be serious."

"I can—"

"With all due respect, your ladyship." Mr. Hobbs's face went red. "What do you know of murder?"

"Quite a lot, actually." My brain was racing to come up with a story about Lady Tabitha's experience with murder investigations.

Hastings reappeared in the doorway. "Excuse me, your lady-ship." His tone was solemn. "Scotland Yard is waiting in the library."

"I thought we had done with the police last night." Lady Sybil threw her napkin on the table and stood up. "The local constable is a friend of my father's. He assured us there would be no scandal."

"May I come with you?" I pushed out my chair.

"Please do." She sighed. "Such a troublesome business. I could use the moral support."

"Of course." I gave her a supportive smile and then followed Hastings to the library. On the way, I steeled myself to see Fredricks pretending to be DI Baker Evans. *I hope I can keep a straight face.*

The library was dimly lit. A mahogany desk sat in the center of the room. Heavy curtains were drawn across the windows. Two walls held floor-to-ceiling bookshelves stocked with leatherbound books. Sofas and chairs were arranged around a fireplace at the far end of the room. I saw the back of Fredricks's head, his thick ebony curls a dead giveaway. With him was another person, much smaller than he. A woman with golden hair pulled back into a messy chignon. Whoever could she be? How did the rascal produce a partner out of thin air? More to the point, I thought I was to be his partner.

Good grief. Dressed in dark tweeds rather than jodhpurs, Fredricks had a freshly bruised eye and split lip. Sitting next to him was none other than Miss Kitty Lane, her frilly pink dress drooling lace where it was torn, and her hair a mess. "Hello, Aunt Tabitha." The girl didn't miss a beat. *What's she doing here?*

"What in the world happened to you two?" I set to work tucking stray hairs back into Kitty's chignon.

Fredricks gave me a sheepish grin. "Ask your *niece*."

"Chasing naughty Poppy, I ran headlong into the inspector." She kissed the furry creature's topknot. "Didn't I, Poppy-poo?"

Footlong, more like. By the looks of Fredricks's face, it had been the recipient of Kitty's boot. She was an experienced foot-fighter. Content with causing him pain, at least she didn't want to kill the man. How did he persuade her to go along with his ruse? And why was she here? Had Captain Hall sent her to babysit me, too? She might be a trained operative, but I was seven years her senior. She was only an eighteen-year-old girl, for heaven's sake.

"Detective Inspector, what can we do for you?" Lady Sybil asked. "I thought our constable took care of everything last night. He determined Dr. Vorknoy died of natural causes."

"Horsefeathers." *Crikey. Did I just say that out loud?* This was the first I'd heard that it had been officially declared natural causes. And I didn't believe it for a second. First, there was the garlic-smelling foam around his mouth. Second, the strange string attached to his wrist. Third, the bit of fabric attached to the trellis. Not to mention a jealous wife, a mournful mistress, a livid patient, a suspicious chimp hawker, and a couple of animal activists who'd just as soon see the doctor cut open himself than any of his animal subjects.

"At Scotland Yard, our motto is *nullus lapis intentatum.*" Fredricks dabbed at his cut lip with a handkerchief.

"No stone unturned," Kitty echoed. "What the inspector means is we need to interview the household to make sure we've done our due diligence." She adjusted Poppy's pink gingham bow, which matched her own pink dress perfectly.

"And you are?" Lady Sybil asked.

"Oh, this is my niece," I intercepted our hostess. "Katherine."

"Your niece?" Lady Sybil scowled. "Do you always travel with an entourage?"

It was a fair question.

"Everyone calls me Kitty." The girl held up Poppy's paws and danced the dog around on her lap. "Right, Poppy-poo?" She giggled and cooed. Was she a silly girl undercover as a sensible one or a sensible girl undercover as a silly one? I never could tell.

Fredricks looked every bit Scotland Yard.

With her ripped ruffles and dancing creature, Kitty was another story. In her case, looks were deceiving. She could test carpet fibers and dust fingerprints with the best of them. Speaking of which, back in my room, I had some nice samples folded in white paper and that bit of fabric in the pocket of my robe.

"Kitty dear." I went around the back of the sofa and put my hand on her shoulder. "Could you come help me for a minute?"

She looked from Fredricks to me and back again.

"It won't take long." She was right to worry. Fredricks had a way of disappearing. "Inspector, I would be happy to show you to the scene of the crime."

"Crime!" Lady Sybil dropped into an overstuffed chair. "Crime," she repeated, this time through her teeth. "The only crime is that my house party has been ruined."

"Indeed." I forced a smile. "It was jolly rude of the doctor to die in your guestroom."

She rang for the butler. "Hastings, bring us some coffee... with brandy."

"If you'll excuse us." I nodded to Kitty. "We'll be back in a few minutes."

Rather than acknowledge me, Kitty cuddled Poppy and cooed. But at least she stood up and lifted her small suitcase off the floor.

"Inspector." My voice was firm.

Fredricks twisted around to face me. "Yes, milady."

"Come along and I'll show you the... er, where the doctor died."

"Perhaps I can join you *after* coffee?" He tilted his head and winked at me.

I narrowed my brows. "Now." My tone was demanding. But I resisted the temptation to stomp my foot. "We can join Lady Sybil

for coffee later." No doubt he was more interested in the brandy
than the coffee.

Fredricks let out a loud sigh but got up off the sofa.

"Hold the coffee." Lady Sybil waved, calling after Hastings,
"Bring the brandy."

19

THE USUAL SUSPECTS

Once I'd herded Kitty and Fredricks into my room, I shut the door —perhaps with a tiny bit too much force. Fredricks sat at the dressing table and used the mirror to examine the damage to his eye and upper lip.

"What happened?" I pointed from Fredricks's black eye to Kitty's torn frock. "Spill it."

"I caught him lurking around outside in the bushes." Kitty shrugged as she put Poppy on my bed. *Really. Did the creature need to soil my bed?*

"And I got a full-booted kiss." Fredricks dabbed at his lip with a handkerchief. "But that you already knew."

"He's a German spy and a criminal." Kitty didn't mince words.

"Yes, well. Right now, we need to work together to find Dr. Vorknoy's killer." I went to fetch my carpet samples from my dressing table.

"Why?" Kitty trailed me across the room. Poppy jumped off the bed and followed her. "Why do we need to work together?"

"By some miracle, Fredricks has convinced Lady Sybil he's from Scotland Yard."

"No miracle." Fredricks tucked his handkerchief into a jacket pocket. "Skill and talent." He stood up and went to the window.

Kitty scoffed, and with one violent gesture, ripped off the torn lace from her frock. Her mistress's force agitated Poppy and the little dog grabbed one of my slippers and ran.

"Everyone, calm down." I held up a finger. "As Lady Tabitha and her niece, we are in no position to investigate on our own. We need him."

"We're in a better position than a known German spy wanted for murder in at least three countries." Kitty flopped onto my bed. With my slipper still in her mouth, Poppy jumped up after her.

"True." I tried to ignore the dirty dog paws prancing around atop my bedspread and rescued my slobbery slipper. "Having Fredricks lead a murder investigation is like asking a poacher to serve as game warden, but in this case, he's our best bet."

"Thank you, ma chérie." Fredricks leaned against the window ledge.

"First things first." I unfolded the paper and flattened it out on the dressing table, exposing the carpet sample. "Why are you both here?" I retrieved the bit of green fabric from my robe pocket and laid it next to the carpet sample.

Silence.

"You first, Fredricks," I said, dropping onto the table the segment of rope I'd found in the bushes.

"I told you earlier." He grinned. "I missed you."

"Poppycock." I arranged my evidence neatly on the dressing table. "What is your real reason for being here?"

He sighed. "Thanks to you, I've forsaken violence in favor of persuasion." He removed his deerstalker and sat it next to him on the ledge. "The Animal Defense Society is one of the most powerful pacificist organizations in Britain. Like you, I'm here to encourage and support them."

Kitty laughed. "The poacher playing game warden indeed." She had a point. Fredrick Fredricks was famous for his hunting prowess, as Clifford so often reminded us with his long-winded safari tales.

"The great South African hunter has forsaken violence?" I raised an eyebrow. "Or just inconvenient violence?"

"Let's not nitpick, shall we?" Fredricks came over to examine the evidence. "Instead, let's put our heads together to find the good doctor's killer."

"Why do you care who killed the doctor?" Kitty asked.

"The same reason you do, *if* you do." He fingered the bit of fabric "As Mr. Lenin would say, peace, bread, land... and of course, justice."

"Justice," I repeated. More than justice, I had a hunch the doctor's death was related to the mole undermining the military animal operations. Yes, his death could have been from natural causes. Or it could have been the result of a homicidal guest, even a crime of passion. But I suspected it had something to do with Porton Down and his monkey gland research. Dr. Vorknoy was trying to create a stronger soldier and a stronger horse. Someone wanted to stop him. Someone connected to the Animal Defense Society, perhaps? The mole-saboteur? Or a known German spy? I leveled my gaze at Fredricks.

He blew me a kiss.

"What about you, Kitty?" I glanced from her to Fredricks. Quite possibly she couldn't tell me why she was here, not in front of Fredricks. No doubt Captain Hall had sent her. She might have important information for me from the War Office. Information about Fredricks.

"We missed you." She smiled sweetly. "Didn't we, Poppy-poo?"

"Horsefeathers. I've seen Poppy every day." I went over and patted the little beast on the head. "Haven't I, Poppy-poo?" The creature licked my hand. I promptly removed a handkerchief from my skirt pocket and wiped it off. "*Uncle* Clifford insisted on bringing her wherever he went, including into the Old Admiralty."

"Heavens." She giggled. "I bet old sourpuss Montgomery didn't like that!"

"He certainly wouldn't like you calling him sourpuss." After I got rid of Fredricks, I would find out why Kitty was here. For now, he was right. We should put our heads together and catch the killer. "Regard the evidence." I swept my hand over the articles I'd placed on the table. "Fibers for you to test, Kitty dear."

With a dramatic sigh, she slipped off the bed and came to look at the fibers. "What sort of tests did you have in mind?"

"The fibers absorbed the victim's saliva, and you should test them for poison."

"You think he was poisoned?" Her countenance brightened. Nothing like a few forensic tests to lift her spirits.

"I don't think he died from Bright's disease." I stood arms akimbo. "His person smelled distinctly like burnt garlic."

"Burnt garlic," she repeated. "Suggests arsenic."

I snatched the fabric away from Fredricks. "Our killer left this on the trellis outside the victim's room. Keep an eye out for a torn garment of the same material." I returned the fabric to the dressing table and picked up the rope. "I found this in the bushes below the victim's window."

"A piece of rope." Kitty took it from me and examined it. "Looped at one end for hanging on a hook."

"Indeed." I slid my notebook and pencil out of my skirt pocket, sat down in the dressing table chair, and made a note: *find hook.* "Now, who had a reason to kill the doctor?" My pencil hovered over a clean page. "His wife, Oksana, and his mistress, Dorothy." I jotted their names at the top of my list.

"Busy man." Fredricks chuckled.

"Cheating husbands are no joke." I glared at him. *And I should know.*

Using my magnifying glass, Kitty examined the carpet fibers.

"Lizzy Lind and Nina, Duchess of Hamilton." I wrote their names in my book. They were adamant about their cause. But would they kill a man to save an animal? "Who else?"

Henry Hobbs had an alibi, which had yet to be confirmed, of course. Who else at Porton Down may have wanted the doctor dead? The exotic animal hunter, Mr. Jäger, looked the part of a killer. And he had been yelling and threatening the doctor over missed payments. Would he kill for an outstanding debt? Private Birdwhistle didn't seem the murdering sort. And yet he had been arrested for striking Mr. Jäger, and the duchess had revealed that the boy was out of jail, and thus available for murder. Wordlessly, I wrote their names in my book. I didn't want to tell Fredricks any more than he already knew about my mission at Porton Down. There, Rear Admiral Arbuthnot could do the investigating.

"What was the name of that patient of his? The unhappy chap here last night?"

My questions were met with blank stares from both Fredricks and Kitty. Right. Neither of them had been here then. I'd have to ask Clifford when he returned from hunting. "Should we start by questioning the ladies?" I closed my notebook.

"Why not?" Fredricks grabbed his hat off the window ledge. "Ladies first."

"I'll stay and test the fibers." Kitty sat her suitcase on the bed and then opened it. Instead of frocks and evening slippers, it contained various colored bottles and an assortment of forensic instruments. "And when you return, we should have a chat." She turned from me to Fredricks and her eyes shot daggers. "In private."

"Excellent idea," I said, stepping out into the hall with Fredricks in tow.

When we entered the foyer, I heard voices coming from the morning room. Lady Sybil, Lizzy Lind, and Nina were sitting around the hunting hounds jigsaw. But instead of concentrating on the puzzle, they sipped brandies.

Fredricks doffed his hat. "Good morning, ladies." He gave a little bow.

"Good morning, Detective Inspector Baker Evans." Lizzy looked up from her brandy snifter and smiled at him. How in heaven's name did she know him as Detective Inspector Baker Evans? How long had he been running around London posing as a detective inspector from Scotland Yard?

"We're so glad you're here." Nina got up, went to his side, and took his arm. "Isn't it ghastly about Dr. Vorknoy? Dying like that in the middle of a house party."

Fredricks and I exchanged glances.

"Quite." He patted her hand.

Women were always fawning over Fredricks. I never understood why. He did have a pleasing face, and gorgeous ebony locks, and a nearly perfect physique. Suddenly, the room was too warm. I fanned myself with my notebook. "Do either of you know why someone might have wanted to harm the doctor?" I asked, pencil in hand.

"Do you have all day?" Lizzy Lind arched her brows.

"Ohhh." Lady Sybil put a hand to her forehead. "Not this again."

"Apologies, milady," Fredricks said, rushing to her side. "Are you quite alright? Do you need another brandy? Or a whiskey, perhaps?"

She looked up at him and nodded.

He left in search of whiskey.

"What do you mean, Lizzy?" I asked encouragingly.

"Not to speak ill of the dead, but he was a despicable man." She shook her head. "What he did to those poor chimpanzees."

"And the horses," Nina added.

The horses. Again, I remembered the conversation I'd overheard between the groom and the jockey. Neither of them was keen to have Dr. Vorknoy operating on Champion. Would they have killed to stop him? I made a mental note to question them both.

"I heard a crash when the doctor fell out of bed." I observed their expressions.

"How terrible," Lizzy said.

"When he died, he fell out of bed, taking the lamp with him."

Nina gasped and put her hand over her mouth.

"That was just before midnight."

"Midnight," Lady Sybil repeated.

"Should we all account for our whereabouts between the time we left the drawing room last night and midnight?" I looked from one to the next. "Lord Kentworthy and I were in our room when we heard the crash next door. What about you?"

"You can't think that we had anything to do with—" Lady Sybil gasped. "Really, Lady Tabitha, you go too far."

"My apologies, Lady Sybil, but surely you don't want a murderer loose on your estate." I put my pencil to paper, waiting.

"We were in our room chatting," Lizzy said.

Nina nodded. "Yes, we were in our room."

"You're sharing a room?" I asked.

They both nodded. Of course, they could be lying.

"We asked for cocoa to be brought up and that lovely kitchen maid, what was her name? Cara. She brought it up." Nina looked to Lizzy. "What time was that?"

Lizzy looked at her watch, as if it could tell her the answer. "Around half past eleven."

I planned to track down this Cara and confirm their alibis. Although I was tempted to cross them off my list because I liked them, my predisposition to trust them was all the more reason for due diligence. I couldn't allow myself to be taken in by their graceful charms and kindness toward me.

"Excuse me, ma'am." Hastings the butler entered the morning room. "Some men from the War Office are here to collect the horses."

"Oh dear." Lady Sybil's cheeks paled. "Father will be beside himself."

Fredricks returned with a glass of whiskey. He handed it to Lady Sybil, who drank it down and then fell into a coughing fit. "Would you like another?" Fredricks asked.

Still coughing, Lady Sybil shook her head. "No. I have to show the War Office gentlemen to the horses." Tears filled her eyes. Wringing her hands, she stood up and went to the window. "Hasn't this horrible war taken enough from us already?"

I remembered what Clifford had said about Lord Rosebrooke closing the front gate forever now that his son, Lady Sybil's brother, had died fighting in Palestine.

"It certainly has," Fredricks consoled her. "Don't worry, ma'am. I'll take care of the War Office."

Whatever did he mean, *take care of*? I frowned. I didn't like the sound of that.

"Would you mind, Detective Inspector?" Lady Sybil put her hand on his sleeve. "My nerves are frayed. I'm going to go out to the caravan."

"Caravan?"

"My friends. They camp out in the far pasture." She rang for her maid. "Being with them relaxes me."

So, it was true. She did travel with the caravan.

"Might you ask if anyone saw someone wandering the grounds last night?" I ventured at the risk of further upsetting her.

"Alright." She closed her eyes. "If it will make you happy."

Her maid entered the room, as stealthy as a cat. "You rang, milady?" She bobbed a quick curtsey.

"Nelly, would you prepare my camping kit?"

"Yes, milady." She smiled, bobbed again, and was off.

"Nelly enjoys our trips to the caravan." Lady Sybil's spirits had already started to improve. "Thank you again, Detective Inspector." She turned back to me and the other women. "If you ladies need anything as you pack to leave, just ask Hastings." She turned to the butler. "Hastings, be so good as to gather donations for the War Orphan Fund from our guests before they leave." As if a weight had been lifted from her shoulders, she bounded out of the room.

Our hostess was fleeing to join a caravan. *Pack to leave.* A not-so-subtle hint that the house party was over. The Friday-to-Monday had been reduced to a Friday-to-Sunday. I hoped Clifford had the requisite donation for the War Orphan Fund.

I followed Fredricks out front where the two men from the War Office were waiting. I'd never seen these soldiers before. They introduced themselves as part of the veterinary service, here to collect the requisitioned horses. So, poor Timmy and the farmers weren't the only ones asked to sacrifice their animals to the cause.

When we reached the stable, Fredricks called out to the groom. But he was nowhere to be seen. We trudged out to the closest pasture. No horses and no groom. On the way back to the house, we poked our heads into the barn again. The groom appeared out of thin air from a dark corner. Had he been there all along?

"These men are from the War Office," Fredricks said. "They've come for the horses."

The groom got a queer look on his face. "Sorry, gents. The 'orses have gone missing."

"The horses are missing?" I asked. "When?" I'd seen at least four horses late last night.

"Early this morning, ma'am." He shifted from foot to foot. "They was stolen, they was."

"More horses stolen?" I squinted at the groom.

How odd... not to mention jolly convenient.

20

THE WIFE AND THE MISTRESS

The barn was huge and held a dozen stalls. Empty stalls. It was hard to imagine hiding a horse. But something odd was afoot. The barn smelled of animals, but none were to be seen. Except the groom's dog. The troughs were full of water. There was hay piled in the corners of the stalls. A sugar lump hung from a hook in one of the stalls. Everything was at it was yesterday, except the horses had vanished.

"Do you mind if we look around?" I asked the groom.

"Suit yourself." He put his thumbs in his suspenders. When he did, I noticed the lining of his jacket had a tear in it. The green silk lining of his jacket. Was he our trellis-climbing murderer? Maybe he was the horse thief too.

"When I saw you out here last night just after midnight, what were you doing again?" I tried to sound nonchalant.

"Tending to the horses." His tone was indignant. Obviously sensing his master's irritation, his dog sat at attention, its ears pricked.

"Then the horses must have been stolen sometime after

midnight?" I walked the length of the barn. Although the stalls were empty, the air still had that warm animal smell.

"Stands to reason, don't it?" He followed close on my heels, and his dog followed on his.

With a look of amusement on his face, smoking a cigarette, Fredricks leaned up against a post and watched. I retracted my lips and silently snarled at him. Was my interview a spectator sport?

"What happened to your jacket?" I asked the groom as I lifted the lid off a large bucket. I immediately regretted it.

"Muck bucket." The groom chuckled.

"That tear in your jacket?" I stopped waving my hand in front of my nose long enough to point to the spot.

"My jacket?" The groom swatted at his jacket as if he'd stepped in a hornets' nest. "Nothing wrong with it." Obviously sensing a threat, the dog moved between me and his master. Had I hit a nerve?

"It's torn." I continued to pick at the lining of his jacket, metaphorically speaking, of course. "You must have got it caught on something."

"Barn's not a place for ladies' finery," he scoffed, his ruddy face turning the color of a ripe tomato. The dog raised its hackles and I backed off.

I didn't want Fredricks to have to come to my rescue. I glanced around. Where was Fredricks? The rotter had disappeared, leaving me alone with a possible murderer and his attack dog. The hairs on my arms stood on end. "Do you have any idea who might have taken the horses?" I headed back toward the door. "The same thief as last time?"

"Yup, same." He'd slowed his pace and I quickened mine.

"Who?" I turned back to him.

"Dunno." He shrugged. "Horse thief."

"Stands to reason." *Horse thief my eye.* He was lying. I could tell by the way he constantly averted his gaze. That and his dog's defensive posture. The groom had hardly given me one straight answer. He was definitely up to something. He was also a large, intimidating man. Next time I questioned him, I'd bring Clifford or Archie or someone more reliable than Fredricks.

Speak of the devil and he shall appear. Fredricks stepped out of the shadows.

"Where have you been?" I brushed hay off my skirt.

"Investigating." He glanced over at the groom, who had stopped to dump a bucket of filthy water. "We make a good team. You distract while I explore."

"How about next time, you distract, and I explore?" I sneezed.

"You're a much prettier distraction." He smiled.

I don't know about that. "No flirting." I stomped a cake of mud off my boot. "We're investigating, remember."

He put his finger to his lips and nodded.

"Where is the jockey?" I glanced around as if he too might appear out of nowhere. I did seem to be conjuring figures from the shadows. When no response came, I repeated, this time louder, "Where is the jockey?"

"Johnny only comes round for the shows or the races." The groom handed his dog what looked like a dead rodent. "Never sticks around."

"He wouldn't have been here last night then?" I stared down at my boots to avoid looking at whatever the dog was eating. "Johnny?"

"No, ma'am." The groom shook his head. "Like I said, Johnny's only here for the shows or races."

I made a mental note to have Clifford follow up on Johnny the jockey's alibi, and I made a circle around the groom. The groom took his dog by the collar and he and the dog both gave me their backs.

"Well, I never." I whirled around and marched out of the barn. Fredricks sprinted to catch up.

"He was lying," I said when I was sure we were out of earshot.

"He certainly was." Fredricks picked a piece of stray hay off my jacket. "I followed some freshly made hoof prints until they disappeared into the wall."

"Disappeared into the wall!" I stopped and stared at him. "That's not possible."

"No, it's not." He picked another piece of hay off my person, this time out of my hair. I swatted at his hand.

"Those horses weren't stolen," he said.

"I concur." I brushed at my sleeves. "But it's not so easy to hide a horse. You can't just tuck it under the floorboards or behind a bookshelf."

"True." Fredricks stroked his chin. "But they don't just disappear either."

"Perhaps we should go back and investigate after the groom and his attack dog have gone to bed." I raised my eyebrows.

He smiled. "Perhaps we should."

When we returned to the house, we found the party assembled in the drawing room. Clifford was holding forth with stories of the morning hunt. I sat down next to him. Rapt with loving attention, Poppy gazed up at him. Everyone else seemed distracted with tea, cocktails, or canapés. Oksana Vorknoy had rejoined the party. Eyes red and puffy, she sat staring at her shoes rather than look across the room at her mirror image, Dorothy, also red-eyed and melancholy. How to approach interviewing two women involved in a homicidal love-triangle? I doubted even the War Office had a brochure for that situation.

Clifford took a break from his tall tales to sip his whiskey, and Oksana quietly turned to Fredricks. "The police told me my husband died of natural causes."

Giving her his full attention, Fredricks pursed his lips.

"Detective Inspector, do you have any more information?" She dabbed her eye with a handkerchief. "He was fine when I left him yesterday." She troubled the corner of the hanky. "We had a terrible row." Tears started flowing. "I feel awful..." Her voice broke off.

Fredricks took her hand in his. "I'm sorry for your loss."

"Rum do, that." Clifford took a seat next to Oksana. He never could resist a woman in distress.

"Such a shame about your husband's struggle with Bright's disease." I picked at a biscuit.

Oksana gave me a queer look. "Sergei didn't have any diseases."

I glanced around. Where was Henry Hobbs? Nowhere to be seen. He'd claimed the doctor had Bright's disease. Either he was lying, or the doctor didn't tell his wife about the diagnosis. "Could your husband have concealed his diagnosis from you?"

"Sergei was fit as a fiddle." She shook her head. "Never sick a day in his life. He took sleeping powders, but nothing else."

Why would Mr. Hobbs lie about Bright's disease?

"I'm sorry to ask, Mrs. Vorknoy." I took a sip of tea. "Might you tell us what your row was about?"

"Good lord, Fi—" Clifford was about to blow my cover. When I scowled at him, he hung his head like a scolded puppy.

Staring across the room at Dorothy, Oksana's jaw moved but she said nothing.

"Me," Dorothy piped up. "Sergei and I were in love. He was getting a divorce so we could marry."

"Lies!" Oksana jumped to her feet. "It was over with you. He'd broken it off. He promised."

"You don't appreciate him like I do." Now Dorothy was on her feet too. "Did." She sniffled.

Fredricks intervened. "Ladies, please..." Standing between the two women, he held out both arms. "He's gone now. There's no use fighting. And there's no bringing him back."

Deflated, both women sat down again.

"Perhaps one of you decided if you couldn't have him..." I stirred my tea for effect. "Then no one could."

"Good lord, Fi, er, Tabitha," Clifford sputtered. "No need to accuse these gentle ladies."

Oksana's eyes went wide. "You killed him, you *shlyukha*." She lunged at the mistress. It was obvious the Russian word was not a compliment.

"You're the tart!" Dorothy growled. "Having an affair with Henry Hobbs."

Oh, my. The doctor's life was something out of a penny dreadful.

"How dare you!" Oksana slapped Dorothy's face.

"I loved him." Dorothy collapsed in a weepy heap on the sofa.

"I say." Clifford blocked Oksana with his body. "Is the bloke really worth fighting over? Fredricks is right. He's gone."

Fredricks and I exchanged glances. No one else seemed to notice that Clifford had called Detective Inspector Baker Evans "Fredricks." I went to Clifford's side and took his elbow. "How about a turn around the garden?" I nodded toward Oksana. "A walk might do us all some good."

"I'd like to collect Sergei's things and go home." Oksana addressed Lady Peggy since her sister and our hostess, Lady Sybil, was still with the caravan.

Lady Peggy rang for the butler and instructed him to bring the doctor's things downstairs and load them into Oksana's motorcar.

"One question before you go, if I may." I stopped in front of Oksana's chair. "Was your husband a fisherman?"

"Good heavens, no." She waved me away. "Sergei hated the

outdoors. He only visited a stable when it would benefit us financially."

"His passing leaves you a very wealthy woman." I leveled my gaze at her.

"Fi, er, Tabitha, really." Clifford was indignant. The poor man had such a thin skin and such a thick sense of propriety.

"Not hardly," Oksana scoffed. "He left me a mountain of gambling debts and no income. The business will go to Mr. Hobbs." She sighed. "I get nothing but the clothes on my back. Even the house will go to our creditors."

Oh dear. Which was worse, a husband who cheated or one who gambled his life away? If Oksana was telling the truth, then far from having a motive to kill her husband, she needed to keep him alive and performing lucrative monkey gland operations. And how about Dorothy? I glanced over at her. She was doubled over on the sofa, holding herself and rocking back and forth. Poor woman. I believed her. She loved the doctor. She didn't kill him.

I made a mental note to cross the wife and the mistress off my list of suspects, at least for now.

21

THE MARSH TEST

I left Clifford and Fredricks refereeing the fighting match between
the wife and the mistress in the drawing room and went upstairs to
see how Kitty was getting along with the fiber tests. When I
opened the door to my bedroom, I was met with the smell of
burning paper. No doubt from Kitty's tests. She lay on my bed, a
fashion magazine in her hands and the dog at her feet. She hadn't
bothered removing her shoes, which had accumulated a great deal
of mud when she'd attacked Fredricks in the bushes. I strode over
to her, lifted her ankles, and moved her feet. After brushing the
residual dirt off my bedspread, I sat at the foot of the bed and
stared at the strange apparatus bubbling away on the dressing
table.

A glass beaker with a stopper and metal funnel was attached
via glass tubing to a small test-tube, also corked, which led to a
glass tube being heated by an open flame.

"What in heaven's name is that?" Poppy gave me her tummy
and I patted it.

"That, Aunt Fiona, is a Marsh test." Kitty dropped her magazine and bounded off the bed. "Watch this." She removed a small

ceramic bowl from her case and handed it to me. Next, she placed the flame near the beaker. "Hold the bowl over the flame."

I came to her side and did as she bade me. As I held the bowl over the flame, she explained the test.

She moved the flame from side to side. "First, I added the carpet sample from the victim's mouth and around his mouth to this glass vessel where I had a zinc and acid solution. If arsenic is present, this produces arsine gas. Look at the bottom of the bowl."

I turned the bowl over. A silvery-black deposit covered the bottom.

"Arsenic." She pointed to the stain. "If arsenic is present, you get that silvery stain. The intensity of the stain determines the amount of arsenic. I'd say your doctor ingested a hefty dose."

"Clever girl." I beamed at her. Now we knew conclusively that the doctor did not die of natural causes. He was poisoned. We just had to determine who administered the arsenic and how.

"I tried a few other tests to no avail." She extinguished the flame. "Then I tried the Marsh test and bingo!"

"So glad you're here." I put my arm around her slim shoulders and squeezed. "Why are you here?"

"Captain Hall sent me to tell you that Fredrick Fredricks was spotted in London." She began disassembling her apparatus. "But I see you already know that." She glanced over at me and raised her eyebrows. "I hear Lieutenant Somersby showed up." She laughed. "Pretending to be your husband." She was laughing so hard she had to brush away tears. "Did you perform your wifely duties?"

Wifely duties. Perhaps my own life was starting to resemble a penny dreadful. Bouncing between Fredricks and Archie and back again. "Settle down." I gave her a side-eye. "Nasty trick telling him I'd eloped with Clifford."

She howled.

"How could you?" I stood glaring at her, my hands on my hips. "It's not funny. He believed you."

"Nooooo." She sucked in air. "You and Uncle Clifford. It's too funny."

"The only way I could get Archie to speak to me again was to promise to marry him." I slipped off my shoes and dug my toes into the throw rug. "And it's all your fault."

"Don't you want to marry him?" Her tone grew serious. "He's kind and very attractive."

"True."

"So why don't you want to marry him?" She took my hand and sat me down on the end of the bed. "Is everything alright? I didn't really ruin things, did I?" She bit her lip. "I didn't mean to, honestly, Aunt Fiona. I was just having a bit of fun."

Sigh. "Let's forget about my marriage prospects and get back to the murder."

"Are you really going to marry him?" She toyed with a bit of lace on her dress.

I retrieved my notebook from my skirt pocket. "The suspects," I said, ignoring her. I tapped my pencil on the list of suspects. "Henry Hobbs is set to inherit the business and yet he claims to have an alibi. He wasn't here. Neither was the doctor's wife, Oksana." I looked up at Kitty. "How long does it take for arsenic to kill a person?"

"Depends on how much they ingest." She sat next to me on the bed. "Judging by the intensity of the stain in the Marsh test, the doctor ingested a lot, obviously a lethal dose. And given that he was in good health until he died, I'd say he was given one large lethal dose, probably thirty to sixty minutes before his death."

"Thirty to sixty minutes," I repeated. "That rules out Henry Hobbs and Oksana since they'd left hours earlier. So had Mr. Jäger." I thought of the chimp and the whiskey trick. Not only was it too early to account for our poison, but also others had drunk the same whiskey. What was I thinking? Dr. Vorknoy murdered by a chimpanzee. How absurd. Although it would be poetic justice.

"Unless." Kitty held up a finger. "One of them put the dose into something he ingested long after they'd left."

"Something like sleeping powders." My pulse quickened.

"Or a late-night brandy or cocoa," Kitty added.

"Oksana is leaving with the doctor's belongings." I snapped shut my notebook. "We've got to stop her and get those powders."

I ran down the stairs and back to the drawing room. "Where's Oksana?" Out of breath, I put my hands on my knees and sucked in air.

"She's leaving," Peggy said. "Hastings is helping her load her motorcar now."

"Thank you." I dashed outside.

Across the driveway, Oksana sat in the driver's seat of her motorcar while a footman loaded cases into the boot. I sprinted to the car. "The doctor's toiletries," I panted. "I need to see his sleeping powders."

Mouth open, the footman stood staring at me. Oksana got out of the motorcar. "What's wrong?" She came around to the back.

"Your husband's sleeping powders. We think that's how the killer delivered the poison."

"Poison?" She put her hand to her mouth. "Why do you say he was poisoned?"

"My associate, er, niece, is an expert in forensics." I pointed to a small leather case. "May I take the sleeping powders to have them analyzed?"

"Who would want to poison Sergei?" She looked stunned.

"That's what I aim to find out." I stepped in front of the footman and lifted the case out of the boot.

Before I knew it, Fredricks and Clifford had joined me.

"I say." Clifford lit his pipe. "What's going on?"

"Kitty determined the cause of death was arsenic poisoning." I opened the case and peered inside. "I'm looking for the doctor's sleeping powders."

"You think the killer added arsenic to the doctor's sleeping powders." Fredricks peered over my shoulder. "That means the killer knew the doctor's routines. It had to be someone close to him." His breath on my neck made me shiver.

Someone like his wife or his mistress. Or... "Who prescribed the sleeping powders?" I asked. "And where did he get them? What chemists?"

"He was a doctor," Oksana said. "He didn't need a chemist. If he ran out, Henry always brought them over for him."

"Henry Hobbs?"

She nodded. "He's a dear boy."

How dear?

"The horrible gossip." Her head jerked. "Dorothy is out of place and dead wrong suggesting there is anything untoward between Henry and me." She huffed. "He's a good friend of the family, like an adopted son. I would never..."

"And now your husband's lucrative practice is his." Perhaps she and Mr. Hobbs knocked off the doctor for romantic *and* business reasons. That was a doubly strong motive.

"In any case, neither Henry nor I were here last night," she said, as if reading my mind.

Convenient. Supposedly, they both had solid alibis. A bit too convenient. Anyway, they could have slipped the poison into the sleeping powders at any time and then left Mentmore Castle to ensure they had alibis.

Aha. I clutched a small brown bottle. "Found them." I held up the sleeping powders. "May I take this?"

"Take whatever you want." Oksana waved me away.

"Who had access to these?" I shook the bottle.

"I did." She gasped. "But I didn't... I couldn't..."

"Who else?" I asked.

"Besides Sergei and Henry." She thought for a second. "No one."

"Thank you, Mrs. Vorknoy." I patted her arm. "We'll let you know what we find out."

Clifford took her elbow and led her to the front of the car. "Would you like me to drive you home?"

"Would you?" She looked up at him with tears welling in her eyes.

"I'd be delighted." Clifford smiled. "Let me fetch my coat and hat."

"I have a for job you," I said, tagging along with Clifford as he dashed back into the house. "A very important assignment. One crucial to our investigation."

"I say, an important assignment." He grinned. "I like the sound of that." He loved to play detective.

"I need you to check up on some alibis, starting with Oksana Vorknoy's." True. She could have poisoned the sleeping powders at any time. But on the off chance the powders weren't contaminated, I needed Clifford to check all alibis. Someone was lying.

"Good lord, Fiona." He tightened his lips. "You don't think that poor woman had anything to do with her husband's death?"

"All wives want to kill their husbands at some point or other." I quickened my pace to keep up with him.

"Fiona, you say the darndest things." His long legs carried him up the stairs two by two. "Anyway, they don't actually do it."

"Some of them do," I called after him. I had to stop on the stairs to catch my breath. I waited for him to come back down and then continued my pursuit. "Ask to go in for tea or brandy or something, a glass of water even, and then ask the staff what time she returned home yesterday and if she went out again last night." I nearly tripped down the stairs trying to keep up with him. He was in such a hurry to help a damsel in distress. "And while you're at it, I need you to check on Johnny the jockey's and Mr. Hobbs's alibis, too. Find out if anyone other than his wife saw Mr. Hobbs last night."

"Oh, alright, Johnny the jockey and Hobbs." He puffed. "It had to be one of those fellows because that poor woman isn't capable of such a heinous crime."

"You'd be surprised." Still clutching the sleeping powders, I left Clifford to escort Oksana into the motorcar. I'd bet my favorite wig these powders contained arsenic. I looked forward to witnessing Kitty's Marsh test in action again.

Back in the bedroom, Kitty was just as excited to perform the test as I was to watch. She arranged the beaker and flame on the dressing table just as before. From bottles in her case, she added zinc and acid to the beaker. Then she dumped in a healthy dose of the sleeping powders. "Watch this." She ignited the gas flame. "Get the bowl."

I did as she bade. The bowl had been cleaned since our last use and sat on a cushion in her case. Just as before, I held it over the flame. After a minute, Kitty and I both examined the bottom of the bowl. There was a sooty stain but no silver tint. "Arsenic?" I asked.

She shook her head. "Afraid not."

"Are you sure?" Blast. I'd been certain we'd found the killer's delivery method. It was perfect. What could be easier than slipping poison into his sleeping powders?

"Absolutely." She extinguished the flame. "The arsenic did not come from this bottle."

"Then where?" I paced the room. "How did the killer get the doctor to ingest the poison?"

"We should ask the kitchen staff if he took anything before

bed." Kitty took a rag from her case and wiped the dressing table, an unusually tidy gesture for her, which I appreciated.

"Good idea." I stopped in my tracks. "And we should reexamine the doctor's room. Perhaps you'll see something I missed." I'd been thorough, of course. But Kitty's knowledge of forensics gave her an expert's eye.

"Right." She picked up Poppy and cuddled her, cooing into her topknot. "You stay here and be a good girl. Mummy will be back in a minute." She gave the creature a kiss, and then accompanied me next door to the doctor's room.

To my surprise, the door was locked. Perhaps Lady Sybil had got tired of us snooping around with a murder investigation that would cause a scandal. I removed my handy lockpick set from a pocket of my bespoke skirt. Clapping her hands, Kitty watched over my shoulder as I deftly maneuvered the little torsion wrench and the rake in the keyhole. A noise from the stairs made me freeze. Before I could remove my tools from the lock and hide them away, Fredricks appeared in the hallway. I breathed a sigh of relief. Honor among thieves and all that rot.

He joined us and watched intently as I went back to picking the lock.

When the door popped open, Kitty stifled a squeal and then gave me a hug. "Aunt Fiona, you're marvelous."

"Isn't she just?" Fredricks's dark eyes danced. "Nothing excites me more than a woman wielding a snake rake."

"You're a snake." I withdrew from Kitty's embrace. "And a rake."

"Ladies." He chuckled and gestured into the room. "After you."

I entered and surveyed the room. An emptiness hung in the air like a melancholy spirit. The bed was neatly made. The closet was empty. The dressing table and nightstand had been wiped clean. Not even a dust mote sullied their shining surfaces.

"Blast." I circled the room. "The maids would have taken away any residual evidence."

Leisurely smoking, Fredricks leaned against the windowsill.

"Move away from the window," I ordered.

Startled, he straightened.

"I think the killer used the window to gain access to the room." I went to the window and pushed Fredricks out of the way—which he enjoyed far too much.

Kitty joined me at the window. "Can I borrow your magnifying glass?" She held out her hand.

"The door was locked from the inside, and Archie had to break it open." I slipped the magnifier out of my pocket and handed it to her. "There's no other way in or out, so I suspect the killer went out through the window." I opened the window and poked my head out. "I found a bit of fabric on the trellis, which makes me think our killer went out the window and then climbed down the trellis to the ground." From my experience, the trellis was too rickety to hold a grown man. A petite woman, perhaps? Someone like Lady Peggy or the duchess?

"Look!" Kitty held the glass to the windowsill.

I bent down and peered through the glass. "A tiny piece of hair."

"And grass." She smiled and held out her hand again. "Tweezers."

I handed her my tweezers, then ripped a blank page from my notebook and sat it on the ledge. Carefully, she picked up the hair and the grass with the tweezers and dropped them onto the piece of paper. I collected the paper and folded it, mindful not to spill its contents.

"We'll know more once I test the hair and the grass."

I held the newfound evidence in both hands like a precious

gem, while Kitty returned my magnifying glass and tweezers to my skirt pocket.

"I'm feeling a bit peckish." Fredricks stretched and yawned. "How about I go interview the kitchen staff?"

"Good idea. Find out if the doctor had anything else to eat or drink before he died." Careful not to drop my cargo, I followed Fredricks and Kitty out into the hall. "But make sure you come back."

"I'll bring back treats, ma chérie."

"Treat. Goodie." Kitty skipped ahead of us. "Don't forget about Poppy. We love treats, don't we, Poppy-poo?"

Fredricks and I exchanged glances.

"Our weekend in the country is coming to an end," I said wistfully. "Which means we only have another couple of hours to find the killer." I walked behind Kitty, carrying my prize flat on my palm. "And to pack." But not before I made one last trip to the stables to find out what that groom was hiding.

22

THE CONFESSION

Back in my room, I sat my suitcase on the bed and quickly packed up some of my things, while Kitty set to work examining the strands of hair and grass. *Impressive.* Turned out, her case had a false bottom and underneath she stored a microscope. She set it up on the dressing table, prepared slides, and using my tweezers deposited the specimens on the slides. *Clever girl.*

At the bottom of my bed lay a book. Kitty never read books. I picked it up. A book by someone called Hans Gross. It had one of those German titles a mile long. "What's this?"

"Only the best forensics handbook in the world." She set up the microscope. "There's a whole chapter on dust. The microscopic debris that cover our clothes and environs are mute witnesses."

"Dust?" I hated to think what a forensics expert could find in my dusty flat.

"You'd be surprised at how much dust can tell you about a person. Where he's been. What he does for a living... and for fun." She smiled over at me.

"Fascinating." I returned her smile. "I'll leave you to your dust. I'm going to snoop around the barn." I exchanged my practical

Oxfords for my sturdy boots. "That groom is up to something and before we leave, I'm going to find out what."

"Right." Bent over her microscope, Kitty didn't look up. "I'll know more by the time you get back."

I threw on my coat and tugged on my gloves. Poppy turned circles around my ankles. "No Poppy, you can't come with me." The creature sat in front of the door and wouldn't let me pass. When I reached for the doorknob, the beast started barking. "Please, Poppy, let me pass." Poppy tilted her head and gave me that irresistible big-eyed pleading look.

"She probably has to go out," Kitty said, still looking into her microscope.

Oh dear. I didn't want any accidents. Poppy didn't have the best manners when it came to her bathroom habits. "Oh, alright."

Kitty fetched a leash from her case. "Be a good girl, Poppy-poo." She called the dog Poppy-*poo* for a reason.

When I attached the leash to the dog's collar, she smiled up at me, her tongue lolling. "Yes, you're sweet." I patted her on the head, careful to avoid the sharp diamond attached to her collar. I'd seen the little beast use it to cut through thick ropes. Her mistress wasn't the only trained espionage agent.

As I turned the doorknob to go, Kitty cleared her throat loudly. I turned around and she wagged her finger at me. "You're not going to get out of it, Aunt Fiona."

"Out of what?" I squinted at her.

"Before we leave, we need to decide what to do about Fredricks." She raised her eyebrows. "He is an enemy spy." More finger wagging. "And Captain Hall ordered us to trail him and get intel."

"I am trailing him." More like *he* was trailing *me*. "Let me worry about Fredricks." I adjusted my hat. *Keep your friends close and your enemies closer* had taken on a new meaning. I gave Poppy's leash a tiny tug.

"I hope you know what you're doing." Kitty shook her head and went back to her slides.

"So do I." Poppy and I stepped into the hall, and I closed the door behind us. *So do I.*

As an afterthought, I dashed back inside and grabbed my handbag. Through the heavy fabric, I fingered Mata Hari's pearl-handled gun. *Just in case...*

The grass was still wet from the constant rain. You need webbed feet for February in England. Poppy didn't seem to mind. She sniffed and ran ahead, pulling at the leash. With every step, my boots stuck in the muddy grass and made an unpleasant sucking sound. When I reached the stables, they were caked with mud. Another pair of boots ruined. I shook my head. Espionage was deuced hard on my footwear.

"Yoo-hoo." Wrapping the end of Poppy's leash around my wrist, I called out into the darkness. "Anyone here?" Holding the hilt of Mata Hari's gun through the fabric of my handbag, I stepped inside the barn. My handbag—and Poppy—leading the way, I patrolled the parameter of the stables. All the stalls were empty. Still no sign of the horses. No sign of the groom or his dog either.

Poppy yanked at the leash. I lurched forward. "Naughty girl." I resisted as best I could. But the leash slipped off my wrist and the little wretch broke free. She ran to a dark corner of the barn where she barked and jumped and carried on as if she'd seen a ghost. Oh, what a gruesome thought. I ventured into the darkness after her.

Kitty would never forgive me if anything happened to her precious little dog. I withdrew the gun from my handbag. Slowly, step by step, I let the darkness swallow me. The further I moved from the entrance and from the light, the thicker the sweet smell of manure hung in the air. A smell that always took me back to my grandfather's farm. So many hours hiding in the hayloft reading Sherlock Holmes stories when I was supposed to be slopping pigs or darning socks.

"What in heaven's name is the matter with you?" I could hear the little creature, but I couldn't see her. Barking and scratching. I hoped to heaven it was the dog and not something other-worldly. "Poppy?" My toe hit something hard. I put my hands out in front of me. A post. I stood a few seconds waiting for my eyes to adjust. "Poppy, get over here and stop that incessant noise." The dog ignored me. In the distance, dim shadows danced across the back wall. I moved toward them, hoping one of them was Poppy.

"Did you know dogs have thousands of times the scent capabilities of humans?" The voice came out of the darkness.

I gasped. Steadying the gun with both hands, I aimed at the disembodied voice. "Who goes there?"

"You should heed the dog's warning," the muffled voice said.

"I'm armed." I waved the gun. Not that it did any good. No one could see a bloody thing back in this windowless corner of Hades. "Show yourself."

Holding a sandwich in one hand and his deerstalker in the other, Fredricks stepped out of the shadows. "Fancy half my sandwich?" He held it out. No wonder I didn't recognize his voice. He was stuffing his mouth.

I shook my head. "What are you doing out here?" And how did he get here so fast?

"Same as you, I expect." He waved the sandwich toward Poppy, who was jumping at the back wall and barking her head off. "I'm serious about the dog. She senses what we can only imagine."

"That's what I'm afraid of." I glanced from Fredricks to Poppy. Filling my lungs with courage, gun first, I went to the dog. "What have you found?" She stopped barking and jumping and sat on her haunches, her tongue lolling. "Well?" I bent down to take her leash. "What is it?"

She ran back and forth along the back wall so fast the leash trailed behind her like a snake slithering away from a cat. Running after her, my foot slipped, and I fell face first into the muck. "You little beast!" The gun flew out of my hand and bounced across the muddy floor. Why was the floor muddy? There was a sturdy roof overhead. Panting, I blew the hay straw out of my face. *What in the world?* A beam of light shone through a chink in the bottom of one of the wall boards. "There's something behind this wall." I scurried to my feet.

Fredricks stood over me holding Mata Hari's gun.

My stomach sank. I'd been in this position too many times before. He'd got the drop on me. But why? I thought we were working together. What happened to Holmes and Watson?

"You dropped this." He stuffed the gun in his jacket pocket and then held out his hand. "Let me help you up."

I reached up and took his hand. In one fluid movement, he hauled me to my feet. He pulled me close. Too close. His heady sandalwood scent gave me goosebumps. Holding me tight around the waist, he whispered in my ear, "You should be more careful, ma chérie." His breath was warm on my neck. "I wouldn't want you to get hurt." It almost sounded like a threat. I wrenched myself out of his arms.

"There's something behind this wall." I watched Poppy, looking for a clue. Barking, she raced the length of the wall. But she always stopped in the same spot, sniffed, and then went back to running. I went to the spot and knelt. Running my gloved hand across the bottom of the wall board, I tried pushing and pulling. Nothing. I continued running my hand up the length of the board as high as I could reach. Above my head, barely within my reach, I felt something. A latch or button. Something hard and metal. "I found something."

Fredricks came to my side. He reached up and twisted the latch-button. The wall panel came loose. When he pushed on it, it moved. The whole panel seemed to be on wheels and pullies.

Light streamed into the barn, and I shielded my eyes. "Oh, my sainted aunt."

"Indeed." Fredricks stepped inside.

On the other side was another barn. A hidden barn. The missing horses happily munched on hay in their individual stalls. Although much smaller than the mammoth barn on the other side of the trick wall, it was amazing that anyone could hide something this size. Half a dozen horses hidden inside a wall. Like something out of a fantasy novel.

"Don't go any further." The groom appeared from behind one of the secret stalls, holding up a pitchfork. "Turn around, nice and slow like." The groom was hiding horses in this secret barn, presumably on Lord Rosebrooke's directive. Hiding their horses from the War Office. Could the groom be the killer? By the looks of it, he would go to great lengths to protect these horses. Did they include murder? He'd threatened me with a gun earlier and now he was wielding a pitchfork. And he'd been lurking around the barn after midnight the night of the murder. Then there was that tear in the lining of his jacket, green lining, just like the fabric I'd found stuck to the trellis.

Poppy ran to my side, stood in front of me, and barked and snarled like a crazed beast. Did she think she was a guard dog? "Poppy, hush." She bared her teeth. Tiny teeth. No match for a pitchfork.

"Blue." The groom whistled. His dog appeared out of nowhere, hackles raised.

I bent down to grab Poppy. But Blue got there first.

"Oh, no!"

Blue went for Poppy's throat. He'd barely touched her when he let out a yelp and retreated. I snatched her up and pressed her to my breast. The diamond on her collar. It was wet with blood. She had the bigger tooth after all. Thank goodness. If anything had happened to her, I'd never forgive myself. "Sweet little Poppy-poo." *Good grief.* I was as bad as Kitty.

Fredricks pulled Mata Hari's gun from his pocket. "Drop that pitchfork and call off your dog."

"Whatcha going to do with that toy?" The groom laughed. "Do you play with dollies, too?"

"I've been known to play with *a dolly* now and again." Fredricks gave me a sly smile.

I scowled.

Wielding the pitchfork, the groom lunged at Fredricks, grunting as he went.

Bang!

The gun went off. The groom dropped the pitchfork and wailed. He held one hand with the other. "You shot me." He sounded incredulous.

Fredricks had shot the man square in the hand.

"He's an expert huntsman." I tilted my head back and sniffed.

"What do you know?" Fredricks chuckled. "The toy shoots real bullets." He helped the groom to a barrel and sat him down. "Time you confessed, sir." He held the tiny gun in the groom's face.

Grimacing and holding his hand, the groom shook his head. "We couldn't let the War Office take them. Them's prize animals. Do you know how the army treats their 'orses?" With pleading eyes, he looked from me to Fredricks. "Do you know how many have been lost?" He sucked in air. "Disease, starvation, abandoned, blown up."

Golly. Was he crying?

"No. Not our beauties." He stood up. "They'll go over my dead body." He puffed out his chest. "I'll not let them be slaughtered like that."

"Calm down," I said. "We're not here to take your horses." I looked at Fredricks. "Are we?"

"Certainly not. He's right. Too many men and beasts have been sacrificed already." Fredricks tucked the gun back into his pocket. "And for what?"

I certainly didn't know.

"You're not going to take the horses?" The groom slumped back against the barrel.

"No." I handed Poppy to Fredricks. "Watch her."

He balked but took the squirming beast.

I removed a handkerchief from my skirt pocket and wrapped it around the groom's bloody hand. "What do you know about Dr. Vorknoy's murder?"

"What?" He flinched. "Murder?"

I lifted the corner of his jacket and pointed to the tear in the lining. "I found green fabric attached to the trellis outside the doctor's window." I tugged the ends of the handkerchief together and tied them in a tight knot.

The groom yelped. "I may not be a gentleman, but I don't kiss and tell."

Fredricks and I looked at each other.

"It's that or a noose." Fredricks patted his pocket where he'd stashed the gun.

The groom closed his eyes and let out a defeated sigh. "Before the party, that were Peggy's room." His face as red as a tomato, he continued his confession. "Peggy and me. That is Lady Peggy. She... I... we..."

Good heavens. No wonder Lady Sybil didn't approve of her

sister's "riding." And no wonder the trellis was worn out and rickety.

"We get the picture," Fredricks said, putting him out of his misery.

I felt in my pockets for another handkerchief or something else to stem the bleeding. Instead, I pulled out the bit of rope I'd found in the bushes. "You wouldn't happen to know what this is?"

He took the rope from my hand. "From a sugar block." He pointed at one of the stalls. Sure enough, a sugar block hung from a hook while a gray mare licked at it.

"Why would it be in the bushes?" I asked.

"No idea." He tilted his head. "A sugar block went missin' yesterday."

"Someone nicked a block of sugar?" Why would someone steal a block of sugar? And what did it have to do with the doctor's murder?

"Sure did." He nodded. "I know 'cos I'd just put a new one in Champ's stall and an hour later it was gone. Vanished like."

"How very interesting." I tucked the rope back into my pocket. "Now, let's get you to a doctor."

He nodded and I helped him up. Fredricks traded me Poppy for the groom, and we made our way back to the house. Blue stayed behind to "guard the horses."

When Lady Peggy saw the blood from the groom's hand, she flew into action. She called Hastings, who in turn called a maid, who fetched hot water and bandages. She telephoned the doctor and then she fawned over the groom until he'd turned the color of an aubergine. The embarrassment seemed to pain him more than the gunshot.

While everyone else was fussing over the wounded groom, Poppy and I went to see how Kitty was getting on with the hair and grass samples.

Poppy burst into the room, yipping and yapping as if she was trying to tell her mistress about our adventures.

"Yes, Poppy." I removed the leash from her collar. "You found the missing horses."

"Oh, what a good girl." Kitty scooped up the dog and cuddled her. "I missed you too, Poppy-poo." The pup licked her mistress's face.

Ahhh. Disgusting, but sweet.

"Did you learn anything about those samples?" I dropped onto the bed and tugged off my muddy boots. Speaking of disgusting.

Kitty danced Poppy around the room. "You'll never guess what I found."

"In that case, why don't you tell me, dear." I rubbed my socked foot. *Sigh. What a day.*

"The grass is actually a bit of hay." She stopped dancing and held Poppy up like a doll. "And remember that hair?"

"Of course." I rolled my eyes.

"It's not human." She wiggled Poppy's feet.

"Not human." I gaped at her.

"It's from a chimpanzee." She kissed the dog's muzzle. "Right, Poppy-poo? A monkey-poo."

Good heavens. "That can only mean one thing." I stuffed my feet into my practical Oxfords. "One of Mr. Jäger's chimpanzees was in the doctor's room. I must get back to Porton Down and find that chimp."

23

THE PARTY'S OVER

As Kitty cleaned up after her experiments, I zipped around the room gathering up the rest of my belongings and stuffing them into my suitcase. While I finished packing, I reviewed the case so far. Last week, I'd gone to Porton Down under orders to find the mole-saboteur. The suspects were Birdy, Mr. Jäger, and Mr. Hobbs. The doctor was dead, so if he was the mole, our problem was solved. And his nurse was more interested in the doctor than his animals, so I doubted she was the mole—although as I was always telling Clifford, never underestimate a woman. It was too late to go back to Porton Down today, but tomorrow morning, first thing. While I was there, I would question Private Birdwhistle and Mr. Hobbs to rule them out as mole-saboteurs.

Before I left Mentmore Castle, I must question Lizzy and Lady Nina about Birdy's involvement with the Animal Defense Society. I knew he was the son of Lady Nina's cook, and he loved animals and hated fighting, but was he sabotaging operations at Porton Down? If Birdy was the mole-saboteur, had he also killed the doctor? Was he perhaps working with Mr. Jäger? Were they both German spies? If I was lucky, tomorrow at Porton Down I could interrogate Mr. Jäger, who had recently moved up my list of suspects for both mole-saboteur and possible murderer. I'd seen his temper when he'd threatened the doctor back at Porton Down. But how was he connected to Lizzy Lind and the Animal Defense Society? Somehow my assignment to find the mole-saboteur was related to the doctor's murder. I had an idea. Perhaps the doctor had discovered the mole-saboteur's identity, and that's why he was killed. If I found the doctor's killer, I'd find the mole-saboteur.

The chimp hair in the doctor's room proved that a chimp was involved in the murder. At Porton Down, I would look for Lazarus the chimp from the evening's performance. If I found him, I might get a clue to how the doctor was poisoned. Lazarus had filled the gentlemen's whiskey glasses and thus had access to the doctor's glass. Yet, since none of the other men fell ill, the whiskey itself was not poisoned. Not only that, but the doctor also drank the whiskey well before the window of death by arsenic, which, according to Kitty, was between eleven-thirty and midnight, when I heard the doctor crash to the floor of his room. There was no evidence that the doctor ingested anything later that night. And yet, there was a chimpanzee in his room. If only I knew what time the chimp had left the room. Before leaving Mentmore Castle, I had to narrow down the suspects. Mr. Hobbs and Mr. Jäger were the persons most directly in control of the monkeys. I would find them and interview them tomorrow at Porton Down.

Satisfied that I had a plan, I went back to packing. I removed my hatboxes from the closet and sat them on the bed next to my suitcase. Next, I retrieved my toiletries bag from the dressing table. Also on the table was Fredricks's slouch hat. Aha. An insurance policy that he would indeed return. Hopefully soon and with news from the kitchen staff. Smiling to myself, I grabbed my toiletries bag, took it to the bed, and then tucked it into my case.

As I surveyed the room for any stray articles that I may have missed, I refocused my mind on the possible connections between the funny business at Porton Down and the doctor's death. The chimpanzee was the missing link. Was Mr. Jäger doing more than delivering animals and putting on shows? The doctor's whiskey had to have been somehow contaminated with arsenic during the monkey show. Mr. Jäger could have done it and left the castle. But why didn't the arsenic take effect until hours later? The show ended at ten and Archie and I heard the doctor crash to the floor at midnight. According to Kitty, the poison should have taken effect much sooner. I rolled up a pair of stockings and tucked them in the corner of my suitcase. There were still so many unanswered questions.

Kitty snapped her case shut and then plopped down on my bed. Poppy jumped up and licked her face, which sent the girl into a fit of giggles. They certainly loved each other. I don't know whether Poppy had a mind or intelligence, but she was jolly clever and full of joy and love. There was more to this Animal Defense Society business than I'd originally thought. Indeed, I hadn't really thought much about animals or their importance to our lives. Again, I thought perhaps I should get a cat.

Come on, Fiona, concentrate. You don't have much time left at Mentmore to solve the murder. Hopefully, Fredricks was interviewing Cara the kitchen maid. I still needed to question Lady Nina about Birdy. I pulled my notebook and pencil from my bespoke skirt pocket and dropped into the dressing table chair. Trying to ignore my haggard reflection in the looking glass, I examined my notes and recounted my list of suspects. Both the wife and the mistress suspected each other. And yet they both seemed sincere in their feelings for the man. What would Clifford find when he checked the wife's alibi? Where in the devil was Clifford? Why wasn't he back yet? Probably still *consoling* Mrs. Vorknoy.

Without thinking, I reached out and caressed Fredricks's hat.

The felt was soft between my fingers. Since Kitty was present, I withstood the temptation to lift it to my nose and sniff. Just thinking about it conjured the scent of sandalwood and manly charisma. *I do wish the rascal would hurry and return from the kitchen. How long could it take to get a snack?* To distract myself from inappropriate thoughts about an enemy spy—a cursed charming enemy spy—I re-read my list of suspects.

Ah. Yes. The groom. I'd circled his name. Although the groom certainly seemed capable of murder, he'd satisfactorily explained the bit of green fabric torn from his jacket. He hadn't climbed up or down the trellis to kill the doctor. Rather, he'd been having an affair with Lady Peggy. And his threatening behavior in the barn had been to conceal the fact that he was hiding the horses to prevent the War Office from requisitioning them. If he was evasive and secretive, it was because he was doing something illegal. But it wasn't killing the doctor. As for the jockey, he wasn't present during the chimp's performance or when the doctor died. *Clifford, where the heck are you?* Hopefully, he'd managed to confirm—or not—the alibis of Mrs. Vorknoy, the jockey, and Mr. Hobbs. I only hoped he returned before Lady Sybil got back from her sojourn with the caravan and threw us all out on our ears.

A rap at the door sent me flying. *Clifford.* I opened it. "Oh, it's you."

"Don't look so disappointed." Fredricks held out a plate of chocolate biscuits. "I told you I'd return with treats." He reached into his pocket and pulled out a napkin. Unfolding it, he laid it on the floor. "For Poppy, as requested." On the napkin were several small bits of meat. Wagging her tail, the pup jumped down and made a beeline to her treat. "And I come bearing news." He stood grinning at me. The bounder knew I'd rather have news than a biscuit.

"Spit it out." The way he teased me, I felt like socking him.

Laughing, he flinched as if I had hit him. "No need for violence, ma chérie."

I stood, arms akimbo, waiting for the news.

"Alright. Cara the kitchen maid told me that the doctor did not take any food or drink after the show, at least not that she knows of, and she appears to know everything that goes on in this house." He bent down and patted Poppy on the head. She licked her chops and smiled up at him. "Why do you think it took me so long in the kitchen?"

"Go on," I said, tapping my foot.

"She also confirmed she took cocoa and biscuits to the ladies at half past eleven and picked up their tray just before midnight." He winked. "And I heard a great deal about Lady Peggy's *riding lessons*."

"I bet." I rolled my eyes.

"Word around the castle is the groom's an excellent teacher." Kitty's bright eyes sparkled. "The parlor maid told—"

Luckily, another, louder, knock at the door interrupted her. I answered it.

Holding a small tray in his gloved hand, a footman stood at attention. "A telegram for Detective Inspector Baker Evans." He didn't make eye contact.

I snatched the telegram off the tray before Fredricks could get to it. Blast. The bloody thing was in Russian. Fredricks came to my side and slid the telegram out from between my fingers.

"What is it?" I glanced over at Kitty, but she was busy playing with Poppy. No doubt the girl had learned Russian, along with a dozen other languages, at her *boarding school* in France. She could translate the telegram.

"Pressing business." Fredricks's expression became serious.

"What pressing business?" I peeked over his shoulder at the telegram, for all the good it did. It was signed V. Lenin. I'd heard of him, of course. The leader of the Bolshevik government. "War business?"

"Just the opposite." He tucked the telegram into his pocket. "Peace business."

"That's what you always say—" I knew better than to believe him.

"That's because it's true." He raised his eyebrows.

"Why are you here?" I blurted out. Of course, I'd been trying to discern his scheme since he showed up at my door dripping blood all over the carpet. And as always, he'd been evasive and never given a straight answer.

"I've already told you, to support Miss Lind and her fellow pacifists." He sighed. "My mission, thanks to you, ma chérie, is to foster peace across the globe."

Thanks to me. What a laugh. "And what of the Animal Defense Society?" I aimed the question and threw it at him like a poisoned dart. He was, after all, a notorious huntsman. Clifford was constantly telling horrible stories about their hunting exploits and all the defenseless beasts they'd killed.

"I believe all animals, including human beings, should be allowed to roam free."

"Except the ones you kill?"

"I only hunt predators that could easily kill me given the chance."

"And when would they get the chance?"

"You'd be surprised." He went over and patted Poppy on the head. "It's a dog-eat-dog world, right, little one?"

"Poppy is an obligate carnivore," Kitty said. "We aren't." What did she mean by that? Come to think of it, I'd never seen Kitty eat meat—or much of anything else except sweets. Had the girl become one of those radical vegetarians?

"I'd love to stay and debate the merits of vegetarianism and hunting..." Fredricks retrieved his slouch hat from the dressing table. "But I'm afraid I'm going to have to leave you now."

"You can't leave." I grabbed his arm. "When will I see you—" I stopped myself and glanced over at Kitty, who mouthed, "Careful."

"Why do you care?" Fredricks smiled down at me. "You're in love with the bad lieutenant, remember?"

"Archie's not bad." I wrenched my gaze away from his annoyingly beautiful face.

"He's not good enough for you." Fredricks took my hand, which was—to my chagrin—still on his sleeve. "Don't worry, ma chérie." He kissed my hand. "I'll stop to say goodbye before I leave town." As he gazed into my eyes, an uncomfortable heat traveled up my neck. "As always, I'll tell you where to find me." He broke away and turned toward Kitty. "Au revoir, Miss Lane." He bowed and doffed his hat. "And Miss Poppy."

Fredricks was barely out the door when Clifford bounded in. "You'll never guess where I've been," he said, out of breath. "I took Oksana home and then questioned her staff. I was right. She told the truth. She was home all afternoon, evening, and night. And didn't go out again until she came back here to Mentmore." He removed his gloves, one finger at a time. "Then I went to check up on our jockey and found him in rather an embarrassing situation with the doorman in his building." His cheeks reddened. "Suffice it to say, he's not left his bedroom since he arrived home." He removed his hat and threw his gloves inside. "As for Mr. Hobbs, this is where things get interesting."

"Go on." I sat on my bed next to my suitcase.

"His wife answered the door but wouldn't speak to me." Clifford shook his head. "Rude woman slammed the door in my face." Given his usual success at chatting up people, especially ladies, that must have been quite a shock. "But his neighbor was more than willing to tell tales."

"Go on," I said, impatiently.

"Mr. Hobbs came home just as he said." Clifford tilted his head and smiled. "But about midnight he went out again."

"Midnight?" That was around the time I'd heard the doctor crash to the floor. If Mr. Hobbs left at midnight, he may have lied about being home all night, but he still had an alibi for the doctor's murder.

"And get this..." Clifford took his pipe from his pocket, clamped the stem between his teeth, and lit it. "Turns out Oksana's butler, Geoffrey, is quite a hunter. He's always wanted to go on safari, you see. And when I told him about the time Fredricks and I were in the Serengeti hunting—"

"What in the world does that have to do with Mr. Hobbs?" I jumped up off the bed.

"I'm getting to that." Clifford had that hurt hangdog look of his.

"Well, get there faster, if you please." I paced a circle around the room. The man tried my patience, to say the least.

"Geoffrey saw none other than Mr. Hobbs visit the house that night after midnight." Clifford puffed on his pipe. "Seems Mr. Hobbs is a regular late-night visitor when the doctor's away."

"When the cat's away..." Kitty giggled.

"Indeed." I stopped in my tracks. So, Oksana and Mr. Hobbs *were* having an affair. That certainly gave them motive to kill the doctor. And yet they both had solid alibis for the entire evening and night the doctor was killed. Since the doctor had to have consumed the arsenic between eleven-thirty and midnight, there was no way either his wife or his assistant could have killed him. The sleeping powders were clean. And there was no evidence that the doctor consumed anything else in his room that night. The last

food or drink he'd taken was the whiskey during the monkey show.
And yet that was well before eleven-thirty.

So, how was he poisoned and by whom?

Lazarus the chimp was key.

24

THE CHIMPANZEE

The next morning, I was happy to wake up in my own bed in my own dusty flat. I got up at dawn and transformed myself into Rear Admiral Arbuthnot. My plan was to make another trip to Porton Down to find Lazarus the chimp. If I could collect a sample of his hair, then Kitty could test it against the hair she found in the doctor's room. Since Mr. Hobbs and Mr. Jäger had the most contact with the chimp, I planned to track them down, too. I had to find out why the chimp was in the doctor's room. There was also the matter of Private Birdwhistle. I hadn't had time to question Lady Nina at length. But before I'd left Mentmore Castle, I had learned that Birdy was an irregular attendee at the anti-vivisectionists' meetings. Lady Nina claimed she knew nothing about his posting at Porton Down. But his association with the Animal Defense Society made him a suspect for our mole-saboteur, if not also the doctor's murder. Hopefully, I could find all three men at Porton Down and solve both the case of the mole-saboteur and the doctor's murder.

After a last look in the mirror to make sure my mustache and beard were on straight, I went in search of Mata Hari's gun. I checked all my handbags. I didn't find the gun, but I did find Archie's telephone number. He'd said to call him when I was back in London. I tucked the card with his number behind my telephone. I'd call him when I returned from Porton Down. I continued my search for the gun. It wasn't until I checked in the oven that I remembered Fredricks had taken it. *Blast him.* I was certain the chimp hadn't acted alone. And while I may not need a firearm to protect myself from a monkey, I would against a very human killer. Without the gun, I'd have to rely on my wits.

My mustache secure and my cap on straight, now I just had to get myself out to Porton Down. Not wanting my investigation to be hindered by chatty Clifford, and so as not to risk him blowing my cover, I had hired a motorcar. Contrary to Captain Hall's opinion, I did not need a chaperone. I was perfectly capable of tracking down a killer on my own. At least, I hoped so.

As the motorcar made its way to the outskirts of London, I contemplated the case. Dr. Vorknoy had died alone, locked in his room. Kitty said the amount of arsenic he ingested would kill him within an hour. Archie and I heard him crash to the floor, bringing the lamp with him, at midnight, which meant he was poisoned between eleven and midnight. Fredricks reported that the kitchen staff did not bring the doctor anything that evening. The last time anyone had seen him alive was at the after-dinner show, which ended around ten. He'd left directly afterwards and retired to his room.

How in the world did he ingest poison alone in his room with no signs of food or drink present and his only medication, the sleeping powders, untainted?

Had someone visited his room, poisoned him, and then climbed out through the window and down the trellis? The trouble with that hypothesis was that the trellis was flimsy and broke under my weight. If the killer weighed less than me, it could not have been a man, or even most of the women at the country weekend. But it could have been a chimpanzee. A chimpanzee trained to kill? Still, how would a chimp persuade the doctor to ingest poison? It just didn't make sense. It recalled Edgar Allan Poe's *The Murders in the Rue Morgue*. Not my favorite. I'd always thought the solution cheating. *An orangutan. Please.*

"We're here, sir." The car stopped in front of the compound gates and the driver twisted around. "Would you like me to wait?"

"That would be splendid." I handed him a tip to encourage him to keep his word. "I shouldn't be more than an hour." *Or two.*

I had to walk from the gates into the compound—the sacrifice I'd made for the peace and quiet of coming alone. Except for the occasional sound of an explosion, as I strolled along the enchanting tree-lined entrance, I could have been on holiday getting fresh air and exercise. After ten minutes of walking, the road opened onto fields on either side. In the distance, soldiers wearing various headgear and gas masks ran around in one field. Closer by, poor unsuspecting goats were tethered in a ditch, no doubt waiting a ghastly fate. I shuddered. I'd never really thought about animals in the military. Or anywhere. So important. And yet so undervalued. I vowed to pay more attention from now on. For Poppy's sake.

This time, no one was waiting for me at the entrance. I let myself into the main building. A uniformed armed guard stopped me and asked for my identification. I produced the card I'd received from the War Office. It worked like a charm. The guard called for an escort. Private Birdwhistle, who was back from jail. Birdy seemed pleased to see me again. He smiled as he gave me a crisp salute.

"Sad about Dr. Vorknoy," I said.

"Terrible news." The private's smile faded.

"The War Office sent me to review his research." My voice

broke and I cleared my throat. "I'll need access to his laboratory and his office."

"Yes, sir." Private Birdwhistle led me down a hallway, to the back of the building, and to the same laboratory where I'd met the doctor on my last visit. "We locked the laboratory after the doctor's death. Only Mr. Hobbs has access now. He will be coming every day to care for the animals."

"Mr. Hobbs. Is he here now?" I would like to interview Mr. Hobbs again.

He shook his head. "Not yet, sir. I don't believe so, sir."

"Were you fond of the doctor?" I tried to sound nonchalant.

"Excuse me?" He stopped in front of the door to the laboratory.

"The doctor," I repeated. "Did you like him?" I observed his reaction.

"I didn't really know him." Now *his* voice cracked.

"You didn't approve of his research, did you?" I held his gaze.

"I couldn't say, sir." He looked at his shoes.

"You can speak freely," I said encouragingly. "In fact, I'd prefer you do."

"It's wasteful and vain." When he glanced up at me, his cheeks were enflamed. "Those poor animals..."

"Is that why you were arrested?" I turned the knob on the laboratory door. "Because you defended the animals?"

"You heard about that?" He looked sheepish. "They're transferring me to the front." He pressed his hands together in prayer. "Today is my last day here."

I hoped by *here* he meant Porton Down and not on earth. "I'm going to ask you something," I said gently. "And I want you to tell me the truth." I took a breath. "Whatever you say will go no further than these walls." If he was the mole and he had sabotaged military operations, I should report him to Captain Hall. But the poor lad was being sent to the front. I couldn't imagine a worse fate.

"Did you do anything to sabotage the military's experiments here at Porton Down?"

His head jerked back. "Sabotage?"

"Perhaps not sabotage." I rephrased the question. "Did you do anything to help the animals here, something the army might not approve of?"

"I snuck extra food to the goats and horses." His lips twitched.

"And what else?" I nodded. "Did you help the chimpanzees or other animals?"

He bit his lip. "I might have freed one or two of the goats." His voice was almost a whisper. "And maybe returned a requisitioned horse to a farmer." In a flash, his countenance went from repentant to defiant. "But that's all. I did not commit sabotage. I'm a patriot."

"Of course you are, Private Birdwhistle." I clapped him on the back. So, Birdy was our mole-saboteur. Except he wasn't working for the Germans. He wasn't even *working* for the anti-vivisectionists. He was merely a young man with a soft spot for animals. I opened the laboratory door. "Did you ever discuss the top-secret research going on here with anyone outside of Porton Down?"

"No, sir." His cheeks reddened. "Not really."

"No, or not really?" I asked, using a friendly tone.

"Well..." He stared down at the floor.

"Yes?" I said, encouragingly.

"My mum works for the Duchess of Hamilton, and she takes care of abandoned animals." He shifted from foot to foot. "And I thought maybe the duchess could help some of our animals."

"I see." Good thing he was leaving Porton Down. "Thank you for your honesty, Private Birdwhistle." I gave him a salute and then stepped into the laboratory. "I'd better get to it so I can finish before lunchtime."

"Do you need my help?" he asked.

"No, thank you." I wanted privacy to snoop. "I prefer to work on my own."

"Very well." He saluted again. "I'll be right out here if you need me."

I nodded and then shut the laboratory door behind me.

With the laboratory empty, I had plenty of time to search—except for my waiting driver. But where to start? I circled the room, taking in the scene. Experiments had been abandoned. Half-empty beakers sat next to hoses and tubes and clamps. All silent as the grave. The smell of sulfur was a mere memory burnt into the walls. In the center of the room, a high table was littered with notes and papers in such disarray I was tempted to organize them. Beyond the main laboratory was a small room where the animals were kept. I went to the door. Locked.

I glanced around to make sure no one saw me and then pulled my handy lockpick set from my pocket. Inserting the wrench and the rake, I thought of Fredricks. It almost seemed as if we were on the same side. *Almost.* I knew better, of course. It took a few tries, but finally the lock gave way. Quietly, I opened the door and stepped inside. Cries and yips filled the small room with the sounds of the jungle.

"Shhhh." I put my finger to my lips. The chimpanzees ignored me and kept up their racket. Their cages were stacked on top of each other in two rows of six cages. Starting with the closest cage on top, I scanned the interior as best I could without getting too close to the agitated creature inside. The cages were lined with straw. They each had some water, but their food dishes were empty. No wonder they were upset. Hopefully, Henry Hobbs would be here to feed them soon. What was I thinking? Hopefully he *wouldn't.* Otherwise, he'd catch me in here spying.

Slowly, I walked the length of the cages, peering inside each one. I didn't know what I was looking for, but I had to find some clues to what happened to Dr. Vorknoy. How did the murderer pull it off?

One of the chimps stuck its hand through the bars and chirped at me. I took its hand. Big mistake. It tried to pull my arm inside. And it was strong. I had to resist with all my might. My face pressing against the bars, I pushed back. The little beast yanked on my beard. "Ouch." That hurt. Once free, I shook my smarting hand and patted my beard back into place. *Little devil.*

To examine the lower level of cages, I had to kneel and then crawl on hands and knees. I hated to think what had been on this floor. Disgusting. Pushing thoughts of chimp poo from my mind, I scanned the interiors of the cages. I recognized the monkey in the corner cage. He had a toy tea set and was pouring out tiny cups of tea from a small teapot. How clever. This must be Lazarus, the fellow who entertained us that night at Mentmore Castle.

"Hello, my friend." I sat down next to his cage.

He looked at me with melancholy eyes, and then held out a tiny cup. How sweet. He was offering me tea.

"Thank you." I took the cup from between the bars and pretended to take a sip.

The creature's lips turned up in a smile and he stuck his hand out of the cage. I knew better than to take it. Instead, I nodded. "You're a very bright little fellow."

He turned his hand over. In his palm he had a sugar cube. He offered it to me. Carefully, I plucked it from his palm. *Wait a hairy minute!* On the underside of his wrist was a tiny black pouch. It blended so well with his fur that it was barely noticeable, even up close.

"What is this?" I touched the pouch. It was attached to his wrist with a small black elastic band. He allowed me to pull it off. In fact, he seemed relieved when I did. I turned it over in my hands. It was a trick pouch. I couldn't figure out how to open it.

My monkey friend tapped his finger into his palm and chirped. Was he trying to tell me something? I watched him for a second and then repeated his gesture. When I tapped on the pouch, it opened. When I tapped it again, it closed. *Interesting.* I tapped it open and looked inside. It was so small that it was difficult to see anything. Retrieving my magnifying glass from a jacket pocket, I looked again. *Blimey.* White powder. I sniffed it. All I smelled were the musky chimpanzees. I tucked the pouch into my breast pocket. I'd bet my mustache that Kitty's forensic tests would reveal the powder to be arsenic.

I recalled the evening's entertainment. Lazarus had delivered whiskeys to the men, including the doctor. Had he also used this clever pouch to deliver something more? A deadly dose of arsenic, perhaps? "So, you're the killer."

The chimp shook his head.

"Who put you up to it? Mr. Jäger?"

A jangling of keys made my blood run cold. Paralyzed, I froze. The chimpanzee and I exchanged glances. *Now what?* There was nowhere to hide in this small room. I scooted into the corner next to the far cage and pressed my back against the wall. With any luck, whoever was out there wouldn't come in here. Then again, I couldn't very well leave here until they were gone. I could be stuck in here until nightfall. I held my breath and listened. Outside the door, footfalls grew louder. I grimaced and pressed harder into the wall. Something touched my hand. I glanced down. A bit of paper was stuck between the cage and the wall. As slowly and silently as I could, I slid the paper out from behind the cage. Moving nothing but my arm, I brought it up in front of my face to see what it was. A receipt from Mr. Jäger made out to Dr. Vorknoy. For six chimpanzees. Dated last month. A handwritten note was scrawled across the bottom.

Oh, my word.

Blackmail won't work on me. Pay up now.

I recalled the dustup between Mr. Jäger and Mr. Hobbs. Mr. Jäger had told Mr. Hobbs that the doctor better pay up. Mr. Hobbs had threatened to go to the police and accused Mr. Jäger of threatening him. Were Mr. Hobbs and the doctor blackmailing Mr. Jäger? Did Mr. Jäger dispose of the doctor to end the blackmail? If so, Mr. Hobbs might be in danger. I needed to warn him.

I stood up and brushed off my trousers. Whoever was on the other side of that door would have to be persuaded that I was sent by the War Office to inspect the chimpanzees. I had a perfectly good reason for being here. Of course I did. I was a rear admiral, after all. I tugged on the hem of my jacket, took a deep breath, and prepared to make my exit.

Before I reached the door, it opened. Mr. Hobbs stepped inside.

Holding a revolver. Pointed at my head.

Bloody hell.

Mr. Hobbs wasn't the one in danger.

I was.

25

THE GAS CHAMBER

The chimpanzees' ruckus was deafening. Some of them hooted and banged on their cages. For a few seconds, I thought they were coming to my defense. Then I realized it was feeding time. The chimps' excitement enhanced their musky smell. The tiny room was filled to overflowing with the sounds and smells of monkeys.

Hands above my head, I conjured my best rear admiral authoritative voice. "See here, Mr. Hobbs." I took a step closer. "There's no need for a weapon." I took another step. "This is a misunderstanding. I was sent by the War Office to—"

"Stop!" He cut me off. "Don't take another step." He waved the gun. "Up against the wall."

I took a few steps backwards until I felt the wall. "Surely there's some mistake."

"Quiet!" His eyes—and his gun—trained on me, he scooped cups of what looked like a dried fruit and nut mixture from a gunny sack and poured them into the empty food dishes. The excited chimps tucked into their lunch, seemingly oblivious to the revolver or the sweat running down my brow.

"May I put my arms down, at least?" I asked, never breaking his gaze.

"No!" He continued filling food bowls until all the animals had their lunch. "Move it." He waved the gun again.

"Where to?" The room was too small to move very far.

"The gas chamber."

"Gas chamber?" My stomach roiled. "You've got to be joking."

"I'm not." He opened the door. "After you, Rear Admiral Arbuthnot. Or should I call you Lady Tabitha?" he sneered.

Holy hell. He'd recognized me. I touched my beard. *Blast.* That bloody chimp had pulled it half off. It was hanging off my face like a rat's tail.

"Keep your hands behind your back where I can see them," he barked.

Once I stepped over the threshold, he poked the barrel of the gun into my back. "Get going."

With the gun against my back, I started walking toward the door of the laboratory. "You won't get away with this. Private Birdwhistle is just on the other side of that door." At least I hoped he was.

"Birdy is out to lunch," he scoffed. "Open the door." The barrel of the gun jabbed me again.

I opened the door. "Now what?"

"To the right."

I turned to the right and he walked me down the long hallway, gun pointed at my back. Could I make a run for it? There was nowhere to go. In this narrow hallway, I was an easy target. Should I yell or shout? The building seemed abandoned. Lunchtime. Everyone was in the canteen. Too bad Kitty hadn't taught me foot-fighting. I could whip around and kick him in the—

"Pick up the pace!"

"Why are you doing this?" I quickened my pace. My pulse was racing.

"You ask too many questions."

Jab. The hard point of the gun against my back. I jolted forward and stumbled.

"Watch it." He grabbed my arm and slammed me against the wall. "Don't try anything or I'll blow your head off."

Gas chamber or gunshot. Some choice. Stalling for time was my best option. He pushed me out the door and followed close on my heels. The air was cold against my cheeks. My torso convulsed in a shiver. I scanned the horizon. On either side were steep ravines. Straight ahead was a small building. No doubt, the gas chamber. At gunpoint, he marched me along the path and into the building.

An acrid smell hit my nose, and I coughed. The room was solid brick. No windows. No furniture. Just a drain in the floor, several vents in the ceiling, and two large levers on the wall near the gas masks.

"Up against the far wall." Mr. Hobbs stabbed me in the back with the barrel of the gun.

Still coughing, I turned around to face him.

He took a mask off a hook by the door. "Move it." His voice was muffled.

The smell of chemicals permeated the room. Even the bricks had absorbed the evil. Pressing myself against the far wall, I asked again, "Why?"

He shrugged.

"You killed Dr. Vorknoy." I had nothing to lose. "Poisoned him with arsenic."

"My alibi is airtight. So, you can't prove it." He fiddled with the gas mask. "Even if you could, you won't be around to testify."

"But you won't be able to cover up my murder as easily." Even though the gas wasn't on in the room, the smell of chemicals was strong enough to burn my eyes and nose. "You'll get caught and hang."

"I didn't kill the doctor. Jäger did." He doffed the animal handler's red cap and then made a show of dropping it on the floor. "Just like he killed you."

"It was you blackmailing Mr. Jäger, not the doctor." If I was going to die, I at least wanted the truth out of him.

"You're wrong," he said, his hand on a giant switch.

I shuddered. The gas switch?

"Oh, hell. Why not?" He leaned against the wall. "You'll be dead anyway."

"Go on."

"Jäger's exotic animal business isn't exactly by the book, if you get my gist." He wiped his eyes with the back of his hand. "The doctor gambled away all his profits to the point of losing his house, the fool." He took his hand off the switch, and I let out a sigh of relief. "The doctor needed money. He couldn't pay Jäger for the chimps. He needed the chimps for the operations and couldn't make money without them. So, he threatened to call the police if Jäger didn't pay up." He shook his head, a tiny smile playing at the corner of his mouth. "No one messes with Jäger. He trained one of his chimps to pour drinks as a parlor trick. Then he trained it to spike the drink with arsenic powder when no one was looking. Very clever, really." He chuckled. "Jäger cues the animal using certain words."

Very clever, indeed. "And where do you fit in, Mr. Hobbs?"

"With the doctor out of the way, I get the business." He straightened. "Damn good business, too. And I'm not going to gamble it away."

"I'd say you've already gambled it away." I gestured around the room. "Killing me, you risk losing everything. Stop now, and you'll have your monkey business, no questions asked."

"I'm not going to let you or anyone else take it away from me." He ran a hand through his hair. "Selling the operation to lords and barons was my idea. And a damned good one, too. We would have been rich if it weren't for Vorknoy's stupid gambling."

"If, as you say, it was Mr. Jäger and his chimp that killed the doctor, then why kill me?" It truly made no sense.

"Jäger and his trained monkey aren't the only clever ones." He raised his hand to the switch again.

A tingling sensation burned through my veins. *Think, Fiona.* There must be a way out. A distraction. Another way to stall...

"I devised our alibi." He smiled.

"The sugar block from the barn," I said. A spark ignited in my brain. He'd used the sugar block as ballast with the rope and the fishing line to break the lamp long after he and Mr. Jäger had left Mentmore. "Very clever, indeed."

"I thought so." His smile broadened. "When the rain dissolved the sugar block, the lamp crashed to the floor, creating the illusion that the doctor had just died—"

"When actually," I interrupted, "you'd arranged the scene earlier in the evening." *Aha.* So that's how he'd done it.

"Exactly." He gripped the handle of the switch.

"Wait!" I took a deep breath. "What about the chimp? We found chimpanzee hair at the scene." I had to keep stalling for time. *Time for what? Time to die?* My palms were sweating, and my breath was coming fast.

"Jäger's not the only one who knows the chimps." He grinned. "Lazarus locked the door after we'd left and escaped out the window, setting up the coup de grace of our little scene."

Lazarus. The chimp from the evening's entertainment. The one pouring the whiskeys. "The locked room." I gave him a few slow claps. "Bravo." Perhaps if I showed the proper appreciation for his genius, I could keep him talking. To what end, I didn't know. It wasn't like anyone was on their way to rescue me. What an idiot I'd been, coming here alone.

He took a little bow. "And now, I must bid you farewell, Lady Tabitha." With a smirk, he grasped the switch. "Sweet dreams."

My heart was racing. What if I told him I was a British agent? What would it hurt to blow my cover now that I was about to die? Then again, would it make any difference? Not to a cold-blooded killer. My only chance was to rush him. The element of surprise. He may shoot me, but it was that or gas. I'd seen the consequences of gas. I'd take my chances with a bullet.

I took a deep breath and ran at him with all my might. I plowed into his torso. He brought the butt of the gun down on my head. The pain threw me to the floor. My vision blurred. I heard the click of metal against metal. The switch. The acrid smell of gas filled my nostrils. *Fredricks.* I'd never see him again. Why in heaven's name was I thinking about him? I held my breath for as long as I could.

I couldn't hold it any longer.

With tears in my eyes, I took my dying breath. "Archie."

* * *

Argh. My hand flew to my aching head. What happened to me? *Ugh.* My stomach roiled, and a nasty bitter taste filled my mouth. When I opened my eyes, the room was spinning. I held onto the side of the bed. *I'm in bed? Where? Whose?*

"Fiona, darling." Someone took my hand. *The hand attached to the voice? Hmmm.* A familiar voice. "I'm here." Warm lips brushed against the back of my hand.

I forced my eyes to focus on his face. The lock of chestnut hair across his forehead. The crooked smile. Those sparkling green eyes.

"Archie." My voice was hoarse.

He nodded. He was sitting next to my bed. I glanced around. Polished floor. The smell of bleach. White walls. A flimsy curtain. A Murphy drip attached to my arm. A hospital room. I was in hospital. The gas. I'd survived. "How?"

"We found you at Porton." Archie's eyes welled with tears. "In one of the testing rooms for chemicals." He grimaced.

I felt my cheeks. "Am I..." I remembered the disfigured men I'd seen at Charing Cross Hospital. Many died in agony from terrible burns. I cringed. And those who survived were scarred for life. Mustard gas should be criminal, even in war.

"You're beautiful." Archie took my hand and kissed it again. "Oh, Fiona, if anything happens to you..." His voice trailed off.

"We'll just have to make sure it doesn't." Kitty appeared in the doorway with Poppy in tow. Pretty in periwinkle gingham, she was a sight for sore eyes. And mine were indeed sore. Burning, even.

"How did you find me?" I was dying to get hold of a looking glass to assess the damage. I may have survived the gas, but there were always permanent scars. If not outside, then inside my lungs. They burned too.

"Your not-so-secret admirer, Fredrick Fredricks." Kitty came to my beside. "He called Archie and warned him that you were in danger at Porton Down."

Fredricks? Fredricks had called Archie? How did he get Archie's telephone number? Had the cad broken into my flat? I'd tucked the slip of paper with Archie's number on it behind my telephone. Fredricks could have found it there and used my telephone. But what was he doing in my flat? He had promised to stop by and say goodbye. In which case, I'd missed him. He could be halfway around the world by now. Or at least to France.

"For once, I'm grateful to him." Archie ran a hand through his hair. "The bastard."

Fredricks had risked his neck to save mine.

"Uncle Blinker sent me and Poppy along." Kitty bobbed a curtsy. "I couldn't exactly waltz into the top-secret military area on my own."

"So, you took Poppy the Pekingese along with you?" I shook my head. Fredricks couldn't exactly waltz into Porton Down either unless he wanted to be arrested... or worse. Fredrick Fredricks. Until now, my only espionage assignment. Would *Uncle Blinker* ever give me another assignment on my own after I'd royally messed up this one?

"Lucky for you I did." Kitty bent down and scooped up the creature.

I tried to sit up in bed, but the room wouldn't stop spinning. I gave up and rested against the pillow, burying my eyes in the crook of my elbow. "Henry Hobbs. He killed the doctor."

"You managed to knock him down and his mask off." Archie chuckled. "And gave him a taste of his own medicine, as only you can do."

"Luckily, the gas they were testing this morning wasn't lethal." Kitty tucked the blanket in around me. "But you were both unconscious when Poppy found you."

"Poppy found me?" I reached out and gave her a scratch under the chin. When she started licking my hand, I immediately withdrew it.

"She's a right little bloodhound." Archie laughed. "Led Kitty right to you. Thank God."

"And where is Mr. Hobbs?"

"In police custody." Archie smiled. "Thanks to you."

Thank goodness.

"He confessed to everything." Kitty brushed an imaginary hair from my face. "Apparently, he and Mr. Jäger used a trained monkey to deliver the arsenic and then made it look like he'd died of natural causes in his locked room."

"Yes, Mr. Hobbs told me." I pushed myself up in the bed and leaned against the headboard. "And what of Mr. Jäger?"

"The police are looking for him." Archie patted my hand. "They'll get him. Don't worry." More hand patting. "Rest now, sweet Fiona."

"Aunt Fiona is strong." Kitty took my other hand. "Isn't she, Poppy-poo?" She kissed the dog's topknot.

"Yes, dears." I smiled up at them. "I'll be fit as a fiddle before you know it."

"You've got a nasty bump on your head." Archie pointed, and I felt my forehead. Ouch. It hurt. And yes, there was a noticeable bump at my hairline, where my wig should have been. I must look a sight. No wig and a purple goose egg on my head. What must Archie think?

"We'll be back in the morning to fetch you for the awards ceremony." Kitty bent down and kissed my cheek.

The awards ceremony. *Crikey.* I'd forgotten all about it. "It's tomorrow?"

"Tuesday, 5 February, at noon." She nodded. "In the meantime, you'd better get your beauty sleep." She pinched Poppy's paw and waved it at me.

I waved back. "I'll need more than sleep to make me beautiful."

"Nonsense." Archie took his turn kissing my cheek. "You're perfect, just the way you are."

I may not be perfect, but at least I was alive.

26

THE CEREMONY

The next morning, Kitty and Archie came to escort me out of the hospital. Kitty brought me my favorite woolen lavender skirt with matching blazer, along with a white blouse and my practical Oxfords. Thank goodness, she remembered my wig. My favorite strawberry-blonde bob. Of course, she brought a hat. Up to that point, she'd been doing so well. A wide-brimmed pink feathery number, the size of a dining table. Whether she intended it as a joke or truly believed it suited me, I didn't know. But I humored her and wore it. Not that I had a choice. It was that or my rear admiral's cap.

"How did you get into my flat?" My cheeks warmed. *Could it be? Was Fredricks still here? Had he let her in? Good grief.* I hope Archie didn't see him. I regretted asking. I preferred not to mention Fredricks in front of Archie. Not that I had anything to hide, mind you. Still, there was no need to get Archie in a lather.

The award ceremony was held in the drawing room of the Old Admiralty. The room had always been one of my favorites in the building. On occasion, I'd retreated to the drawing room to escape the hubbub of Room 40 and sneak a look at the latest Sherlock

Holmes story. Yellow damask wallpaper and gilded furniture created a sunny ambience in the windowless drawing room. Large seascape oil paintings created a sense of expansiveness in the long narrow chamber. Gold satin upholstery shone in the lamplight.

All in all, the room was a cheery space and perfect for a celebration away from reminders of war—except, of course, for all the uniforms in the room. Standing out like roses among ferns, wearing brightly colored frocks, a few women dotted the proceedings. The room was packed. Not just for me, mind you. The public ceremony honored other military officers and even civilians who had served their country with bravery and distinction. I pinched myself in disbelief. Bursting with pride, I could barely keep my blazer buttoned at the thought of being a member of such a distinguished group.

I was delighted that Lizzy Lind and Lady Nina were in attendance. Kitty must have invited them, destroying our cover in the process. With the case closed, obviously Captain Hall had allowed it. Anything for his darling niece. Of course, Kitty wasn't really his niece, but she might as well have been his favorite daughter the way he fawned over her. And yes, thanks to me, the case was closed. I'd convinced Captain Hall that Birdy was not a mole or German saboteur, but rather a soft-hearted young man with a love for animals. Alright, he'd freed a couple of goats and returned a horse to its owner. But he wasn't engaging in sabotage, just sympathy for the poor beasts. With some cajoling, Captain Hall had agreed that Private Birdwhistle's transfer from Porton Down to the front lines should solve the problem.

"So, you're actually a British agent." Lizzy tilted her head and pursed her lips. "You certainly had us fooled." She raised her eyebrows. "Spying on the Animal Defense Society when you should be arresting those knife-happy vivisectionists." I'd given Captain Hall a detailed report on Lizzy Lind and her activities, which from my investigation were all completely above board and legal. Although he wasn't as convinced about Miss Lind, he agreed to take a "wait and see" approach to the Animal Defense Society.

"I don't have the authority to arrest anyone." Although if I did, I was coming around to her point of view and it would be the vivisectionists I'd go after, not her. Still, I wasn't ready to go as far as Kitty and claim that animals were people too. But certainly the creatures could feel pain and didn't deserve the treatment they got at the hands of the vivisectionists, or the military either, for that matter. I was as practical as the next person when it came to our relationship with animals, and I was in no position to judge whether they were put on earth to serve us, but I could not abide cruelty. Not to man nor beast. Well, perhaps to unfaithful husbands.

Changing the subject, I asked, "How is Birdy doing?" While not exactly a spy, Private Birdwhistle had revealed some of the secret goings-on at Porton Down, which in itself could be considered treasonous. Luckily, his transfer to the front lines would put a stop to that and save him from a court martial.

"Poor Birdy out there in the trenches." Lady Nina shook her head. "His mother is beside herself with worry. As a result, her puddings have soured, and her biscuits are hard as bricks." She sighed. "I do hope he comes back safe so I can get a decent meal."

I hoped she was joking. "Just think of the tinned beef and petrol-laced tea poor Birdy will be subjected to and you'll be grateful for whatever your cook prepares."

"I didn't mean—" She waved her hand. "Of course, we are the lucky ones."

"Speaking of luck." Lizzy beamed. "Did you hear about our Timmy's horse?"

"Star?" I had wondered how the boy had fared with his letter to the War Office. If I hadn't been so preoccupied with murderers and spies, I'd hoped to put in a good word with Captain Hall.

"The letter worked." Nina clasped her hands together. "He gets to keep his beloved horse."

"And what of Lord Rosebrooke?" Now that his secret stable had been revealed, would he get to keep his beloved racehorses? It did seem a shame to send those delicate beasts into war. Then again, if the farmers were expected to sacrifice their horses, the lords should have to do the same.

"He will pay a fine for hiding his horses." Lady Nina nodded. "Better to lose a bit of gold than his beloved horses."

There it was. The bottom line. The wealthy could afford to buy their way out of the rules and regulations while the poor farmers had to beg for mercy.

"Sadly, they did take most of them." Lizzy sighed and shook her head. "The irony is..." She grinned. "They didn't take Champion because he'd had that horrible surgery."

Ting. Ting. Ting.

I glanced around. The codebreakers were drinking and laughing. I heard Mr. Knox's loud guffaw above the din of the crowd.

Ting. Ting. Ting.

"Settle down, please." Clifford tapped a knife on his crystal champagne flute. "Captain Hall wants to make an announcement."

The crowd hushed and the captain batted his lashes and cleared his throat. "We are here to celebrate some of the behind-the-scenes heroes—and heroines—of the war." When he nodded in my direction, my cheeks warmed. I wasn't used to so much attention. I had butterflies in my stomach as I waited for him to call my name. Luckily, he went in alphabetical order. "I present the award for valor to Miss Fiona Figg." His lashes fluttering a hearty congratulations, Captain Hall smiled and looped a purple ribbon around my neck. On it hung a heavy gold medallion. The weight of the award secured my arrival into the world of espionage. I'd completed my first solo assignment—with help from my friends, of course. And my past achievements had been acknowledged. Maybe I wasn't such a bad spy, after all.

Once the ceremony concluded, there was a reception in the foyer, where a lovely buffet table of canapés was laid out. As I got closer to the table, I saw the telltale signs of war bread poking out from under bits of cheese and pieces of carrot. *Beggars can't be choosers.* I took up a plate and tried one of each.

"I'm jolly proud of you, old bean." Clifford beamed. "Well done." He clapped me on the shoulder and nearly caused me to eject a bite of war bread.

"You are quite a gal." Archie put his arm around me and squeezed. "The bee's knees." I wriggled loose. We were in a public place. In front of our boss. And I was holding a plate of canapés that were sliding precariously close to the edge of my plate.

"I do feel like I've finally arrived." I couldn't help but smile.

"The harder to break in..." Kitty winked. "The more damage you can do once you get there." Sitting at her feet, Poppy barked in agreement.

I wasn't sure what she meant by *me* doing damage. *She* was the foot-fighter.

"What's that dog doing in here?" Mr. Montgomery scowled. "I thought I told you—"

"I'll have you know—" Captain Hall interrupted. "*That dog* is a certified British agent, who just so happens to belong to my niece." The broad smile on his face amplified the fluttering of his lashes. He was proud of Kitty and so was I. She—and Poppy—had come to my rescue more than a few times.

Mr. Knox appeared with a tray of champagne flutes. "A toast to Miss Figg, master of disguises." He handed round the glasses. "To a beautiful chameleon. As brave as she is changeable."

I rolled my eyes and took a sip. The bubbles tickled my nose. Usually a teetotaler—except when led astray—I didn't go in for drinking. But it was a special occasion. I drained my glass and Mr. Knox handed me another. "Drink up, my dear. It's good for the complexion." Cheeky devil and full of beans as usual.

"Fiona, can I have a word, in private?" Archie bit his lip.

"Can it wait—"

His eyes hardened. *No. It couldn't wait.* I'd asked him to wait too many times already. I sat my glass down on a nearby tray and took his arm. I led him out of the drawing room and into an alcove near the makeshift cloakroom.

"It's just that I'm shipping out again tomorrow," he said apologetically. "And I'm not sure when I'll see you again."

My heart sank. Like every other sweetheart of every other soldier on the eve of every other deployment, it wasn't *when* but *if*. What if I never saw him again? "Soon." I patted his arm. "Very soon." As much as I hoped it was true, I feared it wasn't. "Where are you going this time?"

"Classified." He blushed.

"Of course it is." I gave him my best smile. *And no doubt dangerous.*

"You know what I want to ask you." Holding his cap in his hands, he shifted from foot to foot. "This is the last time. I won't ask you again." He gazed into my eyes, and I knew he meant it. He wouldn't ask me again. "Fiona Figg, will you marry me?"

The scene was set. I'd put him off too many times already. The moment of truth was upon me. My chest constricted. I couldn't breathe. What else could I say? "Yes." I felt the blood drain from my face. "Yes, I will."

He wrapped his arms around my waist and kissed me hard on the lips. "You've made me the happiest man alive." When he twirled me around, my feet left the floor. "Tonight! Let's get married tonight."

I didn't know if it was the champagne, the twirling, or the idea of marriage, but I felt decidedly unwell. My bruised head hurt, and an uneasiness shrouded the moment. I wanted nothing more than to run away, but marriage was for life—or at least it should be. "Not tonight." I put my palm to my forehead. I had just suffered a nasty blow to the head. My head injury. Was that why I said yes? "As soon as you're back." I forced a smile. "We'll do it when you get back."

His arms fell away from my waist. "Why wait?" His countenance went from sunny to cloudy in an instant. "What are you waiting for?" He ran his hand through his hair. "Don't you love me?"

"Of course I do." *I do, right?*

"Then let's get married now before I have to leave again."

Looking into his pleading eyes sent a pang to my heart. "Really, Archie. Tonight?" I took a step backward. "You can't be serious." Why couldn't we wait until after the war? Then, we could have a normal courtship and romance. Long walks along the Thames. Leisurely dinners by candlelight. Reading Sherlock Holmes stories aloud in front of the fireplace. Now, instead, we met in the backrooms of modern warfare. With guns drawn, we held our breath while rounding the next corner, never knowing who might be waiting there ready to do us in. There was no room for love in the midst of war. It was too dangerous. Worse than losing your life, you could lose your heart. It was too much to bear.

"I'm deadly serious." He ran a hand through his hair again. His steely gaze cut me to the quick.

"Then you don't know me very well." With tears welling in my eyes, I turned on my heels. "Good luck on your classified mission," I called over my shoulder. I dashed out of the alcove, my medallion thumping my chest as I ran down the hallway and into the foyer. I stood paralyzed for a moment, looking this way and that. *Now what? What had I done? Where to go?* I brushed a tear from my cheek.

It was true. He didn't know me. How could he? We'd met only seven months ago, and I'd seen him just a handful of times and even then, only for a few stolen minutes here and there. *Oh, Archie.* If it weren't for this bloody war, we might have had a chance.

*   *   *

As soon as I exited the building, the frigid February air hit my face. Within seconds, the bitter breeze penetrated my wool skirt. Not looking where I was going, I stepped in a puddle. Cold dirty water splashed up my ankle, soiling my stocking. I'd left my coat and brolly inside, but I wasn't about to go back in. I couldn't. I couldn't face Archie. He'd meant it when he said he wouldn't ask again. I tried. I tried to say yes. But now I'd ruined everything—forever. The clouds were as dark and threatening as my mood. Before I'd gone another two feet, the sky let loose a torrent. My tears mixed with the pouring rain. By the time I reached the bus stop, I was drenched. Paradoxically, my cold sodden blazer and blouse pressing down on me kept me afloat as I made my way home. The doorman gave me a queer look but didn't say a word as he handed me my key. Water dripped from the brim of my hat. A puddle formed around my feet as I rode the lift to my floor. My practical Oxfords sloshed and squeaked all the way down the hall. Another pair of shoes ruined. My forlorn love life was deuced hard on the wardrobe.

I opened the door to my flat and stood dripping on the threshold. *Good heavens.* What happened here? The place sparkled. The dust sheets were gone, and so was the dust. Every surface shone. Even the windows were clean. Fredricks. What had he done?

As I went from room to room, peeling off my wet jacket, I marveled at the transformation. Red, yellow, and violet flowers adorned every room. Instead of the dreary, lonely flat I'd left last Friday, I'd returned to a bouquet of loveliness. For a villain, he was certainly thoughtful.

"Fredricks?" I shivered as I looked for him—whether from chill or delight, I wasn't sure. The scoundrel had cleaned my entire flat. "Fredricks, are you here?" I thought of Kitty's book on dust. Had Fredricks dusted every surface to erase every trace of his presence? Too bad I couldn't as easily wipe him out of my mind. Cringe. Facing death, Archie hadn't been my heart's desire. My life passing before my eyes, it was Fredricks who came to mind. Deuced confusing. And confounded inappropriate. He was my enemy, after all. *Sigh*. Tell that to my heart. And I did say Archie's name with my dying breath. That must count for something.

In the kitchen, on the table, next to a bouquet of lilies, stood a beautiful chocolate cake. On the counter sat a loaf of bread. Not war bread. But fluffy white bread. How in the world did he do it? I opened the ice box. *Golly*. A small basket piled with fruit, and another filled with French cheeses wrapped in paper. I picked up an orange and smelled it. Heavenly. Standing staring into my well-stocked ice box, I giggled like a schoolgirl. How ever he'd done it, I was the lucky beneficiary. Why me? He could have any woman in the world, so why me?

"Fredricks, where are you?" I searched every inch of the flat. He wasn't here. Deflated, I went back to my bedroom and stripped off my wet clothes. Sliding my feet into my slippers, I wrapped myself in my robe. There he was. Just a hint of sandalwood, lingering on my robe. I inhaled deeply. Fredrick Fredricks, my charming nemesis. When would I see him again? And where? Where would the devil take me next? I smiled to myself. For the daughter of a green-grocer, I'd seen a lot of the world.

As I ran my bath, I reminded myself of how much I'd accomplished since I'd been home: Captain Hall had given me my first solo mission. I'd successfully rooted out the spy at Porton Down. Alright, Private Birdwhistle wasn't exactly a spy. Just a passionate young man with a soft spot for goats. Lizzy Lind and Lady Nina had been vindicated, or at least kept their protests and passions well within the bounds of the law. Henry Hobbs and Mr. Jäger, however, were another story. Along with Dr. Vorknoy, they had been using the secret military base to smuggle illegal animals and swindle rich men out of large sums of money for a phony operation. They had planned and executed the elaborate scheme to murder the doctor with the help of Lazarus the chimp. Very clever to use a sugar block as ballast to delay the sound of the doctor's wrist dropping to the floor and taking the lamp with it. What was left of the melted sugar block must have broken into bits when it hit the window frame. Very clever indeed. But not clever enough to get away with murder.

Yes, I'd say my mission had been a success. My love life was another matter entirely.

I hung my robe on a hook behind the door and then slid into the bathtub. Closing my eyes, I let the hot water melt away the lovelorn shards of failed romance. Perhaps I was destined to spend the rest of my life alone. A widow and a divorcee, not even a proper spinster. *Pull yourself together, Fiona.* A good lather with my rose-scented soap followed by a nice cup of strong black tea and I'd be right as rain. I scrubbed with the vigor of a believer washing away her doubts. If Archie truly loved me, he'd wait to marry me. And if he didn't? I had a successful career in espionage. What more did I need?

By the time the water had gone tepid, I'd quite recovered my equanimity. After a brisk toweling, I retrieved my robe and slipped it on. As I did, something crinkled in one of the pockets. I patted the pocket. A piece of paper? My pulse quickened as I slid the paper out of my pocket. A letter on beige stationery. I sniffed it. Sandalwood. My breath caught as I unfolded the paper.

Fiona, ma chérie,

By now, you are safely in the arms of your beloved Lieutenant Somersby. While I don't understand the attraction, I respect your desire. You want to marry him, and I wish you all the happiness in the world. You deserve it.

Although I can never forget you, I can distract myself by doing what I do best, blowing up something. Perhaps I'll bomb Moscow's Krasnokholmsky Bridge or the Royal Navy's flagship in the Baltic. I hear the Eastern Front is lovely this time of year.

Not to worry. Your benevolent influence continues to touch my soul if not my body. For what is the body but the vanity of the soul? And what of the heart? Your heart. For I know mine. A heart at war with itself is like a country during civil war. Susceptible to corruption. Red bleeding onto white. Your ally falling prey to itself.

Alas. No more riddles. No more games. Just you and me, ma chérie, on the battlefield of the heart. And so, the panther goes back into hiding from your bloodthirsty countrymen who continue to hunt me.

Even if I travel all the way to Siberia, I cannot hide from my love for you.

Yours always,

Fredrick

P.S. Why not "Peace, Bread, Land"?

P.P.S. If you change your mind, join me at Metropol Hotel, Room 315. I offer you only the world.

His panther insignia was embossed on the bottom of the stationery. I moved my finger over the raised insignia and then held the letter to my breast. Where was the Metropol Hotel? My mind raced to decipher the letter. *Civil war. Red on white. Siberia.* Was Fredricks telling me he was off to Siberia?

I tightened the belt on my robe and marched into the kitchen. A cup of tea and fine French cheese would help my concentration. Maybe a slice of bread. *Peace, bread, land.* Mr. Lenin was right about one thing. Everyone was tired of war bread. As I sipped my cuppa, I re-read the letter. How dare he blame me. If he thought he could use me as an excuse to bomb something, he had another thing coming. No more bombs.

Not our ship in the Baltic. Not a bridge in Moscow.

Wait. That's it! Of course. The telegram he'd received at Mentmore Castle. The one from V. Lenin. The bounder was going to Russia. More specifically, to Moscow.

The Metropol Hotel was in Moscow.

I re-read the letter yet again. What did he mean, *a heart at war with itself*? I sat staring down into my cup as if the answer could be found there among the tea leaves. My heart. At war with itself. I didn't know how long I sat there staring into my cup. I'd probably lost Archie forever. Fredricks was gone. My flat was filled with flowers. But that wasn't enough. I wanted more. I took a deep breath. Sandalwood. The lingering scent of Fredricks jolted me out of my reveries. I sat up straight, looked around my kitchen. Yes. I wanted adventure and a mission. With new resolve, I pushed my chair back from the table, drained my teacup, and took the dishes to the sink. The fog shrouding my heart had lifted. I knew what I wanted. And I knew how to get it. It was waiting there for me. I just had to reach out and take it.

Tightening the sash on my robe, I bustled off to the bedroom. "You're burning daylight," my father would say. I threw on the first dress I found, tugged on my stockings, and slipped my feet into my practical Oxfords. I had a busy afternoon of shopping ahead. Harrods, Angel's Fancy Dress, Thomas Cook's Travel. Could I get my hands on an Imperial Russian Army officer's uniform or perhaps one from the Red Army or the White Guard?

As I gathered my coat and hat, I added the library to my list of stops. History books. Fashion magazines. Society pages. What were Russian women wearing this winter?

Next stop, Metropol Hotel.

Where *only the world* awaits.

NOW TURN THE PAGE FOR A SNEAK
PEEK AT...MURDER IN MOSCOW

KITTY'S PROLOGUE
27 FEBRUARY

In Aunt Fiona's kitchen, everything was as immaculate as pent-up passion. No red, or a proper pink, not forest green or even lime. Instead, washed out and muted. Standing in the center of the small room, Kitty Lane glanced around. From the scrubbed enameled stove and the dust-free paraffin lamps to the pale-pink ceiling and mint-green wallpaper, the cramped space exuded repression. Too bad Aunt Fiona had suddenly decided to follow her heart. Never a good idea.

Kitty re-read a line from the letter:

For what is the body but the vanity of the soul?

Talk about vanity. She crumpled up the letter and tossed it onto the table. She took four steps and stopped just short of the window. Hot on her heels, the Pekingese smacked into her foot. "Sorry, Poppy."

Staring at the telephone on the wall, she plucked a piece of paper from behind the box. It read *Archie* and had a telephone number. How sweet. Aunt Fiona had Archie's number tucked between the phone and the wall. Lieutenant Archie Somersby, Aunt Fiona's fiancé. Not anymore. Not after Aunt Fiona's latest stunt.

Should Kitty call him? What would she tell him? That Fiona had run after another man? Aunt Fiona should have stuck with the flyboy. At least he was on our side. No. Fiona had to run after that scoundrel Fritz Duquesne, alias Fredrick Fredricks, a known assassin and German spy. Aunt Fiona had no idea what she was up against. She didn't even know his real name was Fritz Duquesne. It was classified. Beyond her clearance level. And bound to get her killed.

When Kitty pounded her fist on the table, Poppy barked. She bent down and scooped up her little furry friend. The Pekingese had been her constant companion since she'd returned from France four months ago, just before her first assignment partnered with Fiona Figg. She adjusted the pink bow on the dog's topknot. It matched the one she wore in her own hair. Although Poppy's butterscotch hair was a few shades darker than Kitty's, they both looked fabulous in pink.

Kitty reached across the table for the letter and uncrumpled it. She re-read part of the last line:

join me at Metropol Hotel, Suite 315. I offer you only the world.

Snorting, she dropped the letter. *Arrogant arse.* She resisted the urge to kick something. It wasn't her place after all. She tucked the pup under her arm and marched out of the kitchen, back through the flat—stopping only to pluck one of Aunt Fiona's wigs from its stand on the dressing table—and then slammed the door on the way out.

What the hell was she going to tell Uncle Blinker? Uncle Blinker, aka Captain Reginald "Blinker" Hall, head of the War

Office and her boss. He wasn't really her uncle. Neither was Fiona Figg her aunt. At *L'Espion*, Kitty had learned to call anyone older than herself—which meant over eighteen— "aunt" or "uncle." More than terms of deference, they were tools for disarming the enemy. And disarming the enemy was key to defeating them. Lesson number one of spy craft.

She held the dog up and looked her square in the face. Poppy squeaked and squirmed until Kitty put her down. She took up the leash and led the little puffball to the lift. Jamming on the button, she waited for the lift. When the door opened, the pup trotted in. Kitty followed. "Time to face the music, Poppy-poo."

CHAPTER ONE
COUNTESS BRASOVA

A heart at war with itself. For the dozenth time, I repeated the phrase from the letter he'd left in my flat. I shouldn't have followed the bounder from London to Moscow. What was I thinking? Was I completely daft? Concentrating on inhaling and exhaling, I squeezed my eyes shut. At twenty-five, I should have known better. Trailing Fredrick Fredricks for the War Office was one thing—but accepting his invitation for personal reasons was quite another. Even if I didn't end up with a broken skull, I'd end up with a broken heart.

Fredrick Fredricks. South African huntsman, sometimes journalist, and very clever German spy—an enemy spy—who claimed he wanted to stop the war. With his dancing eyes and mischievous smile, he was also too darn charming for his own good—or mine. How could I let myself fall for such a cad? I'd really done it this time.

I took another turn around the hotel suite. Stopping at the desk, I picked up one of the hotel postcards. *The Metropol Hotel, Russia's finest. Sigh.* Like most buildings in Moscow, the hotel had open wounds that would take years to heal. Russia's finest was riddled with bullet holes and littered with bits of plaster. Many of the windows were broken and boarded, and armed guards patrolled every floor. My canopy bed had a bullet embedded in its frame, and the gold satin chairs and matching divan sat proudly in the midst of plaster dust. Like a wounded war hero, beneath its superficial scars the hotel exuded splendor, weary but beyond pity.

Damaged by bombing, the restaurant was closed, but food and wine were served in the private rooms. I felt like a princess locked in a gilded tower waiting for her prince to return. I strolled to the window—the only one not boarded-up. Through cracked glass, I stared out as if I might spot him passing by on the street below. Instead, wearing shabby coats and hats, dozens of women banged on pots and shouted in Russian, their breath freezing into frosty clouds. I guessed they were protesting the lack of food. I shivered just watching them out there in that frigid air. Across Europe and beyond, the war had taken its toll on everyone. Even kings were tightening their belts. Back home, King George V showed off his ration card hoping he didn't end up like his cousin, Tsar Nicholas II, who'd been exiled to Siberia. Some of the codebreakers in the War Office worried what was happening in Russia was a preview of things to come for England. I sincerely hoped not.

In the two days since I arrived, it had become obvious this country was being torn apart by wars both abroad and at home. Things were bad back in England but this was worse. Much worse. Every building within a mile was pocked with artillery shells. Not from the Germans but from civil war. A country turned against itself. And yet, judging by the sounds of music and laughter coming from neighboring rooms at all hours, guests at the Metropol Hotel celebrated like there was no tomorrow.

I dropped the postcard into my skirt pocket. I plopped down into a posh chair, and flipped through an issue of *Moscow Magazine*. The centerpiece was an exhibit by a Russian painter named Wassily Kandinsky, who was recently appointed head of the arts division of the People's Commissariat for Enlightenment. I studied the brightly colored images. A world in motion, a rolling and roiling world of color and shapes, a world turned inside out. Much like the broken city out my window, only more vibrant. I tossed the magazine onto the coffee table, jumped up, and then resumed my pacing.

I'd been here two days and no sign of Fredricks—except fresh flowers delivered daily. He was nothing if not extravagant. While everyone else had to wait for a glimpse of wildflowers in spring and felt lucky to dine on leftover war bread, Fredricks procured roses, red roses, and dined on strawberries and champagne. Upon my arrival, a small card attached to the first bunch of red roses read only:

Back soon, ma chérie

Back soon. Ha! *Back soon* was something you said when you ran down the street for a pint of milk or a bag of sugar, not when you disappeared into the murky political landscape of a war-torn country.

There had to be a clue somewhere in this room. A clue as to why he was in Russia. A clue as to why he invited me here. Not just to Russia, or Moscow, or the Metropol Hotel, but to room 315. I opened the closet again, as I'd done nearly every hour since I'd arrived. A woolen hunting jacket hung over a white ruffled shirt. On the same hanger, completing the ensemble, khaki jodhpurs peeked out below the shirt. Tall black boots stood underneath, creating the uncanny sense of a headless soldier standing at attention. I caressed the sleeve of the jacket. I glanced around the room. Then I leaned forward to smell the collar. Sandalwood, mustache wax, and something else... something stalwart and dark. I slipped my hands into the jacket's pockets, closed my eyes, and imagined an embrace. *Fredricks, where are you? Why aren't you here?*

Wait. *What's that?* My fingertips brushed against the point of something. Something I must have missed the dozen other times I'd slid my hands into his jacket's pockets. I pinched the small box between my thumb and forefinger and withdrew it. A colorful matchbox adorned with a growling tiger. I turned it over. On the underside, in black pencil, were three cryptic lines:

03-03 B-L.
11-03 P-M.
??-?? WRD.

One of Fredricks's secret codes? Not a simple number to letter transcription. *03-03. What was 03-03?* I resumed pacing. It helped me concentrate. Could it be a date? *Third of March?* Four days from now. *What happens on 3 March?* If it was a date, then the second entry would be 11 March. Over one week later.

A rapping at the door interrupted my cogitations. "Fredricks?" My breath caught. He was back. I stuffed the matchbox into my skirt pocket and vowed to get the code out of him if I had to resort to torture—or something more enjoyable. I smiled to myself. Not that torturing Fredricks wouldn't be fun. Quickly, I went to the dressing table and looked at myself in the mirror. I immediately regretted it. My swollen eyes were as purple as two plums, my cheeks as pasty as mealy pudding, and my lips dry and drawn. I patted my wig and adjusted my skirt. Sadly, no amount of patting or preening would make me pretty. Even before lost loves, sleepless nights, and war rations, I wasn't a beauty.

I went to the door and then stood there with my hand on the doorknob. I took a deep breath. Then another. Then another. Was

I ready to face him? One more deep breath. Finally, I turned the knob and opened it.

My heart sank. Not Fredricks, but the aging porter. Trailing him was an attractive woman wearing feathers and furs. With her perfectly oval face, deep melancholy eyes, and long thin nose, she looked rather like a barn owl. Lips twitching, the porter introduced her as Countess Brasova. I peered out the door at her. Why in the world would a countess visit me? And what was proper etiquette when meeting Russian aristocrats? I extended my hand, thought better of it, and bobbed a curtsey. "How do you do?"

She gave me the weakest of smiles.

"I'm afraid there's been a mix up and the countess needs your room." The porter shifted from foot to foot. "I'll have to ask you to vacate within the hour." His white mustache twitched.

"You've got to be joking." I blinked at him. Vacate within the hour. "You're moving me to another room?"

"No ma'am." He grimaced. "We don't have any more habitable rooms." He stared down at his shoes. "I'm sorry."

I felt the blood drain from my face. He was throwing me out onto the street? "Where will I go?" I looked from the porter to the countess. Neither said a word. I squinted at the porter. "Has Mr. Fredricks checked in yet? Fredrick Fredricks?"

"No ma'am." He shrugged. "No one by that name."

"But this room belongs to him. He arranged for me to meet him here. He even put my name on the reservation. Could he have checked in under another name?" Fredricks often used aliases. "Over six feet tall, broad shoulders, long black hair and mustache..." Devilishly attractive and irresistibly charming. "Possibly wearing a slouch hat and jodhpurs, carrying a riding stick." I waved an imaginary stick.

The porter and Countess Brasova exchanged glances. "Duke Zakrevsky," they said in unison.

A Russian duke. What would the cad think of next? Duke Zakrevsky. That name was familiar.

Countess Brasova's eyes lit up. "You know the duke?" She stepped out from behind the porter, removed a gloved hand from her fur muff, and extended it to me. "I'm Natalia Romanov, but my friends call me Natasha."

"Romanov as in Tsar Nicholas?" My mouth fell open.

She put her hand on my arm as if we were best friends. "My husband Michael is his brother."

Golly. The Russian aristocrat was actually Russian royalty. Wait a minute. I seemed to remember something about the tsar's brother being exiled in disgrace for marrying a divorcee. As a divorcee myself, I sympathized. But not enough to accept eviction. I wasn't about to sleep on the street, not even for the tsar himself. "I really don't have anywhere else to go and I'm not about to—"

She squeezed my hand. "Of course, I wouldn't think of letting you give up your room." She smiled at the porter. "Ivan, be a good boy and find me another room." With his white mustache and beard, Ivan was hardly a boy. "And send up some tea." She turned back to me. "And then you can tell me all about your friend Duke Zakrevsky."

Duke Zakrevsky. Aha! I remembered. I'd seen that name on one of Fredricks's fake passports.

Taking my arm, the countess led me back into my room. *My room.* She'd invited herself in for tea. *Sigh.* I let her lead me to the small sitting area near the cracked window. "How long have you known the duke?" Her accent gave her voice a purring quality, like a cat's before it pounced on an unsuspecting canary. "How well do you know the duke?" she asked.

Apparently, I was the only one who *didn't* know "the duke."

The countess took a seat on the divan across from me. "Are the two of you... *close*?" The way she extended the word made it sound obscene.

"Umhmm." I nodded. After all, it was my proximity—or lack thereof—to the duke that had turned the countess from my heartless evictor into my bosom pal. The question was why. What was Fredricks up to now? "How do *you* know the duke?" I asked, relaxing back into the chair. Please, clue me in.

Sprawling across the divan, she crossed her long legs. "I was hoping you might introduce him to me," she said, chuckling. "I've heard so much about him... and about you, of course."

About me? Now, I knew she was lying.

She waved a hand in front of her face like she'd smelled something bad. "You must know *Comrade* Lenin."

"The head of the Bolshevik government?" Why in the world would I know Mister, er, Comrade, Lenin?

"Are you friendly with Vladimir?" She tightened her thin lips, which accentuated her owl-like features.

Should I look for Fredricks in the Kremlin? I shook my head. How did he do it? Ingratiate himself to world leaders from that American president Teddy Roosevelt to the emperor of Austria. Men and women alike loved Fredricks—or the duke—or whatever other alias he was using.

A soft knock at the door signaled the return of the porter with our tea. Scurrying around the sitting area, he sat the silver tea service on the low table and poured us both a cup. Alongside the teapot sat a plate of Russian tea biscuits. Obviously, Countess Brasova merited special treatment. My tea had never been accompanied by sweet biscuits. Nor had it been served in such an extravagant tea service with an ornate silver tray and teapot and delicate floral-patterned china.

"I was hoping the duke might put a word in for my husband." The countess straightened and took up her tea.

I gazed at her over the rim of my cup as I sipped. The Russians did make a fine strong cuppa. Very soothing. Especially accompanied by the fresh cream, no doubt due to the presence of the countess.

"The Cheka arrested him." A cloud passed over her breezy countenance. "It's all a great mistake, of course." She sat her cup on its saucer. "I've appealed to Iron Victor. But he laughed in my face." Her cheeks reddened.

Iron Victor. Goodness. I'd heard of the Cheka—the Bolshevik secret police.

"Evil man." Jerking her head, she brushed a tear from her cheek. "Only Mr. Lenin can help us now, if your duke could put in a good word with him."

"Put in a good word for your husband?" I continued to peer over my teacup. "With Mister... er Vladimir."

"They're together night and day, negotiating with those German *pridurki*." She picked imaginary lint from her muff.

I didn't know what *pridurki* meant, but I knew it wasn't good. Fredrick Fredricks and Vladimir Lenin together night and day negotiating with the Germans. Forget about *pridurki*. This was worse. Much worse.

"I have half a mind to go to Lenin myself." She huffed. "How dare they arrest Michael." Her dark eyes flashed. "With his brother's abdication, he is the head of the royal family." She picked up her tea and stared down at it as if it might be poisoned. In view of the resentments toward the royal family, her fears may be justified.

"Do you know where these negotiations are taking place?" I tried to sound nonchalant.

"It's top secret." She leaned forward and lowered her voice. "But I have it on good authority they're in Brest-on-the-Bug."

"Brest-on-the-Bug," I repeated.

"Brest-Litovsk on the Bug River." She twisted around and

pointed toward the window. "Southwest of here, near Warsaw. Now occupied by those German *pridurki*."

Fredricks was with Lenin at Bug River. My mind was awhirl. I pulled out my notebook and a pencil and jotted down an abbreviated version of the information.

Brest-Litovsk at the Bug River ala Countess Brasova.
B-L. @ B-R ala C-B.

Good heavens. *B-L*. That was the notation on Fredricks's matchbox. *03-03 B-L*. He was in B-L. What was happening in B-L on 3 March?

"I'm sorry to bring you into the middle of this." The countess's eyes were pleading. "But I'm desperate." She bit her lip. "I'm afraid of what they'll do to Michael. The Cheka are brutal."

I shuddered to think.

"I feel so helpless." When she slumped on the divan, her long limbs seemed to fold in on themselves. Her shoulders began to shake. *Oh dear*. Was she sobbing?

"There, there." I went over and sat next to her. "I'm certain the duke will help free your husband." I wasn't certain. In fact, I rather doubted that *the duke* would be inclined to help restore the monarchy if he was busy negotiating with the Germans. If I understood the situation correctly, Mr. Lenin and the Bolsheviks were decidedly anti-tsarists. To them, the royal family represented a threat. I wasn't quite sure about the Bolshevik's stance on Germany. Politics was not my strong suit. Give me a complex filing system any day. Complicated politics gave me a headache. But I was certain of one thing. In the name of peace, Fredricks would do anything to ensure Germany's victory over Britain—an unfortunate sticking point in our relationship. Not that we *had* a relationship, mind you.

I withdrew a handkerchief from my skirt pocket and handed it to the countess. Sniffling, she took it. I put my arm around her trembling shoulders. "Countess, why don't you finish your tea?" I picked up the cup and saucer and held it out. "It will make you feel better." My grandmother always said everything was better with a nice cuppa. But my grandmother never had a run in with the police, secret or otherwise.

Perhaps something stronger would be more appropriate. "Should I call for a brandy? Or a whiskey perhaps?" I usually didn't go in for drinking, especially before noon, but the countess was melting into a messy puddle in my hotel room. "To calm your nerves." I couldn't very well chuck her out, no matter how eager I was to find Fredricks and foil his plot, whatever it was.

Maybe if I found Fredricks and thwarted his plans, then I could redeem myself with the War Office. I cringed. No doubt I'd been sacked. And just when I was getting jolly good at espionage. What excuse could I give for waiting almost two weeks to report in? Kidnapped. I could say Fredricks had kidnapped me, and I didn't have a choice, and I would have called if only I could have. No, I wasn't following my heart but doing my duty. Would Captain Hall believe me?

"Yes, perhaps a brandy would be good." The countess's voice was small. Her demeanor had totally transformed from the confident, entitled aristocrat she'd been when she arrived, to a bereft woman fighting for the man she loved. The war was the great leveler. I plucked a sweet biscuit from the plate. At least in some ways.

Thud. Thud. The porter's knock was harder than before. Perfect timing. I could order that restorative for the countess and then get rid of her. I patted her arm and then went to the door. When I opened it, a bearded man barged inside the room. He looked menacing in his black leather jacket, tall black boots, and a woolen mariner's cap. In the hall another uniformed man armed with a bayonet stood at attention.

"Natalia Romanov." The bearded man barked out her name. "*Vy arestovany.*" He glanced at me. I didn't understand what he'd said, but I knew from his tone it wasn't good.

"Under arrest!" The countess jumped up. "But why?" She'd knocked her cup and saucer to the floor. At the sound of the breaking china, the armed guard dashed into the room, bayonet aimed at me.

"*Vy oba.*" The leather-clad brute grabbed my arm. "*Vy arestovany.*"

"Both of us, but Miss Figg hasn't done anything." Arms akimbo, the countess stared them down as she spat something at them in Russian.

I yanked my arm away. "I'm a British citizen, a visitor from London."

"*Zalmochi.*" He shoved me toward the door.

I lost my footing and fell to the floor.

"Don't tell her to shut up!" The countess ran to my side. She yelled something in Russian.

One of the Cheka pointed his bayonet at me.

"I've twisted my ankle," I whined. Holding my ankle, I rolled around on the floor.

The countess kicked the Cheka in the shin. He grabbed her by the hair and she screamed. Both guards were on her now. I took advantage of the distraction and slipped my notebook out of my pocket. Quickly, I scrawled *CHEKA* in big letters and then skated the notebook under the nearest piece of furniture. An armoire that stood next to the door. A big hand was around my upper arm. The Cheka yanked me to my feet. His partner seized the countess around the waist and dragged her from the room. Struggling, she managed to knock his hat off. But that only made him angry. He threw her against the wall and then brought the butt of his rifle down on her head. She fell to the floor in a heap.

I gasped and my hand flew to my mouth. Good heavens. These Cheka *pridurki* were going to kill us.

Thwack. What felt like a horse's kick to the skull threw me to the ground. Holding my head in both hands, I moaned. My vision blurred. Then everything went black.

A NOTE FROM THE AUTHOR
FUN FACTS

Many of the characters in this novel were inspired by real people. Emilie Augusta Louise Lind af Hageby, known as Lizzy Lind, was a Swedish-born animal activist who founded the Purple Cross for horses and started the first veterinary field hospitals for military animals. She did enter medical school at the University of London to expose their vivisectionist cruelties. And she co-founded—with Lady Nina Douglas, Duchess of Hamilton—the Animal Defense Society with an office on Piccadilly. Nina used her estate at Ferne as a sanctuary for animals abandoned during the war, especially World War II when food was in such short supply that many pet owners could no longer afford to feed themselves and their pets.

The character of Sergei Vorknoy is inspired by Dr. Serge Voronoff, known as the "monkey gland expert" and the "monkey gland doctor." Dr. Voronoff grafted tissue from chimpanzee testicles onto wealthy men and their horses. He claimed the operation would restore youth and vitality and boost intelligence. He performed his operations mostly in France, but also in England.

The codebreakers in Room 40 are all loosely based on real codebreakers: Nigel de Grey, Dillwyn Knox, and William Montgomery, Captain "Blinker" Hall was the head of the War Office in the Old Admiralty Building.

Lady Sybil is very loosely based on Lady Sybil Grant, daughter of Lord Archibald Primrose, Earl of Rosebery, who served as the prime minister of the United Kingdom in 1894–1895. He did close the gates to one of his estates, The Durdans, when his son left to fight and never again reopened them. And after his wife, Hannah de Rothschild, died, he wore mourning for the rest of his life. He was also an avid horse lover and owned several stables and racehorses. He did not, however, hide horses from the War Office and neither did his groom. Lady Sybil was known for her unconventional ways, including climbing trees and issuing orders with a bullhorn and traveling with the caravan of Romani she allowed to camp on the estate.

Fredrick Fredricks is inspired by real-life spy Fredrick "Fritz" Joubert Duquesne, the South African huntsman who escaped from prison several times in outrageous ways, adopted several personae, and generally charmed his way through high society posing as a journalist, a British army officer, and a duke. One of his aliases was Fredrick Fredricks. He was also the leader of an infamous spy ring in World War II until his capture in one of the largest espionage convictions in United States history.

ACKNOWLEDGMENTS

A hearty thanks to the Boldwood team. You all rock! Thanks to my critique group (Benigno, Fred, Lorraine, and Susan). They always read the first chapter and help get me off to a good start. And as always, I'm grateful for my family, furry and otherwise—thanks Dad, Moneca, Ruthy, Chuck, Teri, Beni, Mischief, Mayhem, and Mr. Flan.

ABOUT THE AUTHOR

Kelly Oliver is the award-winning, bestselling author of three mysteries series. She is also the Distinguished Professor of Philosophy at Vanderbilt University and lives in Nashville Tennessee.

Sign up to Kelly Oliver's mailing list here for news, competitions and updates on future books.

Visit Kelly's website: http://www.kellyoliverbooks.com/

Follow Kelly on social media:

twitter.com/KellyOliverBook

facebook.com/kellyoliverauthor

instagram.com/kellyoliverbooks

tiktok.com/@kellyoliverbooks

bookbub.com/authors/kelly-oliver

ALSO BY KELLY OLIVER

A Fiona Figg & Kitty Lane Mystery Series

Chaos at Carnegie Hall

Covert in Cairo

Mayhem in the Mountains

Arsenic at Ascot

Boldwood

Boldwood Books is an award-winning fiction publishing company seeking out the best stories from around the world.

Find out more at www.boldwoodbooks.com

Join our reader community for brilliant books, competitions and offers!

Follow us
@BoldwoodBooks
@TheBoldBookClub

Sign up to our weekly deals newsletter

https://bit.ly/BoldwoodBNewsletter